Who Is Emerald Monday?
Roz Denny Fox

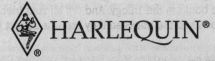

ISBN 0-373-70984-6

WHO IS EMERALD MONDAY?

Copyright © 2001 by Rosaline Fox.

This edition published by arrangement with Harlequin Books S.A.

® and TM are trademarks of the publisher. Trademarks indicated with ® are registered in the United States Patent and Trademark Office, the Canadian Trade Marks Office and in other countries.

Visit us at www.eHarlequin.com

Printed in U.S.A.

Who Is Emerald Monday?

CHAPTER ONE

EMMY MONDAY leafed through a three-week-old Shreveport newspaper in search of the classified ad section. Steam curled from her coffee mug, dampening the lower edges of the paper as she considered whether to stay in Louisiana or not. Fortunately, she was resilient. When it came to school, jobs, men, you name it—she had long ago developed the ability to shrug off disappointment and move on. And May, according to her horoscope, was a season of renewal.

Where *were* those ads? Depending on what jobs were available, she'd have to revise a résumé that was already eclectic by most employment standards. During her thirty-two years she'd dabbled at a variety of jobs. She'd waited tables, cleaned houses, traveled with a circus, worked as a gardener, a camp counselor and most recently, dealt blackjack, a job she had a knack for and enjoyed while it lasted.

Letting the paper slip, Emmy scooped four heaping spoonfuls of sugar into her thick black coffee. As she stirred, she mulled over the past day's events. Richard Parrish had knocked on her door at 2:00 a.m. Not late for him. He owned the casino where she worked, and for three years they'd dated at odd hours. The loose arrangement suited them both, she'd thought, even if Richard had broached the subject of marriage now and again. Emmy had never taken his proposals seriously.

Her mistake, he'd said. A point he made just before he announced his intention of marrying Melanie Fletcher, Emmy's co-worker. A croupier. A woman Emmy had considered her friend.

Right!

Emmy could have—would have—accepted the marriage. She didn't love Richard. In fact, she tended to scoff at love and happily-ever-after, which had been another of Richard's observations. Last night he'd felt compelled to list what he deemed her shortcomings. *She didn't let anyone get close. She'd fenced off sections of her heart. She was afraid of commitment.* Finally, he said none too gently, "Emmy, you've gotta find out who the hell you are and exorcize all that nonsense about how there might be evil lurking in your genes. Because," he'd added, "If you don't lay those ghosts to rest, you'll never find happiness. And it's not fair to any man who really falls for you."

Then he'd fired her! Oh, he couched the dismissal in sympathetic terms by handing over a severance check that was unprecedented in the field. Or so he'd said. Emmy saw right through him—the weasel. What it boiled down to was the fact that his soon-to-be-wife viewed Emmy as a threat. Melanie had delivered an ultimatum. "Get rid of Emmy." Which Richard had done, just like that. Emmy snapped her fingers.

The sweet coffee helped cover the bad taste lingering in her mouth. But it did nothing to silence Richard's accusations. They ran rampant through her head. *Who is Emerald Monday? Who is she, really?*

The cup wobbled, sloshing sugary brew all over the paper. As she leaped up and tore a paper towel off the dispenser to blot up the spill, headlines on a wet article jumped out at her, putting a stranglehold on her heart.

Mystery Bones Discovered Near East Texas Lake

Below the headline a town was named. Uncertain, Texas. Emmy's breath came out in short gasps. Her heart hammered erratically. Were her eyes playing tricks because Richard had probed deep into old wounds?

She dropped the soggy paper towel, grabbed the newspaper and quickly read the entire article. "Uncertain, Texas. The mystery of Frannie Granger's disappearance may finally be solved. The forty-seven-year-old Harrison County woman vanished nineteen years ago this spring. Her remains were recently found close to an Indian burial ground near Caddo Lake. She is believed to have been murdered."

A cry burst explosively from Emmy's tightly compressed lips. She forced herself to continue reading, even though her hands shook so hard she had to lay the paper flat on the table to steady the print.

On March 28 of this year, upon the discovery of human remains obviously not those of a Caddo Indian of the early nineteenth century, archaeologist Tessa Lang turned the skeleton over to the authorities for identification. This week, comparison with local dental records proved the bones to be those of Frannie Granger, a widow who was housekeeper for various local residents and who provided foster care for unadoptable children in her own home in Uncertain. Granger was well-liked in the community, and her sudden disappearance caused quite a stir. Sheriff Logan Fielder could not be reached for comment. The question remains, who murdered Frannie Granger, and why?

Emmy reread the coffee-marked column, stopping to haul in a deep sob at the part about Frannie taking in unadoptable children. Emerald Monday had been one of those children. The first of three. It'd been a while since she'd allowed intrusive thoughts of her foster siblings, Jed and Will. Or of Mom Fran, for that matter. Emmy had, in fact, worked hard to wall off that portion of her life. Because recalling how it had once been—well, it was just too painful.

Until this moment, she'd never known for sure why Social Services had abruptly jerked her out of the only home she'd ever known to dump her with strangers in Houston. A family whose two natural daughters hated having a new kid in their lives even more than Emmy hated being there.

Mom Fran had left for work one day and didn't come home. By noon the following day, a woman from the agency had collected Emmy from school. They hadn't let her say goodbye to Jed Louis or Will McClain, her foster brothers. Until now, Emmy hadn't known that Mom Fran had never returned home. After her bitter experience of the system, Emmy had judged Fran Granger just another cop-out. Now she felt guilty for those thoughts.

But good grief! She'd tried hard to learn the truth. Twice she'd run away and been caught hitchhiking back to Uncertain. Three times the state had shifted her into new homes, each a bigger disaster than the previous one. Finally they'd parked her in a group facility in Corpus Christi, and that was the last straw. The fight had gone out of her, leaving only underlying anger. She'd given up on Jed or Will or Frannie ever finding her. Assuming anyone had looked. That, she saw, was at the core of her restlessness.

It was clearer now. Each move she'd made after her mad flight from the group home the day she'd reached legal age had brought her closer to her beginnings. Her roots, murky as they were, lay hidden across the border in Texas.

Emmy hadn't cried in years. And she didn't now, because she'd dealt with the grief of losing Mom Fran long ago. But there remained a need to possess the facts. Facts about her past that might come to light if the local sheriff dug for clues to Fran Granger's murder.

Two days slipped by before she managed to sort things out in her mind. She supposed she owed Richard Parrish—or more likely, Melanie Fletcher—for unwittingly providing her with the time and the resources to go back. Back to a town whose very name described her past, present and future—Uncertain.

It took her five days in all to pack and leave Shreveport. Even then, all her worldly possessions fit in a dozen cartons stacked in the back of her aging Ford Ranger pickup. But hadn't she always traveled light? Anyone who'd bounced around the foster care system for long knew it was asking for heartbreak to get attached to…things. All Emmy had of her past was a single item the caseworkers had inadvertently allowed her to keep. The social worker who'd yanked her out of school and packed her stuff at Mom Fran's had thrown Emmy's clothes into what she assumed was a laundry basket. A deep, oval basket in which Emmy had been found as an infant. If she had any link to her past, it was that. She'd clung to it stubbornly—to the point of bloodying one foster brother's nose when he tried to carry some stupid project to school in her basket.

Emmy smiled at the memory while checking in the

rearview mirror to make certain the box containing her treasure was still wedged against the tailgate.

It was.

Her gaze swerved to watch Shreveport, her home for the past few years, recede into the distance. A car horn honked, reclaiming Emmy's attention. She realized her knuckles were white from gripping the steering wheel so tightly. Part of her wanted to stop, turn back and hide out in her old apartment. Ahead lay unknown risks. It had been infinitely easier to think of Mom Fran as endlessly missing.

But murdered... Emmy shivered. It hurt to think that someone she'd once cared for deeply had been reduced to a pile of bones, her remains unceremoniously dumped in an old Indian burial mound. Who was Tessa Lang, and why did she have to expose a private person like Fran to the prying eyes of the world?

Murder, a little voice nagged. *Don't you want the person responsible to be found?* She did; Emmy wanted the person who'd killed her foster mother and shattered her own idyllic childhood to pay and pay big-time.

Jed and Will would want that, too.

Heaven only knew where they were. So many nights she'd waited, expecting one or the other to find her and take her back to Mom Fran's, where they'd be together again. Jed had assumed the position of man of the family from the moment he'd arrived to live with them at age six. He was solid, reliable. Emmy had liked that about him. Will, a surly thirteen when he came, at first hated everything and everyone in town. He'd pretty much considered Emmy a pest until the three foster kids had forged an us-against-them bond. Will became Emmy's fierce protector if anyone at school picked on her. The summer before life fell apart, the three had made a pact to stick together no matter what. So why hadn't Jed or Will come for her, or called, or written?

And what about Riley Gray Wolf? Emmy's heart skipped a beat even now as she conjured up images of Riley. His family were descendants of the Caddo Indians for whom the lake bordering the town was named. Lord, but she'd had the worst crush on Riley. Literally from the age of nine, when she'd seen him at school defending a handicapped kid. Riley hadn't noticed Emmy nearly as soon, but to her great delight, he'd begun hanging out with Will and Jed. For years, Emmy had tagged along.

Almost overnight, her relationship with Riley had changed. If she let her mind drift, she could still feel the first time he'd kissed her. A kiss that had started out tentative, but quickly became more. She'd been thirteen.

Mom Fran was forever scolding Emmy about sneaking off alone with Riley. A few nights before she disappeared, Fran had run Riley off the property, ordering him to stay away from Emmy—who never saw Riley again. But for a long time she'd expected him to turn up like a white knight to save her from a terrifying situation. Jed, Will and Riley had all let her down. Counselors had repeatedly told Emmy to forget the boys. In time, she'd managed to stuff memories of them behind a barrier. It hadn't been easy then. Or now, as the images crowded back.

Richard obviously didn't know how painful it would be for her to go rooting around in her past or he wouldn't have so blithely suggested it. Not that he was the first to recommend she get off her duff and research her background. A professor in a college sociology course had said it was simple these days, with the aid of computers, to find someone who'd put up a child for adoption. He'd offered to help her—said if she found the answers she

needed, she might lose her attitude. She'd declined, dis-
playing a lot of the attitude he'd been talking about.

Emmy hadn't been adopted out. She'd been left in a
basket at First Monday Trade Days in Canton, Texas. *Left*
like some garage sale item to be sold or traded. That was
what people did at Trade Days, billed as the largest flea
market in the world. So no, Emmy hadn't been quick to
search for the woman who'd abandoned her. In fact,
she'd quit the stupid class and dropped out of college.
That was her second, and last attempt at getting a degree.

Maybe she'd mosey over to Dallas now and enroll in
classes. Thirtyish wasn't too old to graduate in something
worthwhile.

It surely wasn't. But instead of keeping on toward Dallas, Emmy slowed her pickup on the outskirts of Marshall
and made the turn that led straight to Uncertain.

When she reached her destination, the town seemed
little changed from what she remembered. An unexpected
wave of nostalgia hit Emmy. Her throat clogged and she
blinked rapidly as her eyes stung. Tears? *Impossible.* The
Emmy Monday she'd become had shed her last tear the
day the state removed her from private foster care. That
was when Emmy had left foolish, girlish tears behind.
And dreams.

Apparently leaving here a girl and returning a woman
had triggered a battery of strong emotions. But she could
handle this. In a life filled with ups, downs and doubts,
this homecoming could be either a ripple or a wave.
Emmy hauled in a deep breath and forced an iron grip
on unguarded feelings.

She couldn't decide what to do first. Find a place to
rent, pay a visit to the sheriff—a duty call Emmy didn't
find particularly appealing—or buy herself lunch. It was

past noon. Maybe the knot in her stomach simply meant she was hungry.

Before doing anything, though, she wanted to drive past Mom Fran's old house—if it was still there.

It was. Just seeing the little house looking homey with lacy curtains—someone else's curtains—caused a surge of darker sentiment. She didn't know why it hurt to see a new roof and freshly painted clapboard siding. Emmy's fingers flexed on her steering wheel. Several moments passed before she realized there was a For Rent sign in the front window. On legs not quite steady, she climbed from her pickup and followed a winding flagstone path to the porch. She copied down the telephone number of a rental agent—or maybe the owner. The sign didn't specify.

The house was larger than Emmy would need. There were three bedrooms. Jed and Will had shared the largest. The boys were of such different temperaments that Fran had felt each needed his own space. She'd hired a contractor to close in the porch for Will. Not at first, because Will had a tendency to sneak out at night. But later he'd earned Frannie's trust. Emmy and Jed had both been envious over that remodeling job. Had it ever been completed? She decided to find out.

She picked her way to the backyard through overgrown shrubs. From there, she could smell the swampy odor of decay. Part of the property sloped to marshy Caddo Lake and part climbed to a vacant lot next door. Only the lot wasn't vacant anymore. A redbrick house sat smack in the middle with a chain-link fence surrounding its immaculate lawn. As she stared at this unexpected sight, a stern-faced woman pulled a curtain aside and stared right back. Emmy gulped and waved, garnering no response.

The last thing she wanted was for someone to call the sheriff and accuse her of trespassing. Anyway, she'd satisfied her curiosity. The porch room had been completed. It held a white wicker settee and a profusion of plants. "Good," she mumbled aloud, hurrying back to her pickup. "The place seems to come furnished. Now, if only the rent is reasonable…"

Emmy soon discovered more than mere price was attached to renting Mom Fran's home. Standing at a pay phone, she felt her stomach churn. Sweat popped out on her forehead even before she'd punched in one number. A hypoglycemia attack, she figured, backing out of the booth. She'd skipped breakfast to load the last of her belongings and it was well past lunch. Surely there wasn't such a huge demand for rentals here that she couldn't grab a bite before she made the call.

She avoided Catfish Corner where Fran used to take them to celebrate special occasions like birthdays or when Jed won musical awards. The Ferguson family who owned the restaurant had been frying fish there since before the town was named. Emmy preferred not to run into anyone who might recognize her. She was still too shaken by her trip down memory lane, so she chose instead the Caddo Kitchen, which used to be a favorite burger joint of local teens. Tips weren't great and waitress turnover was high. High-schoolers worked there. Or they did, anyway. With luck, not a soul would know her.

The place was nearly empty. Two men sat at the Formica counter drinking coffee, and a woman with a baby and a boy of about five were seated in the first booth. The woman and boy shared a large chocolate sundae. The baby slept in his carrier. All were strangers. Relieved, Emmy slid across the vinyl bench seat of the last booth. Surveying the café's interior, she noticed that the decor had changed dramatically. Mounted bass replaced posters of rock stars, and fishing rods and tackle hung on the walls. Netting fluttered under the breeze of overhead fans. The jukebox was gone. Obviously the clientele had changed, or aged. Bass fishing had always been a steady tourist industry for the otherwise sleepy town.

A gum-chewing waitress slapped a glass of water, napkin-wrapped silverware and a menu in front of Emmy. "Homemade chicken noodle is the soup of the day. Hey!" The gum cracked twice. "Don't I know you? My God, it's Emmy Monday! I never forget a face. I'm Cassie. Cassie Ames, now Morris," the woman said, plunking herself down on the bench opposite Emmy. "I look different. Got contacts and had my teeth straightened. Oh, and my hair used to be cow-pie brown, not red." She giggled as she patted her hair. Seemingly oblivious to the fact that Emmy sat there frozen, the woman rattled on, "Look at you, girl. Haven't changed a bit. That naturally blond hair was the envy of every girl in town. You're still model-thin—except for the right amount of curves." Pop went the gum again, and Cassie licked a pink bubble off her lower lip. "That's why all the girls hated you— especially those in the in crowd."

Emmy blushed and murmured a protest, which didn't stop Cassie. "You had the greenest green eyes. The rest of us were stuck with blah brown or boring blue. Course, those eyes are what got you the name Emerald, right?" Cassie propped her chin in one hand. "Personally, with a name like Emerald Monday, I always figured you'd end up a movie star."

Emmy tried not to grimace as she finally stammered out a greeting. Most people thought her name was a result of her eye color. They couldn't be more wrong. She had no intention of enlightening Cassie or even saying that she hadn't landed in Hollywood. "The Caesar salad sounds good. I believe I'll have that and iced tea."

"Um, sure." Cassie tucked her gum into the side of her cheek and called Emmy's order in to the cook. With barely a pause, she babbled on. "Too bad you didn't drop into town last month, Emmy. We held our first-ever high-school reunion. Of course, the girls who dreamed up the idea were the only ones who had time to diet down to the weight they used to be. Amanda Jennings, but you probably guessed that." Cassie sucked in her cheeks and crossed her eyes. "She's dumped three husbands. Other than that, she's the same old Amanda."

Amanda's family owned the local bank. Even as a kid she'd used the power of the Jennings name to her own advantage. She'd lived in a pretentious house, one which Mom Fran cleaned. A fact that never stopped the status-conscious Amanda from shamelessly chasing Jed and Will. Emmy had heartily disliked her. Not solely because she'd let Emmy know she was socially inferior, but also because she'd made fools of Jed and Will. Even Riley had danced to Amanda's tune. Emmy had never understood what the boys saw in such a phony.

"I wouldn't have been invited to the reunion," she admitted guardedly. "I never attended high school here."

"I started to ask what brought you back," Cassie interjected. "But I guess it's because you heard Jed's the prime suspect in Frannie Granger's murder."

"What? Jed? But—but," Emmy stuttered. "That's impossible." She almost dropped the silverware she'd unwrapped. Emmy, who'd wanted the talkative woman to shut up, now waited impatiently for Cassie to elaborate. But the cook yelled, "Order up," and Cassie went to retrieve it. However, she didn't miss a beat after setting the salad and frosty tea glass in front of Emmy. "Yep,

Jed's number one on Sheriff Fielder's list. Some folks think Logan ought to track down Hank Belmonte. He was the town drunk, remember, who did odd jobs? He did some carpentry work for Frannie and for Amanda's dad, Ray, around the time Frannie disappeared. Hank never finished either project.''

"Then isn't he the logical suspect?" Emmy stabbed a forkful of salad. She wanted to ask more about Jed. She didn't have to; gossip flowed from Cassie. "I guess you know Jed inherited Beaumarais, his uncle's estate. After college, Jed turned into a regular entrepreneur. His wife is real nice. And brave. I don't know that I'd marry someone suspected of murder. But marry him she did, about a week ago. Still, she had to know what she was letting herself in for."

Jed married and living at Beaumarais? Emmy swallowed hard. "The sheriff has questioned others besides Jed, I hope."

"Sure. All the families Frannie cleaned houses for. Oh, and Riley Gray. But he had an iron-clad alibi."

"Riley Gray Wolf?" Emmy's heart stumbled and beat faster.

"He dropped the Wolf part of his name when he became a big-shot business attorney. Now, there's a guy who *looks* the same, but who's really changed. He got married. Has a daughter. A real cutie. She's four or five—I forget which."

Emmy felt a kick in her midriff. *Riley and Jed both married.* "Uh…did…Riley marry Amanda?" Emmy asked weakly. She didn't think she could stand it if the answer was yes, and yet she had to know.

"Lord, no! And after her last divorce Amanda took back her maiden name. Some people say it's so her mom will still foot her bills. About Riley…he married an outsider he met in Oklahoma. Lani Sky. Shortly after you left town, Neva Gray Wolf took sick, couldn't work and ended up losing the house. She went to live in Oklahoma with her brother. On a reservation, with the last of the Caddo tribe. Riley moved here about six years ago...." Cassie glanced away. "I, uh, don't like talking about his wife. Something happened there, and he's split with his whole family."

"So his sister Josey's still in Oklahoma? Neva's okay? You don't mean she died? Losing his dad in Vietnam put such a hardship on the family, and especially on Riley. He suffered so much. I can't bear to think how he'd handle losing his mom."

"Oh, Neva recovered. And Josey moved back here, too, but I rarely see her. She's a master potter at the factory over in Marshall."

Emmy's senses were on overload. She'd heard enough. Too much. Folding her napkin, she extracted money from her wallet to cover the bill and tip.

"No wonder you're still skinny," Cassie said, eyeing Emmy as she stood. "I can have that boxed to go, if you'd like."

Emmy shook her head. "Thanks, but I have to stop at the bank and then find a place to stay tonight. It's been great, though, Cassie," she said politely.

"The Kit and Caboodle Cottages are clean and nice and the owners will give you a break on monthly rates. They're across from the St. Cloud Marina. Layla St. Cloud runs it now. Actually, she's Layla Santiago. She married Rico. Too bad you don't have more time—that's another interesting story. I'm sure you remember them."

"I do. And thanks for the info on the cottages. I have no idea how long I'll be in town."

"Then I'm glad you stopped here today. Although,"

Cassie said ruefully, "next time you'll have to tell me what y'all have been doing. Whatever, it's agreed with you. You look like a million bucks."

Emmy felt the heat rise to her cheeks again. "Um...I've done a little of this and a little of that. I can't claim any marriages, though."

Cassie walked Emmy to the door. "Kevin and I have five kids. The oldest is in high school, would you believe? We've been married sixteen years this May."

Emmy vaguely recalled Kevin Morris, a chubby boy who always had his nose in a book. Emmy couldn't even imagine being a waitress while raising five kids. She'd waited tables and it was hard work. If she did eat here again, she'd be more generous with her tipping. If she stuck around, she'd have to find a job—but not in a restaurant. Main Street, tree-lined and sleepy, had revealed some new touristy businesses. With summer coming, someone might need extra help.

Emmy needed to find a quiet place to digest all of Cassie's gossip. But the afternoon was slipping away. She had to deposit the check Richard had given her and find out how to transfer her funds from Shreveport—if she decided to stay more than a few weeks. After that, she'd call and inquire how much Fran's house would cost to rent.

The lobby of Cypress Bank and Trust smelled old and musty. Emmy had been there a few times with Mom Fran. If memory served, it hadn't changed. The bank and the building itself had all belonged to Amanda's maternal grandfather. Emmy recalled hearing stories that Ray Jennings had married Catherine for her money. Surely her good looks had played a part. Ray's wife had been an older, classier version of Amanda, who overdid makeup and bleach. At least she used to.

As Emmy waited to be helped by a teller, Ray Jennings exited his office with an elderly man, a rancher. Ray studied Emmy in passing. His eyes remained on her even after they'd reached the door. Amanda's dad hadn't changed at all. He still acted pompous, and he still had a roving eye. The old goat.

Emmy attended to business, which took longer than she'd expected. In her rush to leave and find that pay phone again, she dashed from the bank and nearly bowled over a man headed in.

"Whoa! Sorry. I didn't look where I was going." The man adjusted his tie as he stepped back and flashed Emmy a dazzling grin. In addition to the knock-out smile, he had liquid black eyes that cruised over her with interest as he gazed down from a lean, six-foot height. The sun blinded Emmy before she had time to assess much more—or to put on her sunglasses.

"Emmy? Holy smokes! Where...when...?" The masculine voice rose excitedly.

Finding herself snatched close to a broad chest and whirled completely off her feet, Emmy finally managed to identify a once-familiar face. *Riley! Lord in heaven, it was Riley.* Emmy was quite sure her tongue was glued to her teeth. She barely managed a garbled greeting. She'd known, of course, given the size of Uncertain, that there was a likelihood of their paths crossing if she planned to stay in town. She'd thought she'd have more time to prepare.

"I can't believe it's really you," he said, still hugging her tight. Before reluctantly setting her away, he repeated several times how great it was to see her. Even then, his eyes lingered on her face. "Where have you been? *How* have you been?"

"I'm, uh, okay." Except it was a lie, because right

now, *okay* was the last thing she felt. *Overwhelmed* was more like it. Breathless, she could do nothing but stare up at a face she'd imagined only in her dreams for nineteen years. She recognized the lock of straight black hair that fell across his forehead and caught on his impossibly long eyelashes. That hadn't changed. Lord, the man fulfilled every fantasy she'd ever had of what Riley Gray Wolf would look like as an adult. But, according to Cassie, he'd shortened his name to Gray—and he was no longer Emmy Monday's best pal. Riley was married and had a child. A coldness she couldn't explain seized her, and Emmy moved out of his reach.

Riley, who still wore a stunned grin, checked his watch. "I was going to make a deposit, but that can wait. We have half a lifetime to catch up on. God, Emmy, just give me a minute to get my breath. I feel like I've been hit by a truck. Listen, why don't you join me for a cup of coffee? We'll stretch it to include dinner if you're free."

In this town of rumormongers? With no mention of his wife joining them? Emmy dragged down the sunglasses she'd shoved up into her hair when she'd entered the bank. She had to cover her eyes before they revealed too much pain. "I'm sorry, Riley," she said coolly, sidling past him. "I've got a list of things to do. Maybe some other time." Then—to ensure that she wouldn't break down and say to hell with caution—Emmy all but ran to her vehicle.

With jaw slack and hands in the pockets of his trousers, Riley watched the woman who had haunted his dreams for years vault into a beat-up yellow Ford pickup. The tailgate was caved in on a row of boxes that lined the metal bed. At least the old vehicle had a roll bar, he thought. *Damn, but Emmy looked great.* She'd grown into a beautiful woman, as he'd always known she would. Riley shaded his eyes against the blinding shaft of sunlight. *She was real, wasn't she? She hadn't been a mirage?*

A heavy hand clamped his shoulder, breaking into Riley's confusion.

"Appears you've lost your touch with the ladies, Gray." The bank president's narrow salt-and-pepper mustache twitched with humor. Ray Jennings followed Riley's gaze as the battered Ford pulled away from the curb. "I saw her inside the bank. She looked familiar, but I'll be damned if I can place her."

"Emmy Monday," Riley murmured, still shocked by their chance encounter. "She was one of Fran Granger's foster children. I suppose she's come to help Jed."

Ray dropped his hand and turned to peer at the truck until it disappeared around a corner. "Do you reckon Logan tracked her down and brought her back for questioning? Is he also looking for Frannie's other riffraff foster kid? What was his name?"

"Will. Will McClain. He'd had some bad breaks, but he wasn't riffraff."

"Says who? Doesn't matter. I figure he's in prison by now. If we're lucky," Ray said around a snort. "Jed's the best of the lot. He'd do well to forget he ever knew those other two. Same goes for you, Gray. A man in your position has to think twice before getting too friendly with a little blond nobody." As abruptly as he'd appeared, Ray stomped back into the bank.

Riley mulled over his parting shot. Jennings had never had much use for the Native American blood that ran in the Gray Wolf veins. Riley found it almost comical that after all these years, Ray would overlook his origins—

now that he didn't give a damn what Jennings or anyone else in Uncertain thought.

He shouldn't give a damn that Emmy Monday had given him the brush-off, either. But it was hard to forget those weeks nineteen years ago when he'd gone crazy trying to locate her after Social Services had taken her away. Riley recalled creating such a commotion in the Family Counseling offices, they'd called the police and had him arrested for disturbing the peace. His poor mother had to borrow money to bail him out. If it hadn't been for old Hamish Abrams, the lawyer who'd been his mentor and whose practice he'd later bought, Riley would have ended up with a juvenile record.

Though he wanted to go after Emmy and demand to know why she'd dropped completely out of sight, Ray might have a valid point. What did anyone know about Emmy Monday? Why had she never tried to contact him or Jed? Granted, they'd both gone off to college within the year, but neither would have been terribly difficult to find. Anyone in town could have pointed her in the right direction.

No, he didn't know squat about the woman who'd dismissed his offer of coffee and catch-up so easily. And he had a daughter to think about now. To say nothing of a solid, hard-won law practice. One look at Emmy, and he'd apparently forgotten both. Scowling, Riley stalked into the bank to make the deposit he'd been so willing to delay for a woman who obviously didn't care to renew their friendship.

Hell, it'd been more than mere friendship for Riley. He might've been only sixteen, but he'd been head-over-heels in love with Emmy Monday. If she could so easily cast off all they'd meant to each other, then she hadn't turned into the woman he'd imagined she'd be. Lucky for him that she hadn't taken him up on his offer.

CHAPTER TWO

ON THE DRIVE to the phone booth, Emmy's thoughts were consumed by Riley. How good he looked. How successful. How difficult it would be to see him around town. Living in a small town increased the odds of future meetings. Darn, why hadn't she asked him for Josey's address? At one time, Riley's sister had been Emmy's best girlfriend. Josey threw pots and wove wool and baskets. She and Emmy had spent hours on crafts. The girls had been friends before Emmy took notice of boys. Of Riley in particular.

Angling into a parking spot on the street adjacent to the booth, Emmy deliberately thrust Riley Gray Wolf, or Gray as he called himself now, firmly into the past where he belonged.

The number she punched in rang three times at the other end before a woman's lilting voice sang out, "Hello."

"I'm calling about a house you have for rent. A small place off Moss Road. Is it available? It seems vacant."

"It is, although there are still boxes in a bedroom that need moving. The home belongs to my husband. He's away on business, but I expect him back by dinnertime. Say, seven-thirty, if you'd care to call then."

Emmy twisted the phone cord. "Oh. Perhaps I'll just go ahead and rent one of the Kit and Caboodle cottages then."

The owner's wife sounded curious. "You'd rent a house based on a drive-by?"

"I—uh," Emmy stammered, "—know the place. I used to live there. Although it looks nicer now than it did then."

"Are you sure you have the correct house in mind? Jed, my husband, has owned the place for some time. He grew up there himself."

"Jed? Jed Louis is your husband? He owns the old Granger house?"

"Yes. You know him? I don't believe I caught your name." The voice sharpened, unless Emmy imagined it.

"He probably had no reason to mention me. My name is Emmy Monday. A long time ago, we both lived there as foster kids."

"Emmy!" A happy cry followed. "Jed's told me about you. Oh, he'll be so pleased when he hears you've come home. I know he'll want you to stay at Beaumarais with us."

"Oh, I couldn't." Emmy recalled what Cassie had said about Jed's recent marriage. "I heard you're newly married. Besides, Jed and I haven't spoken in years. We're virtual strangers."

"I guess I understand how you feel. But you two have so much catching up to do. Tell you what, I'll meet you at the rental. Jed would never forgive me if I turned away the only family he has." She lowered her voice. "I'm assuming you've heard what a mess he's been thrown into?"

"Bits and pieces. Enough to know that what they're accusing him of is totally absurd. I'm not Jed's only family, by the way. There's Will. Will McClain. Is he around?"

"No. But I'll let Jed fill you in on everything that's

happened since you, Will and Frannie all disappeared. If you won't stay with us, Emmy, promise you'll at least come to dinner tonight. Eight-thirty. I'm ten minutes from the rental. If we meet now and you find the house suitable, that'll give you time to unpack and rest a bit before dinner.''

"Wait. I'd love to see Jed, but I'll have to reserve judgment on renting the house.'' Emmy felt bowled over, and yet her words reflected a smile.

"Fair enough. A warning, though. I can be very persuasive."

Throughout Emmy's drive to the town's outskirts, she tried not to form any opinions about Jed's wife. As it happened, Mrs. Louis beat Emmy to Frannie's place. Technically Jed's, but to Emmy the house would always belong to Mom Fran.

She took her time climbing from the pickup and used the extra moments to inspect the woman her foster sibling had married. Before hanging up, Jed's wife had said her name was Gwyneth; please call her Gwyn, she'd added.

Emmy didn't know why, but she hadn't expected her to be so tall. Gwyn topped Emmy's five foot five by at least four inches. A thick auburn braid slapped a slender waist as she turned the key in the lock. The main thing Emmy noticed was that although Gwyn wore faded blue jeans, dusty boots and a plaid, western-style shirt, she had the carriage and bearing of someone born to wealth. Casual elegance. The kind enjoyed by women who strolled through the Shreveport casino shrouded in an aura of money and power. The genuine article. Not someone out to impress.

Emmy's instant perception was that Jed was a lucky man.

Gwyn's "Hi" wafted across the lawn in a low contralto as she beckoned Emmy through an already open door. "We're birds of a feather, I see." Gwyn pointed to Emmy's pickup, then to her own green Land Rover parked by the neighboring fence. "We truck women have to band together. I hope you're a coffee drinker, too. I brought a thermos and two mugs." She had them hooked on three fingers of her left hand. A hand flashing a gorgeous diamond wedding set.

Somewhat tongue-tied, Emmy merely nodded. Jed's wife was a bit of a whirlwind.

Gwyn disappeared into the kitchen, saying she'd pour their coffee. The distinctive aroma reached out to Emmy. Exactly what she needed to fight off waves of nostalgia that struck the minute she stepped inside. Although the living room carpet was new, the furnishings different, the decor modernized, memories of her life here catapulted Emmy back to childhood. Standing there, she realized again that those years had, without doubt, been the best she'd ever known. Why had she waited so long to come home? Only it wasn't her home—not really. Where *did* she belong?

"Emmy?" Gwyn extended a steaming cup. "Are you all right? I'll, uh, wait in the kitchen if you'd prefer to explore on your own."

Accepting the mug, Emmy swallowed several times and shook her head. "It's very different from my recollections. Smaller, for one thing." She rolled stiff shoulders.

"I found it comfortable enough for me and my animals." Gwyn laughed. "The cat and dog didn't fight me for the only bathroom. How ever did four of you manage, though?"

Relaxing minutely, Emmy sipped the strong, black coffee. "We had a schedule. Mom Fran and I showered at night, the boys in the morning. Jed always complained that Will hogged the bathroom and used all the hot water."

"Jed talks in fits and spurts about that time in his life. Finding your foster mom's remains on his property was a horrendous shock."

"I can imagine. No, that's not true. I can't imagine it. How did that archaeologist come to be digging there?"

"My fault, I'm afraid. I leased pastureland from Jed for the miniature horses I raise. When he first discovered they were miniature, he hit the roof. He doesn't consider the breed a horse. You may not know, but Jed raises mammoth Percherons. Tessa Lang, the archaeologist, wanted to dig for Caddo Indian artifacts. Jed believed her excavation would spook his herd, so he refused her request. He and I argued a lot back then." She grimaced slightly. "I thought Tessa's project had merit. She had a grant, and a deadline. Jed's decision seemed unfair, so I suggested she petition the court for the right to search for artifacts. I felt absolutely awful when among the first things Tessa found were Frannie's bones. I'm still sick over it, but there's no reversing what's happened."

"The article I read didn't mention it was Jed's land. Oh, Lord, poor Jed."

Gwyn paced the perimeter of the room. "Yes. Fielder's convinced the reason Jed made such a fuss over Tessa's dig was because he killed Mrs. Granger."

"That sheriff's a fool. He can't know Jed if he thinks that."

Worry lines creased Gwyn's smooth brow. "The evidence keeps mounting. Do you remember Amanda Jennings, Emmy?"

"Hard to forget Uncertain's Dolly Parton lookalike."

"Yes, well, there is that. According to Fielder's old

notes, Amanda reported that Jed skipped school the day Frannie disappeared.''

"I'll bet Amanda made that up. She used to tell lies about people to get them in trouble. Then she'd stand back and smirk.''

"She didn't make it up. I'm sure he'll tell you himself, but Jed's felt guilty for years over that. He and your foster mom argued the morning she vanished and he took off for the day. He's found it really hard, knowing that the last time they parted was in anger.''

"They argued?'' Emmy frowned.

"Yes. Some ongoing spat about Jed applying to Juilliard. I gathered Frannie thought music was a big waste of time.''

"And money,'' Emmy agreed slowly. "But no one was prouder of Jed's awards.'' Her frown deepened. "Gosh, I may have told the sheriff that Fran fussed at Jed that day. Until you brought it up, I'd forgotten Fielder came to school the next morning and questioned me. I was scared to death.'' Emmy ran a finger around the rim of her cup. "Will and I were always slowpokes. Fran was late for work, I think. Jed had a permission slip he wanted signed. Yes, now I do remember. They were turning the air blue as they walked out the back door. I dashed out the front to catch my bus.'' Emmy lifted her eyes to meet Gwyn's. "Will would have covered for Jed if he missed roll call. Will sometimes ditched class. Highly unusual for Jed, though. What's his story?''

"He took his boat out on the lake and spent the day cooling off. Apparently no one saw him. Without witnesses, it makes him look bad. If you can remember anything else…'' Gwyn pleaded.

"I wish I could. It happened so long ago.''

Gwyn turned to dump her coffee down the sink. She

stared out the window, saying nothing, but her shoulders were bowed.

"I'm glad Jed has you in his corner," Emmy said softly. "I don't know much about the law, Gwyn. Does Jed have a good lawyer?"

Nodding, Gwyn faced Emmy again. "Riley Gray handles Jed's business needs. The second time Sheriff Fielder questioned Jed in conjunction with the murder, Riley recommended Jed hire someone more experienced in criminal law. I suggested an old family friend, Dexter Thorndyke. He's well-known for winning difficult cases. Thorny agreed to advise Jed."

Emmy got hung up on the part about Riley doing legal work for Jed. Back when they all built forts and pretended to be pirates conquering the Caddo swamp, had the boys sneaked off by themselves and discussed what they'd be when they grew up? Emmy had daydreamed about marrying Riley Gray Wolf and caring for their kids while he went off to work. Those were secret dreams she hadn't shared with a soul. Funny thing about dreams—they hardly ever came true.

"Emmy? You seem miles away."

"What? Oh." She blushed. "I...er...don't think I've ever heard of Mr. Thorndyke. Isn't the evidence Sheriff Fielder has on Jed circumstantial? Surely a good attorney will get him off."

Gwyn sighed. "I hope so. Anyway, I've probably bent your ear enough. Jed can answer any other questions you might have. If the house meets with your approval, I'll take off and let you get settled. I'm on my way into town. Now, don't forget—dinner at eight-thirty. I assume you know how to get to Beaumarais?"

"Yes." Emmy pictured the big white mansion on the hill that Jed used to say would eventually belong to him.

Everyone but Will and Emmy had laughed at his prediction. The families of the other kids in the area were involved with timber, oil or cattle. Who could blame them for thinking throwaway kids would never have two dimes to rub together? So true in her case. But Emmy had no clue as to her ancestry, while Jed had always known he was the illegitimate son of a mother whose family was filthy rich.

"Gwyn, shouldn't you wait and discuss my coming to dinner with Jed? Not to mention the possibility that I might be renting our old house... Give him time to adjust to the idea of dealing with another ghost from the past?"

Gwyn paused at the door. "Frankly, Jed will be overjoyed to see how flesh-and-blood you are, Emmy. Since we got back from our short honeymoon, he's talked about trying to locate you and Will. I'm not sure, but he may be scared to death Tessa will unearth you and Will from that site next. Of course, Fielder hasn't given her permission to reopen her dig, although she's hounding him to lift the ban."

Emmy followed Gwyn outside. "Since I first read the article, I've had a difficult time believing it's true. I feel as though it happened in another life." She shook her head. "I was just a kid, but I know Mom Fran was well-liked. She worked hard. Work and us three kids were her life. I've racked my brain and I can't fathom why anyone would murder her."

"Nor can Jed. He said if it happened today, he'd guess a random act of violence. Nineteen years ago, he said, Uncertain was as safe as any place could be."

"I'm glad you were here to help Jed through the funeral. I know it's belated, but I'd like to take flowers to the cemetery if you'll direct me to her grave."

Gwyn's lips contorted. "Fielder refused to release

the—the—remains. There hasn't been a service yet, which makes it doubly hard on Jed."

"Gwyn, that's terrible! You know, I haven't been sure about sticking around. But how can I *not* stay and support Jed?"

"Oh, Emmy…"

A child's voice interrupted Gwyn's struggle to complete her thanks.

Emmy glanced around and saw a little girl hanging over the fence. She had hair the color of midnight gathered on either side of her head in two corkscrew ponytails. Blue jeans tapered over scuffed white sneakers. A frilly pink blouse enhanced a delicate bone structure.

Emmy smiled at the girl. She was no judge of children's ages, but this one couldn't be more than four or five.

Gwyn returned the girl's wave. "Hi, Alanna."

"Miss Gwyn, are you moving back to the little house?"

"No. Remember, I married Jed Louis? You were the flower girl at our wedding. This is Emmy Monday, Alanna. She's going to live here."

"We didn't discuss price," Emmy protested. "I may not be able to afford it."

"Fiddlesticks." Gwyn brushed aside Emmy's concerns. "It's up to Jed, but I'd be surprised if he lets you pay."

"I'm not here to freeload," she said firmly. "I have money. Just not a lot. Depending on how long I stay, I'll probably need to find a job."

The child at the fence prattled on. "Emmy's a nice name. And you look nice, not grumpy like Mrs. Yates. Tonight I'll ask Daddy if you can baby-sit me instead of her."

Emmy cast a startled glance at the child, then appealed to Gwyn for aid. Emmy had once worked for a temporary agency in Galveston who'd sent her to fill in for a sick nanny. The children were younger than this girl, one a baby and the other a toddler. Emmy had enjoyed the assignment, but she'd never had occasion to repeat it. "Who is this precocious child?" she muttered out of the side of her mouth. Louder, to the little girl, she said, "Your name is pretty, too."

"Emmy, meet Alanna Gray," Gwyn said, handling the introductions. "I believe I mentioned her dad is Jed's friend and attorney on business matters," she added.

"Riley lives next door? In that house?" Floored by the news, Emmy gaped at the child. *Riley's daughter.* She supposed that if she compared them feature for feature, she'd see a resemblance to Riley in the smoky-black eyes and impish grin. The boy Emmy recalled so well had been wiry but strong. Totally masculine. Riley had always walked with an inherent male swagger. Alanna's girlish attributes obviously came from her mother. *Her mother! What had Cassie said about Riley's wife?* Something vague; Emmy couldn't quite recall it.

"Miss Emmy? Will you ask Mrs. Yates to let me come over and play with your kitty and doggie?"

Still reeling, Emmy responded too sharply. "I don't have any pets."

"She'll be so disappointed," Gwyn whispered. "Mrs. Yates is terribly allergic. Alanna loved my animals. I'm afraid I let her pretend one of my kittens was hers while I lived here." She raised her voice again. "Oh, I forgot to say, in addition to raising miniature horses, I'm also an animal agent." When Emmy failed to comment, Gwyn explained. "I supply many of the pets used in local TV commercials or magazine ads. I'm like a casting agent. I negotiate fees and monitor work hours and schedules. Animals are a lot like child stars. I make sure they're not exploited.''

Finally, slowly coming out of her stupor, Emmy darted a surreptitious glance at Alanna Gray. "You have an unusual job, Gwyn. It sounds very interesting. I… ah…assume if Alanna stays with a sitter it's because her mom also works. What does she do?''

Gwyn pitched her reply an octave lower, although Alanna had dropped from the fence to chase after a squirrel. "Her mom died. When Alanna was a baby." Gwyn followed the child with dark, sympathetic eyes.

"I didn't know." Emmy's brows drew together. "Cassie—someone I knew from before—works at the café in town. She said Riley had gotten married and that he had a child. I wish she'd told me his wife passed away. I ran into him at the bank. Literally ran into him. He asked me out for coffee. I'm afraid I acted rather rude when he didn't suggest having his wife join us.''

"You thought he was playing around on her?" Gwyn exclaimed in surprise. "I haven't known him long, but that doesn't strike me as Riley's style. He's devoted to his law practice and to Alanna. Jed's had to pry him out of the house for anything social.''

"Obviously he's changed. The old Riley dated two or three girls at once. Even when he was underage, he played pool and threw darts four or five nights a week at Crazy Jake's Pub. He was exceptionally social back then.''

The little girl again appeared to swing on the fence. She chimed in on the conversation. "My daddy's got a pool table and a dart board. I can't play. Only big people can." She issued a tragic sigh that made Gwyn and Emmy grin.

"Your daddy taught me to throw darts when I was a kid," Emmy said. "Because I bugged him. He's patient, though. He never made fun of my mistakes. Once you're a bit older, Alanna, I'm sure he'll teach you."

"You knew my daddy when you were little?"

Emmy nodded, sharp memories propelling her back to a time when she'd followed Riley around like a stray puppy. He'd eventually grown tired of having her always at his heels, and had taught her to throw darts so she'd give him some space. It had the opposite effect. He'd finally noticed her—noticed she was growing up.

Standing here looking at the child he'd created with another woman, Emmy forced her mind off Riley and onto darts. In later years, the game relaxed her, had carried her back to happier times, so she made it a point to play regularly. With each match, she captured bits and pieces of Riley. His muscular brown arm reaching around to steady her hand. His gravelly voice whispering in her ear.

Darn, this wasn't smart.

Alanna spoke, distracting Emmy from a bout of melancholy. "That's cool. Did you know my daddy then, too, Miss Gwyn?"

"No. I was raised in a city a long way from here." Gwyn glanced over Alanna's head, toward the house. "I hear Mrs. Yates calling you. Tell her I was introducing you to your new neighbor." Gwyn wagged a hand at the waiting sitter.

Alanna appeared reluctant to leave. She turned several times and resorted to skipping backward on one foot, continuing to wave at Gwyn and Emmy.

Then the older woman came down the steps to meet the girl, and after the two of them had disappeared, Gwyn released a pent-up breath. "If you don't like children,

Emmy, you'll have to set firm limits. Alanna is grown-up for her age, but she's lonely. Mrs. Yates is getting on in years, and Alanna wears her out. I'm afraid I allowed her to run in and out of my place at will.''

"What makes you think I don't like children?'' A breeze had sprung up and Emmy had to sweep strands of her silvery-blond hair away from her eyes in order to see Gwyn.

"I wasn't being judgmental, Emmy. But it wasn't my imagination that you stiffened up when I introduced Alanna.''

Emmy realized she probably had stiffened up. It was a major shock hearing Riley lived next door. That didn't mean she cared to tell Gwyn Louis every detail involving her history with Riley Gray Wolf. Indeed, the good memories might have existed only in Emmy's imagination, so the less she said about him the better. Still, knowing how rumors swept through Uncertain, Emmy hated to leave Gwyn with the impression that she didn't like Riley's daughter. "I've never really known any kids. I spent the last five years on a floating casino dealing blackjack during the witching hours,'' she explained. "Otherwise, my experience with kids is limited to those I met briefly when I toured with the circus. She seems a darling girl.''

"A blackjack dealer and circus performer? Quite a mix of talents. I definitely want to hear more at our next visit. Call me nosy, but…when you raised your arm a minute ago, the neck of your blouse drooped. Well, there's no way except to ask straight out. Is that a real tattoo you have…there?'' Gwyn's lips twitched as she brushed a forefinger along the upper edge of her own breast to indicate where she meant.

Emmy rolled her eyes, then laughed. "It's real. Please don't tell Jed.''

"Why not? To borrow a phrase from Alanna, it's cool! Goodness, I really have to run." Gwyn checked a serviceable watch that was at odds with the rings she wore. Emmy accompanied her as she hurried to the Rover and climbed in. Before closing her door, she impulsively reached out and squeezed Emmy's hand. "I can't wait to tell Jed who's going to be living in his rental. He'll be so happy." Her expression grew bleak for a moment. "I'm afraid happiness is something he's lacked for too long. He still feels he has something to prove to the residents of Uncertain, if not the world. I'm counting on you to help me show him how to have more fun, Emmy. It'll be good for all of us to have family around." She nodded. "That's what you are—his family. And now, mine, too."

Emmy said little. She pulled her hand away and shut Gwyn's door. Staring after the rumbling vehicle as Gwyn backed down the lane, Emmy felt the tic beginning under her right eye. For years she'd been plagued with a jumpy nerve. It came whenever tension built. As pleasant as Jed's wife seemed, Emmy couldn't buy into the bubbly prediction that the three of them would be a family. The spiraling sense of letdown clutching at her stomach was something she'd had to contend with ever since Social Services dragged her away from here. Jed, at least, had roots. She'd never really belonged anywhere.

As Emmy hauled the first box of her things into a house filled with ghosts, she renewed an earlier vow to initiate a search for her birth parents.

No sooner had the thought struck her than a tan-and-white county police car roared off the main road and came to a halt behind her pickup. The very presence of a police vehicle in this particular drive set Emmy's nerves roiling.

Hoping she gave an appearance of unconcern, she stacked boxes on her pickup's tailgate. She manhandled three into the house, recognizing an older Sheriff Fielder as he and a deputy climbed from the car. In spite of knowing she'd done nothing wrong and had nothing to hide, Emmy's heart sped up. Sweat broke out on her upper lip and her palms.

The leathery-faced sheriff hitched his pants up lean hips and closed a gnarled hand over a holstered service revolver. His scowl hadn't changed, Emmy thought, but his face had grown craggier. He didn't wear a hat today, and she saw that his brown hair was now liberally streaked with silver.

"Moving in or out?" the deputy asked inanely.

Emmy supposed she shouldn't smart off under the circumstance, but she wasn't known to suffer fools lightly. "Given the efficiency of the rumor mill in this town, I think you already know the answer to that question."

She bit her lip. Darn, but Fielder had always had the ability to make her feel guilty just by staring at her from faintly accusing eyes. Maturity hadn't changed that reaction, either. Emmy's knees knocked inside her jeans.

"Are you the Emerald Monday who lived here with Frannie Granger?" Fielder asked in a gruff voice.

"Yes." She found her mouth too dry to expand on that.

"My daddy always said bad pennies have a way of turning up again. You've been gone a good piece, little lady. What brings you back now?"

"I'm not a *little* lady, Sheriff. I'm full grown. Thirty-two if Fran got my birthdate correct. That's one reason I'm here." She glanced toward the house. "I read a news article that said you'd found my foster mother's body. I'd hoped while you're investigating who killed her, some clue might turn up as to who I was…uh…who I am.''

The sheriff gave her his famous blank stare. ''So that's your story? Seems odd you'd suddenly get an urge to know at thirty-two. Why not when you came of age?''

Emmy crossed her arms and leaned a shoulder negligently against the door casing. She hadn't invited her surprise guests inside, nor would she unless they insisted. ''At eighteen I worked two jobs to keep from starving. Finding the person or persons who dumped me at Monday Trade Days ranked sort of low on my list of priorities.''

''Humph.'' The sheriff feigned interest in a notebook he'd pulled from his shirt pocket. ''Where you been living?''

Emmy thought about telling him to find out himself if he was such a hotshot investigator. She discarded that idea almost as quickly as it had come. ''Shreveport,'' she said. ''I worked in a casino owned and operated by Richard Parrish. He's in the phone book if you'd like to check that out.''

''Don't think I won't, missy.'' He grunted. ''Can't say I'm glad to see you. Trouble had a way of following you, Louis, Gray Wolf and that McClain kid. I suppose he'll show up next.''

''I wouldn't know. I haven't been in contact with my foster siblings since I left town. If you've got no other questions…'' Emmy made a point of checking her watch before brushing past the sheriff to drag another box from the bed of her pickup.

''Where were you the day Frannie Granger vanished?''

Emmy felt her slippery, sweaty fingers lose their grip on the box. Carefully, she tightened her hold. ''When she left for work, I was heading out the front door to meet my school bus. I think you know Jed called all over town that night when she failed to come home. I was terrified. We all were.''

"Why did you three go off to school the next day as if nothing was wrong?''

"Joleen Berber, Fran's best friend, notified the police. They said we should go on about our business. It was you. You said it.''

"On day two, Jed managed to attend his classes, yet he was truant the day before.''

"I don't know about that. We attended different schools.''

"It says here you were thirteen. Old enough, I'd think, to ask why the woman who'd served as your mother would just up and run off.''

"Oh, I asked all right. I asked the social worker who yanked me out of class because *you* reported us. She brought me here and packed my things. I cried. I begged. I demanded to know what was going on. I was told nothing. Zero. That's it, Sheriff. That's all I know. Until a week ago I didn't even know Mom Fran never came home.'' Emmy's voice thinned at that point. She stopped speaking.

"Why did Jed wait so long to phone Joleen? Was Frannie in the habit of staying out? Did she often leave you three kids on your own to fix supper?''

Emmy opened her mouth to flatly deny the last two questions. As to the first, she was thrown painfully back to the night they'd all been so frantic, when Fran hadn't phoned or come home. Emmy had to clear her throat twice to control her temper at Fielder. She steadied the box filled with her cooking spices and kitchen utensils against the porch railing. ''From the tone of these questions, I think I'd prefer to have an attorney present before I answer anything else.''

Fielder slammed his black notebook shut. ''Suit yourself. I suppose since you're moving in next to Gray Wolf he's probably advised you already. From where I sit, clamming up only makes matters worse. I *will* get answers.''

''Riley hasn't advised me. Anyway, I understand his expertise is in the field of business law. I'll ask Jed to recommend someone when I see him tonight.''

''Your unwillingness just drives another spike in Jed's shaky defense.''

''That's ridiculous! You can't blame him because I want representation. Jed was plenty worried when Mom Fran didn't come home. But he was the oldest. He had to act brave so Will and I wouldn't fall apart. What would *you* have done at seventeen, Sheriff? Jed was very responsible for his age. Now, excuse me, I'm finished with this interview. I'll phone your office tomorrow and leave the name of my lawyer.''

Sheriff Fielder shook a finger at Emmy. ''Just see that you don't take a hike. Not until I'm satisfied I have answers to every last question. Somebody killed Fran Granger in my town and I'm damn well going to find out who did it.''

''I hope you do, and I mean that sincerely.'' Turning her back on the men, Emmy pushed open the screen door with her foot and carried the box into the kitchen. She didn't realize how hard her hands were shaking until she heard Fielder's car start and she couldn't lift the curtain aside to watch him go.

Emmy unloaded the carton she'd brought in, thinking all the while how foolish she'd been to pull up stakes on a whim. The sheriff wasn't going to help her find out anything about her background. He only seemed bent on pinning Fran's murder on Jed. Did that mean Jed was in a more serious predicament than Gwyn had indicated?

"Lord," Emmy groaned. Whatever had possessed her to treat the sheriff in such a cavalier manner? Now he thought she was hiding something. She wasn't. And she didn't exactly have the funds to hire an attorney.

On her return to finish unloading her pickup, Emmy was surprised to again see Riley's daughter draped over the fence.

"Are you in trouble?" the child asked in hushed tones.

"No, honey. The sheriff stopped by to say hello."

"He sounded mad."

"I guess he did. But don't you worry about it, okay?"

"My daddy helps people who got problems. I can ask him to help you."

"No, don't," Emmy said harshly, grabbing for a small box that tumbled from the stack she'd gathered. "I...mean, don't bother your daddy. I'm sure he has more than enough on his hands."

"'kay. Mrs. Yates is washing windows. She said since Miss Gwyn knows you, I can visit. I could help you unpack, Miss Emmy," the child said in a wistful voice.

"Call me Emmy without the miss, Alanna."

"That's not proper, Daddy said."

"Um." *Manners.* Was it moving into this house that reminded Emmy of how hard Fran had worked to teach the three of them proprieties? At times it must have seemed a daunting task. Emmy capitulated with a smile. "By all means, tell Mrs. Yates that *Miss* Emmy cordially invites you to assist me with the task of moving."

"Huh? So, can I say you want me to help you unpack?"

Emmy bobbed her head, remembering too well what

it was like to be a lonely kid. "I'm only going to unpack my clothes, though. Gwyn invited me to dinner, so I have to allow enough time to shower and dress."

"You got a pretty dress?" Alanna asked, cocking her head to one side.

"A dress?" Emmy halted on the lower step and half turned, causing her stack of boxes to wobble. She had worn uniforms of a sort at the casino. The few dresses she owned were glittery cocktail wear.

"Me'n Daddy ate there when Miss Gwyn and Mr. Jed got married. Daddy wore his best suit. He bought me a pink dress with lots of ruffles."

Emmy heaved a sigh of relief as she set the boxes inside the house. "Weddings call for special dresses, Alanna. When you just go to someone's house for dinner, a fancy dress isn't necessary."

"Oh. I like dresses. My prettiest ones are too little now." She dropped to the ground. "Daddy told Mrs. Yates to take me to the store to buy some. She bought me overalls." The girl gave a disgusted sigh. "Now I look like a boy."

Emmy laughed out loud. "No one would ever mistake you for a boy, Alanna. You're a girlie girl."

"I am?" she asked, raising her voice to be heard over the noise of an approaching car. "Hey, my daddy's home!" Alanna ran to the edge of the driveway, jumped up and down and waved madly.

Far from ready to chat over the back fence with Riley Gray Wolf, Emmy hurried inside with the last of her boxes. She peered at him through a crack in the kitchen curtains, taking care to not be seen.

A midnight-blue Chrysler convertible slowed dramatically. When Riley parked and leaned over to open the passenger door for his daughter, Emmy saw he'd re-

moved his suit coat and had the sleeves of his white shirt
rolled up above his elbows. The man had nicely muscled
arms. Emmy had always thought that. She'd been crazy
about Riley's body. There had been something about the
broad set of his shoulders and the narrowness of his hips;
even at the age of sixteen he'd turned female heads.

Emmy let the curtain fall. She was dwelling far and
away too much on the adult Riley's body. Did he work
out to keep fit? Had he grown chest hair? If he ever found
out she'd eavesdropped on him and Will one evening,
when the two boys were discussing Riley's lack of chest
and facial hair, she'd die of embarrassment. Jed and Will
both shaved early. Riley envied them in the worst way.
Emmy had felt bad for him. She'd baked his favorite
peanut-butter cookies to console him, then lacked the
nerve to tell him she'd spied. He'd thanked her for the
treat with the half grin that always made her insides
queasy. She paused in shuffling boxes to speculate
whether peanut-butter cookies were still Riley's favorite.

"Enough already," Emmy grumbled, striding into the
bedroom to sort out something to wear to Jed's. She
made every effort to blank her mind to all memories out
of the past as she let hot water from the shower massage
her tight neck.

After trying on and discarding several outfits, she settled on toast-brown linen pants and a buttery-yellow
blouse. She clasped her hair at the nape of her neck with
a broad gold clasp, and chose a gold herringbone neck-
lace and bracelet Richard had given her for Christmas.
She dug a brown cardigan out of a box. It was cash-
mere—in case Alanna had been right about dinner at the
Louis home being dressy.

Emmy started her pickup and let it cough itself into
running smoothly before she backed out of the drive. She

saw someone lift a blind in Riley's house. Had Alanna told him she'd moved in next door? Probably. The kid was a chatterbox. Emmy chuckled; people used to say the same about her. She still ran off at the mouth when she got nervous.

Ten minutes later, when she guided her old pickup through the impressive, monogrammed wrought-iron gates at the bottom of the hill leading up to Beaumarais, Emmy's nerves were jangling. She didn't recall the house being quite so intimidating. Maybe because, as a kid, she'd only viewed it from afar. No one liked Jed's Uncle Walter, the old geezer who owned the property. Least of all Jed. He'd felt cast off by his mother's brother, who referred to Jed as a bastard. Yet now, this all belonged to him.

Horses grazed contentedly in an adjacent pasture. A dog frolicked in the side yard. Lights blazed from tall, mullioned windows, and if she looked closely, she could count the many chandeliers.

Emmy's battered pickup looked out of place in the broad circular drive. Her knees banged together as she walked to the door to face a man she hadn't seen in almost twenty years.

Family. Jed is family. And you're the poor relation, a little voice whispered.

When Emmy's tentative knock was answered by a regal-looking woman who bade her come in and have a seat in the parlor, Emmy was positive she didn't belong. She ought to have her head examined for accepting Gwyn's invitation.

From the parlor, Emmy could see into the dining room. Tapered candles lit a gleaming mahogany table elegantly set with crystal goblets and eggshell-white china. "Alanna was right," Emmy muttered. This house called for a pretty dress.

CHAPTER THREE

HER STOMACH too jumpy to let her sit on the ornate peach couch or either of two spindly chairs, Emmy walked around and studied the room. She desperately hoped it would give her a clue as to the man Jed Louis had become. Under her feet was an oriental rug that picked up shades from the couch, chair cushions and heavy satin drapes. Light spilled from a gorgeous old Tiffany lamp, softening the hues. But nothing here connected with the Jed Emmy remembered. The tidiest of the three kids, Jed had gravitated toward stark black shirts and pants. His side of the bedroom, furnished sparsely as they all were, had been decorated in black and red.

Fran might have selected the curtains, but Emmy thought Jed had gone with her to Tyler to pick out his own bedspread and sheets. Will had scoffed at choosing stuff to sleep on. Will had been happy just to have a bed.

Hearing the approach of heavy footsteps, Emmy spun away from a landscape watercolor she'd been examining. Goose bumps rose on her arms. She clutched the empty arms of the sweater she'd draped around her shoulders, and tried to ward off the chill that came with the anticipation of their first meeting.

Jed strode into the room, his cocksure walk so familiar to Emmy in spite of the tears distorting her vision. Though his image had suddenly blurred, his lanky six-four frame appeared little different from the way he looked in a dog-eared photo she carried in her wallet. He was deeply tanned, and his angular features still set off his mesmerizing blue eyes.

He stepped fully into the room and gripped the hands she fluttered toward him. "Emmy." He expelled the single word with a gust of emotion. Jed's throat worked as his grip tightened. "You grew up fine, little sister. So very fine." He hesitated briefly, then gathered her into a hug. "I can't begin to tell you how I've missed you, Emmy-M." His gruff voice sounded close to disintegrating as he called her by the nickname he'd chosen for her as a kid.

Emmy fought against the tears scalding her eyelids. The way Jed ran her first name and last initial together made it sound like M&M's—the brightly coated chocolate candies Jed used to give her as a treat. Wresting herself away, she picked up her fallen cardigan and dropped it onto the purse she'd set on the couch. "Then why—tell me why—you didn't find me and bring me back?"

Jed scraped a hand through his short-cropped hair. "Lordy, Emmy, if you only knew how hard I tried. I got home that day and found a terse note from someone saying the state had taken you. Will read it, panicked, packed his duffel bag and lit out for the territories." Will McClain had always reminded Emmy and Jed of Mark Twain's characters. An amused quirk of Jed's lips aided his feeble attempt to joke, and Emmy smiled briefly, too. "I must have made a hundred phone calls after that, trying to find you. Everything here was in chaos." He paced to the window and propped a hand against the casing. "Try to understand, Emmy."

"I guess I never thought about how tough it must've

been for you. But later, Jed, after things settled down. Couldn't you have tracked me down then?''

''I tried. So did Riley. He stormed the office of social services in Tyler. They tossed his butt in jail. I didn't have the money to bail him out. His mom borrowed from her brother to post his bond.''

''Riley did that for me?'' Her eyes teared and her voice grew high and shaky.

''He did. He acted like a wildman. But his run-in with the law really cooled our heels. As it was, I was just weeks away from graduation, and everything was going down the tubes. Ray Jennings surprised the hell out of me. He stepped up and lent me a hand. I figured out later he didn't want to lose the Beaumarais accounts. At the time, all I knew was that he saved my bacon.''

Emmy released a long, shuddering breath. ''Sorry for coming on so strong. There's no need to belabor this, Jed. I know the struggle it takes to survive. I ditched my last foster placement the second I turned eighteen. I hitchhiked to Florida where I ended up working with a lion tamer in a traveling circus.''

''You traveled with a circus? God, Emmy. I may have stayed here, but that's not to say I ever understood why you and Will never bothered to see what had become of me. Or of Frannie.''

Emmy winced. ''I can't speak for Will. But I worked hard to wall off every trace of my life before Houston. You know, with the passing years, pain and frustration subside and memories fade—at least a little. Enough to allow you to function in a new life. You must've experienced that, too. Where's Gwyn? She and I talked a little bit about that.''

''She wanted to give us time alone to sort out the past.'' Jed's full smile softened his hollow cheeks. ''Isn't

Gwyn something? The best thing that's ever happened to me since my mom died and Frannie took me in."

"Jed," Emmy said hesitantly. "What do you think happened to Mom Fran?"

"It's a relief to know you don't accept the consensus around town that I did her in."

"Never," she said fiercely.

He tucked his hands into his pockets and rocked back on his heels. "I've lain awake nights trying to reconstruct the weeks leading up to the day she disappeared. You may remember she and I quarreled over a stupid permission form that morning." Jed removed a hand from a pocket and swiped it over his jaw. His eyes turned bleak. "It hasn't been easy living with that guilt."

"I don't imagine it has," Emmy murmured. "They *will* get to the truth, won't they?"

"They would if Fielder wasn't so focused on me." Jed sounded bitter.

Emmy's voice was far from steady. "Ri-ght before I came here tonight, the sheriff and a deputy paid me a visit. I—I answered a few questions. Then Fielder took out a notebook and started grilling me about stuff that happened back then. I refused to answer without having an attorney present. I don't have a lot saved up, Jed. Can you recommend a competent but not-too-expensive lawyer?"

Before Jed had an opportunity to answer, the woman who'd ushered Emmy into the house reappeared. Jed glanced at his watch. "June, why are you still here?"

"Miss Gwyn told me to leave on time, but I wanted to fix a special meal for you tonight. It's ready in the oven. I'm leaving now."

"Why, thank you. I appreciate your thoughtfulness and I know Gwyn does, too. Emmy, June and her husband worked for my uncle. I couldn't have managed the estate without them, especially in the early years when I was a greenhorn. June, Emmy is the long-lost sister I told you about.''

The woman issued a warm greeting before she donned a light jacket and hurried out the front door, leaving Jed to show Emmy into the dining room.

Gwyn appeared at the bottom of a winding staircase. Stepping down, she accepted Jed's outstretched hand, all the while glancing expectantly between her husband and Emmy.

Jed ushered both women into the dining room and pulled out cane-backed chairs on either side of where he'd sit at the head of the table. "Don't look so worried," he told his wife. "Emmy and I talked through some old stuff. As you'd expect, there are regrets on both sides." He squeezed Emmy's hand as he seated her. "If only we'd been older and more in control of our lives. Hardly a day goes by that I don't start a sentence with *if only....*''

Emmy unfolded her napkin and spread it across her lap. "My stock phrase is *what if?* Like, what if I was really a princess stolen at birth? Stuff like that," she said with a self-deprecating laugh.

Jed accepted the basket of rolls Gwyn passed him. "I feel I should apologize because things worked out so well for me, Emmy, and you've had it rough," he said, handing her the silver basket.

"Don't be silly. After the rotten way your uncle treated you and your mom, Jed, you deserve good things. Not that I call being a murder suspect good. But at least you know there aren't any criminals in your background." She broke off a corner of her roll. "What's my recourse if Fielder tosses some accusation like that against me?"

Gwyn gasped. "He wouldn't...couldn't do that. Jed?"

Her light-blue eyes sought concurrence from Jed as she set a platter of fish on the table.

He served the main course, while Gwyn retrieved two side dishes. "Tracing roots is supposedly easier now, Emmy, with the Internet and everything. Have you tried? I know the uncertainty, the doubt, always bothered you, even as a kid."

"That's one reason I'm here," Emmy admitted. "I've imagined finding my birth parents for so long and did nothing. When I read the article saying…that archaeologist found Mom Fran's, uh, bones, my circumstances had just changed. For the first time, I had the freedom—and the money—to return and possibly mount a search. Now I'm seesawing again. Since I've decided to hire an attorney, I may have to forgo hunting for my parents. It was probably a dumb idea, anyway. I haven't got the foggiest notion where to start."

Gwyn sat, still holding a steaming dish of asparagus tips. "Maybe you could do both for one fee. An adopted friend of mine began her search through a lawyer. Why not hire Riley? For a nominal retainer, wouldn't he accompany you to Fielder's office?"

"Oh, I couldn't ask him." Emmy's mouth twisted. So did her heart. "Anyway, Gwyn, you were the one who said his field is more business-oriented."

"It is, but Riley counseled Jed at first. Fielder hasn't accused you of anything, has he, Emmy?"

She shook her head. "He said not to leave town. Right after he said trouble followed me. Of course, he included Riley and Will in that remark. I frankly doubt it would improve my circumstances to show up at Fielder's office with Riley in tow."

"I'm in no position to offer you an opinion," Jed said. "But if you're strapped for cash, I'm sure Riley would help as a favor. For old time's sake. Otherwise, you'll need to hire someone from Jefferson or Tyler. Those guys charge transport fees to come here, on top of high hourly rates.'' Jed touched a napkin to his lips and cleared his throat. ''In case you can't tell, this is the voice of experience speaking.''

Emmy knew Jed and Gwyn thought she ought to contact Riley. They wouldn't understand her reluctance. Nor did she want to go into her reasons. Trying to explain the mad crush she'd had on Riley at thirteen sounded like a lame excuse for not seeking his help all these years later. Even to Emmy.

Although, goodness, the man hadn't lost all that much sleep over *her*. Forget what Jed had said about Riley spending a few nights in jail for trying to locate her; clearly, he'd wasted little time in finding someone else to fall in love with and marry.

In all fairness, though, Emmy couldn't hold that against him. Her memories of Riley hadn't stopped her from entering an occasional relationship. Nor had he been the main reason for her never taking the matrimonial plunge. That came down to an unrelenting fear of the gaps in her ancestry. But people who hadn't actually walked in her shoes would never understand the ongoing worry that something horrid might lurk in her genes— waiting to emerge in the next generation. It was a fear that struck every time Emmy moved to a new city and changed doctors. Their forms asking for family history remained painfully blank.

Richard insisted she could undergo blood tests to see if she carried something like hemophilia. But what if her father had been a rapist or if her mother had been mentally unbalanced? Blood tests wouldn't disclose those facts.

"Thanks for the advice," she muttered. "I'll give it serious thought." And she turned the problem over in her mind as talk about law and lawyers continued throughout dinner. Jed and Gwyn ate as they talked. Emmy picked at her food.

Gwyn finally pushed back her chair and folded her napkin. "Let's have our coffee and dessert in the library. We'll discuss happier subjects than our need for lawyers."

"Good idea." Jed got to his feet. "I'll bring the coffee," he said, opening the door leading to the kitchen.

"What you ate tonight wouldn't feed a sparrow," Gwyn fussed as she hooked an arm through Emmy's and aimed her toward the back of the rambling house. "I hope meeting Jed didn't make you too nervous to eat."

Emmy gave her new friend an impulsive hug. "At first, maybe. But Jed's exactly as I recalled. Oh, I wish we had some way to locate Will. Who knows if he even stayed in the state? He mentioned joining the marines."

"Hmm. Maybe he just thought it sounded macho."

"I don't know what Jed's told you, Gwyn, but Will wasn't nearly as tough as he let on. Fran knew it was all a big act. She had a way of relating to troubled kids. It's sad that her life was cut short." Emmy sighed unhappily.

"Hey." Gwyn shook Emmy's arm. "We were going to change the subject, remember?"

Emmy stopped to stare when Gwyn snapped on several lamps in the massive room she'd called the library. Shelves of books did dominate, but unlike the parlor, the furniture here begged to be sat on. Two creamy leather couches flanked a ceiling-to-floor marble fireplace. A huge round glass top rested on a polished burl that served as a coffee table between the two couches. A comfortable-looking plaid chair with matching ottoman completed the arrangement.

A big cat sprang off a pillow on which she'd been napping and wound around Gwyn's legs. A dog, the sheltie she'd seen in the yard earlier, rose from his bed on the floor and came to sniff Emmy. "Oh, aren't you beautiful," she murmured, patting him as she slipped to her knees to look more closely at the regal cat.

"Watch Jed accuse me of having an ulterior motive for wanting coffee in the library. She's seal point Siamese. I'm weaning her kittens. Cleopatra is an excellent show cat and I bred her to pass on those qualities. The problem for a breeder is that not all of a litter is necessarily up to show standards. Cleo's awards and her pedigree ensured the sale of the best kittens but I've got a couple left." She rolled her eyes. "I believed my vet, who said Siamese tend to have small litters. Wouldn't you know, Cleo gave birth to six." Gwen held up six fingers.

"Are they terribly expensive? I'd love a kitten if they're not." Emmy absently stroked the dog's furry ears. "I don't care if I have a show-quality cat."

"If I say they're free, will you take two? It's certainly less lonely living by yourself if you have animals. Frannie's house is set so far off the main road, I was glad to have both a cat and a dog. I feel guilty shoving kittens at you. Maybe you'd rather get a dog."

"I've always thought I'd be more of a cat person, Gwyn. That probably sounds foolish, since I admitted I'd never owned either."

"Of course not. I love all animals, but some people lean toward a particular species. After we have coffee and a piece of the luscious pecan pie June made today,

I'll show you the two kittens and you can decide if you want one or both.''

Jed carried in a polished silver tray filled with a coffee service and three plates of pecan pie. ''I knew I shouldn't leave you two alone. Has my lovely wife twisted your arm to get you to take a kitten, Emmy?''

''There was very little arm-twisting going on. I practically begged her.'' Emmy grinned as she plumped the pillow Cleo had so recently left. ''And Alanna will be ecstatic if I come home with a cat. I think she was ready to trade me for Gwyn once she found out I didn't have any pets.''

Jed and Gwyn both chuckled. ''So you've met Riley's precocious offspring,'' Jed mused.

''I did,'' Emmy said. ''It's hard for me to think of Riley having a daughter. Somehow I imagined him with a houseful of boys.''

''Alanna has him wrapped around her little finger.'' Jed set the tray on the glass-topped table.

''Did you know Riley's wife?'' Emmy inquired casually.

Jed bounced the tips of his fingers together. ''I saw her a couple of times. She didn't much like Riley's friends. Not just me, but Rico and Jake, too.''

''Goodness,'' Emmy exclaimed. ''Did she think you bachelors would lead him astray?''

''I don't honestly know. And Riley's completely closed off that part of his life.''

Emmy said no more as she sat thinking that Riley must have loved his wife to distraction. It would be like him to deny his own pain.

Gwyn busily arranged the coffee cups and plates of pie so that the three of them sat in a cozy triangle. ''If you want to wash the animal hair off your hands, Emmy, you'll find a bathroom two doors down on your left. Pop into the room across the hall and see the kittens.''

Jumping at the opportunity to get off the subject of Riley and his child, even though she'd been the one to keep it alive, Emmy excused herself at once. She found the room with no trouble, but hesitated to touch the gleaming gold faucets. The bathroom was as grand as the rest of the house. The entire bathroom in her last apartment wasn't as big as this glassed-in shower stall. In fact, her whole apartment would probably have fit in this room, she thought as she left and shut off the light, then peeked at the kittens next door.

"They're adorable, Gwyn. But I can't choose. Maybe I'll take them both.''

Gwyn gave Jed an I-told-you-so grin.

The hour grew late as the three discussed Jed and Gwyn's horses. Jed and Emmy also reminisced about people from the past, while Gwyn listened, obviously captivated. After a while, Emmy caught herself yawning in spite of her interest and the help of strong chicory coffee.

"I think we need to call it a night,'' Gwyn said. "Why don't I drop by your house tomorrow with the kittens, Emmy? I have extra food and a cat bed in the barn that I'll bring, too. Shall we say late afternoon? That way, if you find anything that needs fixing in the house, it'll give you time to compile a list.''

"Speaking of the house,'' Emmy said, after gathering her purse and sweater, "we never discussed the rent.'' She pulled out her checkbook. "I assume you'll want the customary first and last months?''

Gwyn fell back, letting Jed escort Emmy to the door. "Call me sentimental,'' he said, after clearing his throat. "The place was as much a home to you as to me. Probably more so. You were there first, and if Frannie'd had the means, she would've tried to adopt you. She'd be very upset with me if I charged you to live in her home. And I'd like to pay for your lawyer, too.''

As if she understood that her husband's gesture had overwhelmed Emmy, Gwyn punched him on the arm. Then she grinned. ''He had no compunction about charging me. Grab the deal and run, Emmy.''

The tension shattered, they all laughed. Emmy rose on tiptoes and brushed a kiss on Jed's cheek. Then she turned and hugged Gwyn. ''Both of you—thanks. You shouldn't make me too comfortable—I may stay here forever. I can't accept your offer to pay for an attorney, though, and if you ever change your mind about the rent, I promise there won't be any hard feelings.''

''Scram, kid. I'm not going to change my mind.'' Jed slipped his arm around his wife, and they waved from the steps as Emmy climbed into her truck. She navigated the circular drive and blinked her lights in a final goodbye.

On the drive to the place she'd always considered home, Emmy basked in the warmth from her visit with Jed and Gwyn. After nineteen years apart, she and Jed could so easily have found their reunion awkward, or worse. This was the kind of homecoming she'd often envisioned with her birth parents.

For years after Emmy had been ejected from the only home she knew and loved, she'd made up elaborate stories about Frannie Granger being her real mom. Even though she knew it wasn't true.... Fran had retold the story of her rescue many times—how Joleen Berber, a nurse and Frannie's best friend, had chanced upon Emmy at the back of an antique booth at Monday Trade Days. For a while, Emmy had convinced herself the two women had concocted the story to cover an illegitimate pregnancy. Reflecting on Frannie's life, Emmy saw the fallacy in her childish dream. Fran Granger cleaned homes for some of the town's most prominent and gossipy residents. Inside of six months, everybody for miles around would have known if she was pregnant.

Emmy slowed to turn into her driveway when it struck her that she had nothing in the house for breakfast. It was ten o'clock, so she doubted the town's general store would be open. But she'd prefer driving somewhere tonight over having no coffee, juice or toast in the morning. Admittedly, she was not a morning person.

She remembered passing a Winn-Dixie on her way into town. Stepping on the gas, Emmy drove on past her place, and also Riley's. She couldn't help noticing that his midnight-blue convertible wasn't where he'd parked it earlier. *It's in his garage,* said the voice of logic.

Yeah, right. More like he had a hot date. Gwyn had described him as a stay-at-home. But did Gwyn really know his habits?

Emmy had no problem finding the store. The lot was surprisingly full, considering the lateness of the hour. Stifling a yawn, Emmy grabbed a cart and took stock of the various aisles. She didn't intend to spend half the night tracking down a few items. As dairy products were on the far right, she elected to start there. Rounding the corner, she pushed her cart into someone else's. "Sorry," she gasped. A teasing quip about grocery shopping in her sleep died on Emmy's lips as she glanced up and into Riley Gray's dark eyes. She groped for something—anything—less inane to say. All she managed was a few unintelligible squeaks.

"Emmy." Inclining his head, Riley started to move around her.

Still off guard, she shuttled in the same direction and their carts again collided. Now her heart got into the act. It beat like a marching band.

Riley untangled his full cart from her nearly empty one, mumbling, "Two accidental meetings in one day could only happen in a town the size of Uncertain." In a cool offhand voice, he added, "Alanna tells me we're going to be neighbors. I should've known you'd go to Fran's. Listen, my daughter gets her feelings hurt easily. So, do us both a favor and don't encourage her visits. Now please excuse me, I have Mrs. Yates on overtime."

He whipped out of sight before Emmy corralled a sudden, wicked thought. Wicked because she pictured her and Riley making love on the floor between the dairy products and frozen foods. *Heavenly days! Where did that come from?* Quickly harnessing hormones that had run amuck, Emmy rushed after him, needing to make amends for her earlier rudeness at the bank. By the time she'd turned the unwieldy cart around, he was nowhere to be found. And she still owed him an apology.

Or maybe now Riley owed her one. Don't encourage Alanna, indeed. His daughter was lonely, for pity's sake. Surely Riley didn't think she'd be unkind to a kid.

Somehow, Emmy had lost her zeal for shopping. She continued down aisles, though, until she had everything she'd come for. There was still no sign of Riley when she checked out, or when she loaded the sacks into her pickup.

At home, his car again sat in the spot where he'd parked after work. Emmy thought about his work while she unloaded and stored her groceries. Considering the cold shoulder he'd shown her tonight, there was no way she'd ask him to represent her. She'd have to call Fielder in the morning and request additional time to hire counsel. Shoot, why not set her alarm and get up early and go tell Fielder to his face? Emmy didn't want the sheriff getting any idea that she was trying to weasel out of his questions.

IN THE MORNING, she followed through. But who should she meet walking out of the police offices as she headed in? Riley, that was who. "Not again," she muttered under her breath. Lord, but a man had no right to look so good this early in the morning. Sun glinted off the black hair he wore so much shorter these days. The natural bronze of his skin contrasted perfectly with a pale yellow shirt. His three-piece suit could only be termed professional, yet dashing.

Emmy was so thunderstruck, she stood like a ninny blocking his path.

A lopsided smile flickered on Riley's mouth. "Three people phoned this morning to see if I knew you were back in town. I didn't tell any of them how hard it would be to miss you. Are you stalking me, Ms. Monday?"

Folding her arms, Emmy measured his changed mood through half-closed eyes. "Are ladies in the habit of stalking you, Mr. Grrr-ay?" She stumbled, almost calling him Gray Wolf.

He clapped his right hand over his heart. "It's a cross we celebrities have to bear."

"Celebrity? Have I missed something?"

"The morning news?" He straightened his already straight tie and gave her a cocky grin.

"All right. Stop with the guessing games, Riley. Why were you on the news?" Emmy knew he wasn't putting her on. Men carrying cameras emerged from the side of the municipal building. Two or three of them packed equipment into the back of a van sporting the logo of a neighboring town's TV station.

"Does the name Porter Ashton ring a bell?"

Emmy filtered everyone she knew from their past through her brain and came up blank. She shook her head slowly. The way her response deflated Riley, Emmy wished she'd known the name.

"Obviously you haven't lived in Texas these last two years. Ashton has been running insurance scams in small towns from Brownsville to Uncertain. Up to now, he's successfully covered his tracks. Logan Fielder first alerted me to the fact that Ashton was in town. According to the FBI, he always hired a local attorney to handle his affairs. The feds suspected he paid big under the table to make sure he looked clean. This time he picked the wrong man. Last week I turned his falsified tax records over to the feds. We nailed him on twenty-four counts of tax evasion, fraud and numerous other infractions."

"Congratulations." Emmy felt deeply proud of Riley. More than she ought to feel considering the distance she'd been careful to put between them.

"You say that like you mean it." Riley sobered and ran an assessing gaze from her head to her toes. His dark eyes kindled with interest.

"Why wouldn't I mean it? You think I'm lying because I wasn't familiar with Ashton's name? Louisiana's been my home for the last few years. Anyway, I'm not an avid news fan. It was purely accidental I happened to see the article on Fran. The paper was outdated, at that."

Riley shoved his hands in his pants pockets and rattled his keys. "Will you answer one question, Emmy?"

Squinting up at him, she lifted a shoulder casually. "If I can."

"Why didn't you come back sooner? Even if you

weren't in a position to leave wherever the state placed
you, you might have written to let me know you were
okay. You up and fly off one day and you're able to
forget about me and everybody else you left behind?''

"No! It wasn't like that," she blurted. "I tried to run
away so many times. The first foster family drove me to
and from school and locked me in my room at night.
There were bars on the window, and they tore up the
letters I tried to send. The second family used a belt to
keep me in line. The third and fourth families had other
devious ways of ensuring that I stayed put. By the time
they moved me into the group home, I'd learned how to
bury any mention of my previous life.'' Silent tears
slipped from her eyes and slid over her cheeks, but she
didn't make any move to wipe them away.

Riley did it for her. He clasped her face gently between
his hands and smoothed his thumbs across her cheeks.
"Erase everything I said, Emmy. I should have known
you weren't the type to go quietly. Hell, I did know.''
Dropping his head, he planted a kiss on her silvery bangs.
Straightening, he met her shimmering eyes. "I'd like to
start over. Do you think we can pretend you just blew
into town and this is our first meeting?''

Unable to speak, Emmy nodded. A lot churned through
her mind. An apology for her first brush-off. Asking Riley if he'd sit in on Sheriff Fielder's questioning her
about Mom Fran. Hiring him to probe her background.
All impossible favors to ask of someone merely extending the hand of friendship. What Emmy wanted from
Riley was far more. She wanted his touch. His love. She
wanted the years that had been stolen from them.

"Good," he said, brushing her damp cheeks one last
time before he took his hands away to check a flat gold
watch hidden beneath the cuff of his yellow shirt. "I have

an appointment in half an hour, so we can't go for that belated cup of coffee just yet. This afternoon I have papers to file at the county seat. That means I'll be late getting home." Pausing, he pulled a slim day planner out of his inside pocket and flipped through a few pages. "Tomorrow," he said brightly. "If you're free at five, we could meet at Crazy Jake's for a drink."

"Do you still play darts there?" she asked, regaining her equilibrium.

"Not nearly as much as I used to. Don't tell me you still play?" His eyes gleamed, the way a man's eyes did on encountering a challenge.

"Some," Emmy admitted.

"Then it'll really be like old times." Riley rubbed his hands together as he backed toward the street where Emmy saw he'd parked his car.

"Sure, like old times," she agreed. "Except I've grown up, Riley. Tomorrow you won't get away with buying me a cola."

His smile widened into a feral grin. As he vaulted over the door into the front seat of the convertible, Emmy thought he might have said, "Hey, kid, I've missed you." With the roar of the car's powerful engine, she wasn't sure. Watching him drive off, she felt a soul-deep yearning. Yet she wasn't altogether sure that agreeing to meet him in a dimly lit bar was the smart thing to do. Riley hadn't given any reasons for not playing darts as much as he used to. But she knew why. He had obligations. He was a family man. No amount of wishing would recapture the years they'd lost. And Emmy seriously doubted he put as much store in their upcoming meeting as she did. If he had, he would've called it a date.

It wasn't a date. The sooner she stopped thinking

about it as one, the better off she'd be. Drawing in a ragged sigh, Emmy trudged inside to see Logan Fielder.

Fielder wasn't happy. He wasn't particularly nice. He did, however, grudgingly agree to give her an extra week to seek counsel. Darn, Emmy had hoped he'd say she didn't need a lawyer. Technically, she didn't. She couldn't shed any light on her foster mom's disappearance or her subsequent murder. Emmy shivered as she stepped out into the fresh air, but she was determined that no one in this backwater town was going to walk on her or bully her.

Furthermore, someone around here knew who she was, and by God, nothing would deter her from finding the truth.

CHAPTER FOUR

FOLLOWING HIS LAST meeting with Emmy, Riley expected to be too involved in work to think about her or their proposed date. He had back-to-back appointments with longtime clients. Nice guys who insisted they couldn't possibly owe the government more than they'd already shelled out quarterly for taxes. It wasn't that Riley didn't like talking tax strategy, but it did get boring to cover the same ground with the same folks year after year. Some never seemed to get the concept of taking steps to shelter money before, not after, the fact—when it was too late.

It wasn't until the last rancher left that Riley realized he'd doodled Emmy's name around the edges of five pages of tax notes. The woman scrambled his brains as surely as he did Alanna's breakfast eggs. She always had. His high-school teachers had taken him aside to discuss the sketches on his homework—his clever attempts to entwine Emmy's name with his. Then, as today, he'd been mortified when faced with the facts. Although it troubled him more today.... Not only did he no longer have the excuse of being a teenager, Riley was shaken to discover that lust could hang around so long.

And he'd admit that in his misspent youth, he *had* lusted after Emmy Monday. Maybe the fact that he'd never acted on his feelings was the problem, Riley mused as he wandered from his office into the conference room to refill his coffee cup. On his return, he tucked the damning evidence in his middle desk drawer, then sharpened a new set of pencils in preparation for his final meeting with the FBI.

The doodles continued to plague his thoughts. One of his college roommates who was prone to pontificating, had once told him that guys forgot their high-school conquests but they never forgot the girl who got away.

Emmy didn't exactly fit that description. Riley had never really looked at her as a possible conquest. He hadn't pursued her. Because of her age he'd gone to great lengths to maintain a hands-off policy.

"Hmm." Tilting back his chair, Riley laced his fingers over his stomach and smiled at the memory of how dismally he'd failed on that score. On her thirteenth birthday he'd broken his code of ethics and he'd kissed her. And brother, did she kiss him back. He should have felt guiltier that she was such a quick study. But there'd been no shred of remorse in spite of his knowing that Jed or Will would've ripped him apart if they'd had any inkling.

From the moment their lips touched, Emmy's heart, soul and body had been his for the taking. The power in that knowledge allowed Riley to draw a line he never crossed thereafter. His respect for her—rather than any threat of being beaten to a pulp by his best friends—set the boundaries.

His intercom buzzed. Riley jerked forward in his chair. *Damn!* The fibbies were here to put a cap on the Ashton case and he'd spent the last half hour daydreaming. Over a woman. He'd promised himself after the bad match he'd made with Lani that he'd never again allow a female to be the center of his attention. Other than his daughter. Huh. Considering the history he had with Emmy Monday, it was a good thing she'd suggested they engage in something competitive on their first date.

Meeting, he corrected, scowling as he flipped the intercom. "I'm ready for the agents, Marge. Show them into the conference room. I'll get the coffee. You can lock up and go to lunch. We'll close out the case and probably grab a bite afterward."

The intercom crackled as Riley waited for signs of agreement from the competent legal assistant he'd inherited from the former owner of his practice—a man now happily retired on a gulf coast beach.

"The agents aren't here. Uh, Riley, I just fielded an odd call. A woman, I can't place the voice, called to inquire about your hourly rates."

Riley laughed. "It's odd because she asked in advance about rates instead of throwing a fit after receiving our bill? Or odd because there's actually someone in town you haven't met? I know, she's an alien. Her spacecraft accidentally landed on Caddo Lake. The water's so low she's mired in lily pads. Taxes are due on Plutarium and she wants me to file an extension for her."

"Stop, Riley. You are so bad." His assistant tried hard to remain serious. "Didn't your professors tell you comedy and finance don't mix?"

"All the time. I've had numerous lectures on the subject. Okay, no more joking."

"Good. This caller evaded every one of my standard questions. But I haven't been in this business thirty years for nothing." Marge sounded smug. "After my bully tactics, she admitted to having two matters that may require legal services. One investigative. One criminal."

Riley had no idea why Emmy immediately came to mind. Except that Marge did know everyone. But she wouldn't know Emmy's voice. "Criminal, you said? You explained I don't handle criminal cases unless they involve tax evasion?''

"I did. I think the news went in one ear and out the other. Without missing a beat, she asked if you'd ever done genealogical research, and what it cost.''

His stomach plunged. Riley released the intercom button. *It had to be Emmy.* Was she being furtive because he'd try to talk her out of digging in her past?

Leaping from his chair, he went out to question Marge further. "Did the caller leave a number where she can be reached?''

"No. Get this—I didn't give her a lick of information, yet she thanked me sweetly for all my help, and then hung up.''

"You've fielded hundreds of queries. Why did this one stand out?''

"At first I thought she might be a reporter after inside information on the Ashton case. But she sounded too sincere. Gosh, Riley, I can't explain any better.''

He shoved his hands deep in his pockets. If Emmy needed help in a criminal matter... *Hell, it'd have to be connected to Fran Granger's murder.* "You referred her to the law registry?''

"She never let me get that far. Um...you saw Logan earlier. Has he turned up any new evidence in the Granger murder?''

That was where he'd bumped into Emmy. Outside the municipal building. Surely Logan wasn't questioning her. She'd been only thirteen when Fran disappeared. She couldn't know a thing.

"Riley?''

"Frannie Granger's foster daughter is back in town. She was a kid at the time the ME dated that murder. I doubt Emmy's under suspicion or Logan would've dropped a hint. He knows I was close to all three of Frannie's foster kids. Since I'm not one of his favorite people, if he had something—anything—on Emmy Monday, he'd have been sure to rub my nose in it.''

''Okay. Another possibility is Tessa Lang. I'm not sure I'd recognize her voice. And yesterday, when I had my hair done, Jessie Bond told everyone in the shop the archaeologist is getting on Logan's nerves. Could he be hassling her over permits or something?''

''Word is, it's the other way around. Tessa is badgering Logan to let her reopen the site. Unless she's hatched a plot to do in our illustrious lawman, I see no reason she'd need legal advice regarding a criminal matter.''

Marge snickered. ''Ms. Lang might have to stand in line to get to Logan. He's making an ass of himself over this case. It's his last big hurrah, you know, before he hangs up his spurs. Or should I say his star? Uh-oh—'' she lowered her voice to a whisper ''—your men in black are here. And I don't mean the undertakers.''

''I see I'm not the only comedian in this office. Pull my file on the Ashton case, would you? Seat the agents in the conference room, and tell them I'll be right with them. Oh, and Marge, if your caller phones back, interrupt me, okay?''

''Sure enough, boss.'' Marge snapped him a quick salute.

Riley stepped into his office to retrieve his suit jacket. By the time he joined the two men from D.C., the call she'd brought to his attention had flown from his mind.

EMMY ANSWERED a knock at her door. She greeted Gwyn Louis through the screen, juggling a pitcher of iced tea and a handful of lemon slices. She ended up using her elbow to release the latch.

Gwyn was weighed down, too, with an empty cat litter box in which a cute Siamese kitten scrambled around batting a ball. She also lugged a full bag of cat litter and a sack of kitten food. "Look at us. Two obsessive-compulsives. We have to do everything at once instead of taking things one at a time."

"Speak for yourself." Emmy held the screen open with a toe and motioned Gwyn in. "I'm perpetually late because I'm the biggest procrastinator in the world. We'll have to drink this lukewarm. I got busy unpacking and just remembered to bring in the sun tea jar." She screwed up her nose. "You get to choose whether or not you want your tepid tea with or without lemon."

"With, please. And isn't that why someone invented ice cubes? For busy women who do everything at the last minute?"

"I give up. You're too fast with the comebacks." The screen banged shut. Emmy and Gwyn walked into the sunny kitchen, where Gwyn deposited the box and sacks with a sigh.

"I thought you were bringing both kittens," Emmy said as she pulled two glasses out of the cupboard and poured the tea.

"I intended to, but as I was loading my pickup, a woman dropped by. The family came last week to see the kittens and said no. Since then, they'd changed their minds and wanted the little female. I suspect their kids badgered them into it. Even so, I'm satisfied they'll follow through with shots and spaying."

"So this is the last one? A male, you said." Emmy set her glass on a colorful place mat and picked up the tiny fawn-colored ball. The kitten stared trustingly at Emmy out of bright blue eyes. His purr revved to a rasp that shook his scrawny frame.

"He's the runt of the litter. Undoubtedly why no one wanted him."

Emmy rubbed her cheek over the points of the soft brown ears. "Then he and I are two of a kind." The kitten straightened, butted his head against Emmy's shirt and meowed loudly. "He reminds me of the cats carved on Egyptian urns. Runt or not, I'm giving him a lofty name. Meet Egypt."

Gwyn chucked the kitten under his chin. "He'll never make a show cat, but from the way you two are bonding, he'll be a great pet. Uh, Emmy, I'm bothered by what you said about you and the cat being two of a kind. What makes you so positive your birth mother *wanted* to give you up?"

"Did Jed fill you in on how I came to live with Frannie? I certainly didn't walk to that booth at the Monday Trade Days. It's a huge flea market—you've heard of it?" At Gwyn's nod, she continued. "What people do at the trade days in Canton is buy, sell and trade junk."

"Have you ever attended one of their sales? I have, several times now. A lot of expensive antiques change hands during the meet. I've seen some pretty classy stuff. And well-heeled people flashing big bucks around."

Emmy set the kitten down to explore. She filled the litter box from the bag Gwyn had brought, then tucked it into a quiet corner opposite the pantry.

"I guess this sudden attempt to busy your hands means you don't want to talk about other possibilities." Gwyn let another moment tick past before prodding again. "Have you decided whether or not to contact Riley about initiating your search?"

Emmy washed her hands and found two plastic dishes in a box. She filled one with water and the other with kitty niblets and set both on the floor. "I did phone Riley's office to inquire. His secretary wasn't very informative. She asked me more questions than I asked her.''

''That sounds like Marge. Riley acquired her with the practice. She knows everyone and everything in this town. In fact, she might remember particulars dating back to when Frannie took you in, Emmy.'' Gwyn looked thoughtful. ''I'm not sure of Marge's age—late sixties I'd guess, with a mind like a steel trap.''

Emmy wandered to the table where Gwyn sat squeezing lemon into her tea. ''Quite a few people in town might be able to help me if I could figure out where to start and what questions to ask.''

Gwyn set her lemon rind on a napkin. ''First and foremost, Emmy, you need to ask yourself if this is really, truly what you want to do. My friend who went through it hit brick wall after brick wall. She got plenty discouraged along the way.''

''But she was ultimately successful?''

''Yes,'' Gwyn said carefully. ''She found her birth mother.''

Emmy pursed her lips. ''Was, uh, did they get along and…everything?''

Gwyn's pause was significant. ''The truth is, Emmy, some people simply don't want to be found. My friend was terribly disappointed. She said one good thing did come of her persistence. Her attorney was able to obtain her medical history.''

''Even that would be a big relief. You can't imagine how hard it is not to know the most basic things other people take for granted. A certain part of your life just doesn't exist.''

''That would be hard to accept. I wonder why so many of us have screwed-up lives?'' Gwyn gazed out the window and idly swirled the ice in her tea. "Having a family sometimes isn't all it's cracked up to be, you know."

"I'm sorry, Gwyn, I didn't stop to think that your life might not have been all rosy."

"Compared to yours and Jed's, mine was a piece of chocolate cake. At least on the surface. I grew up privileged. Suffice it to say that comes with its own set of problems."

"Ah. Poor little rich girl?"

"I'll have to think about it. I'm not sure that applies to me. It's more that my privileges came with a rigid set of expectations. By refusing to live up to them, I've caused hard feelings and let a lot of people down."

Emmy would have said something sympathetic, but she was interrupted by a knock and a small voice calling, "Hello," through the front screen.

"It's Alanna." Gwyn started to get up, then sank back down. "It's your call whether or not to invite her in. She must've seen my pickup and asked Mrs. Yates to let her come over."

Emmy sprang up. She smiled at the child, who had her nose pressed tight to the screen. "Hello yourself, Miss Gray. Does your sitter know where you are?"

The dark head bobbed up and down. "She said I could come." Fumbling in her pants pocket, the girl pulled out a folded note. "Our phone number. She said you should call her if I can stay, 'cause she needs to go out for groceries."

Emmy opened the screen and took the note. "I'm afraid I haven't got a phone yet. Go on into the kitchen and ask Gwyn to give you a glass of milk. I'll run over to introduce myself to Mrs. Yates and find out what time she plans to be back."

Just then the kitten ran out of the kitchen, chasing a

leaf Emmy recognized as part of a silk arrangement she'd taken out of a box and left sitting on the floor.

"Oh, what a pretty kitty! I thought you didn't have pets," Alanna exclaimed, plopping down on the floor to gather the kitten in her arms.

"Gwyn just brought him. His name is Egypt. Play carefully, okay?"

"I'm always careful," Alanna promised, gazing at Emmy out of solemn dark eyes. Something in her look reminded Emmy so much of Riley—especially when he used to try to convince her he hadn't dated Amanda Jennings—that Emmy gave a start.

"I'll take your word for it," Emmy said, tripping on the doorjamb as she backed up. "Don't forget Gwyn's in the kitchen. You're not allergic to milk or chocolate, are you?"

"Nope, I'm not 'lergic to anything. So can I eat lunch here?"

"One thing at a time, young lady. First, I need to meet your sitter."

"She'll say okay. 'Cause she watches TV at lunch and she says I talk so much she can't hear the program. But it's boring. *You* don't watch boring TV when you eat, do you?"

"No. I don't own a TV." Emmy's head swam a little from trying to keep up with Alanna's chatter. Emmy would enjoy having Alanna stay for lunch, but the comments Riley had made at the grocery store played in her head. He'd said not to encourage his daughter's visits, although that had been before they bumped into each other this morning and he'd suggested starting over. Still, she didn't want to deliberately oppose him if he harbored reservations.

"Tell you what," she said. "Let's not plan lunch today. I have several errands to run. Oh, that reminds me. Gwyn,'' Emmy called. ''There's no phone jack in the bedroom. Is it okay if I have one installed? The only jacks are in the living room and kitchen.''

Gwyn stepped to the door, her glass of iced tea in hand. ''I always intended to ask Jed to have a phone outlet put there. There's no need for you to foot the bill. I'll get Jed on it today.''

''It's no trouble for me. The telephone office is next door to the library. Signing up for a library card is already on my list.''

''Okay, but charge the installation fees to us. Alanna, why so glum? I happen to know Emmy has chocolate milk in the fridge.''

''I wanna eat lunch here,'' the girl answered with a pout.

Emmy retied one of Alanna's hair bows that had worked loose. ''I know you're disappointed. Me, too. But try to understand, honey, I already had a list of things planned.''

Alanna nodded, although she remained downcast.

Nevertheless, Emmy wanted to speak with Riley before she got too involved. ''Alanna brought a note from Mrs. Yates. I need to go see her, Gwyn. Would you give Alanna a couple of cookies to go with her milk? There's a brand-new bag of Oreos on top of the fridge.''

''Oreos?'' Gwyn grinned. ''I knew we were soul sisters. I can make a meal out of chocolate milk and Oreo cookies.''

Emmy knew Gwyn was trying to be funny. Yet as she crossed the property to Riley's home, Gwyn's statement brought Emmy's thoughts back to her secondary reason for being here. For all she knew, Gwyn might be her biological sister. Well, no, she didn't *really* believe that, but in fact it was entirely possible that she had unknown siblings living nearby. The idea sobered her. And made her wonder why she'd waited so long to start finding answers.

She didn't know why it hadn't crossed her mind before. Did Fran have old records that might shed some light on her origins? Emmy didn't have an actual birth certificate, as far as she knew. Didn't you need one to register a child for school? Perhaps Jed would know, or maybe he'd even kept Frannie's important papers. She'd ask him this afternoon. If there *were* records, she might be able to launch her own search and thus avoid making an appointment with Riley.

Feeling better, Emmy rang his doorbell with more verve than necessary.

A matronly woman opened the door. "Mrs. Yates?" Emmy smiled. "I'm Emmy Monday from next door. Alanna's note says you wanted me to call, but I haven't bought a phone yet."

"If the girl's a bother, send her home."

"Oh, she's not…any bother." Staring at the woman's stern features, Emmy arched an eyebrow. "I'm merely explaining why I'm at your door instead of phoning. Alanna said you were going grocery shopping. I ran into Riley at the store last night and his shopping cart was overflowing. I…well, I wanted to be sure Alanna hadn't come up with that story so I'd let her stay longer."

The woman's jaw tightened visibly. "Did I tell her groceries? No. You're quite right. Her father did stock up. It's an appointment. For me. Sorry to have troubled you. Just send the girl home. I'll drop her off with a friend for the hour or so I'll be tied up."

"You misunderstood. I have no objection to watching

her that long. Gwyn Louis just brought me a kitten. He'll entertain Alanna for a while.''

''I suppose that means she'll come home with cat hair all over her. And I'll have to get my allergy medication filled again.''

''Oh. Well, it would be impossible to keep the two apart. If you don't want her around the kitten, then perhaps she'd better go with you.''

''She'd just call her dad and beg to stay with you. That one's a willful child and her father spoils her rotten.''

Emmy's snap judgement of Riley's housekeeper-sitter was that she was a bit of an ogre and probably didn't like children much. ''Please honk when you get home, and I'll make sure Alanna gets here safely.''

''Well, I see you're not one to gossip over the back fence. A friend of mine said you're a hometown girl who ran off to live in the city. What brings you back?''

''Business,'' Emmy said. Turning sharply on her heel, she retreated, wondering why Riley had hired this woman.

Alanna and Gwyn were still seated at the kitchen table. A pile of the chocolate cookies lay before each. A third stack sat on a napkin at Emmy's place, along with a fresh glass of tea.

Gwyn smiled as Emmy settled in her chair and immediately broke open a cookie. She licked out the white frosted center.

''So, now you've met Lucille Yates,'' Gwyn murmured.

Emmy caught herself before she gave away her true feelings. ''Um…yes. Alanna, Mrs. Yates will honk when she drives in. Will you help me listen?''

''Maybe she won't come back.''

Emmy's heart contracted. Did Alanna worry about being abandoned? She'd lost her mother, and her dad worked long, erratic hours. "She'll come back, Alanna."

"Oh. Well, I like staying here."

"So you're okay with her going off and leaving you?" It was Gwyn's question.

Alanna slurped her milk. "I think Mrs. Yates is gonna see somebody about a job. I heard her talking on the phone, but she doesn't know it."

"You shouldn't have listened in on a private call," Emmy chided gently. "You could be mistaken. Anyhow, I'm sure she'd give your dad plenty of notice. Caregivers don't go off and n-n-ot come ba-back." Emmy sucked in a deep breath. It surprised her that after all these years the subject affected her this strongly.

Alanna seemed not to notice Emmy's distress. She polished off the last of her milk and asked to visit the kitten again. "He's sleeping in that funny chair you have."

"Funny? Oh, you mean the one filled with beans. It's a relic. I should get rid of it, but I hate to throw anything out."

"Are the beans cooked?"

"No, honey. They're probably not even beans. More like those little foam peanuts used for packing breakables."

The girl ran off giggling.

"Are you all right, Emmy?" Gwyn whispered. "Innocent comments sneak up and bother Jed, too. And speaking of Jed, he sent you a list of competent attorneys." Gwyn dug a folded paper out of her back pocket. "I never had a chance to ask if the sheriff agreed to an extension to hire counsel."

"Yes, but I could tell he wasn't happy about it. Not that I can blame him." Emmy wrapped her hands around her glass. "We all want this murder solved ASAP."

"No one more than me," Gwyn said. "For Jed's sake." She sighed and shook her head. "What type of evidence hangs around for nearly twenty years?"

"I don't know. I'm not well versed on murder." Emmy shivered.

"I guess that means you haven't remembered anything that might help clear Jed." Rising, Gwyn carried her glass and Alanna's empty one to the sink.

"I'm sorry, I wish I could come up with something."

"I know, clues don't lie there, just waiting to be found. But I keep hoping...."

"Gwyn, does Jed still have Mom Fran's stuff? You know," she said, when Gwyn looked blank. "Papers or such? She had a desk in her bedroom that was off-limits to us kids. It's where she put bills, the checkbook, stamps, warranties—that kind of stuff. I was going to call Jed and ask if he has anything stored. If he does, I'd like to take a look."

"He may have something, Emmy. Jed acquired this house long before he met me. Drop by later. He's overseeing the replanting of several fallow pastures today. I have a noon appointment scheduled with an ad man from Beaumont. He'll arrive soon, so I need to get going. Shall I tell Jed you'll be stopping by? If he has Frannie's things put away, it's possible he's forgotten about them."

"I hate being a pest, but yes, tell him I'll drop in tonight. Maybe I'll eat out and come around nineish. Will that allow you to get your dinner out of the way?"

"This is June's day off. Since I'm the world's worst cook, I'm doing deli salads. While you're out, grab a loaf of French bread and join us. Say, eight-thirty again."

"Gwyn." Emmy sounded exasperated. "You've been married—what? two weeks? Jed may have his own plans for tonight."

"We always have our nights. Think how much sweeter it'll be if I make him wait." Gwyn's cheeks blossomed pink, which did nothing to dim the devilish twinkle in her eyes.

"Point taken. All right, I'll see you at approximately the same time as last night. But if Jed throws me out on my ear, I'm saying I told you so."

The two new friends shared laughter all the way to the door. Gwyn stopped long enough to hug Alanna good-bye. Emmy latched the screen and stood in the filtered sunlight until Gwyn's green Land Rover reached the main road.

"Baby kitties sure sleep a lot," Alanna said fretfully.

"No more than you did when you were a baby, I'll bet."

"Huh. Babies crawl and play with toys. And they like to ride in strollers. I wish I had a baby sister. I keep asking my daddy," she said, frowning. "All he says is maybe I'll get one someday." Alanna flopped on the floor and propped her chin in her hand.

Emmy wasn't about to touch *that* subject. However, she couldn't help wondering—was Riley being vague simply to put Alanna off or did he want more children? And if so, did he already have a prospective mother picked out?

Although she had a perfect opportunity to pump Alanna about any woman in her father's life, Emmy would never stoop that low. Obviously she needed to think about something other than Riley.

"I have three boxes of books." Emmy pointed. "Would you like to help me arrange them on the shelves, Alanna?"

"'kay. When we're done, will you read me a story?"

"Alanna, these are all books for big folks. Next time,

bring one of your favorite stories and I'll read it. Or, we can check kids' books out of the library," Emmy said, remembering fondly the many happy hours she and Mom Fran had spent there. Almost instantly, Emmy realized what she'd said to Riley's daughter, forcing her to hastily add, "I mean, we could go if your dad says it's okay."

"Why wouldn't he?" The child cocked her head prettily to one side.

"Because...because I'm new in town. Parents have to be very careful who they let their children go off with."

"I know. Daddy told me to not take candy or go with strangers. But you aren't a stranger, Emmy. Miss Gwyn knows you, and so does Daddy. Mr. Jed phoned this morning. I heard Daddy talking about stuff him and you used to do."

"Ah," Emmy said. "I really think you should quit that listening in when adults are on the phone."

Alanna looked sheepish as she shrugged. "I wouldn't listen, 'cept nobody ever tells me anything."

She sounded so vexed, Emmy had to chuckle. "Come on, little Miss Pitcher With Big Ears. My books won't shelve themselves." Emmy directed Alanna to start with the bottom rows. As they worked, they talked about games and dolls. Time ticked by fast. The child was an absolute joy. She handled the books with care, and placed them according to height. She even read a few words in some of the titles which impressed Emmy. Neither was ready to end the day when they heard several long blasts from a car horn.

"Rats, she's back." Alanna poked out her lower lip.

Emmy glanced at her watch and was surprised to see that two hours had slipped by. "Actually, she was gone longer than she said. That'll put me behind on errands.

Tell you what, I'll leave the rest of these until Mrs. Yates lets you come again.''

Since Emmy still sat on the floor, Alanna scrambled over and threw her arms around Emmy's neck, followed by a smacking kiss on the cheek.

Emmy, who'd long ago rejected the idea of having her own children but who'd never imagined she'd regret the decision, was moved by Alanna's display of affection. She not only hugged the girl back, she walked hand in hand with her to the door.

The good feeling lasted as Emmy went about her business that afternoon. It lingered even after she pulled into the circular drive at Beaumarais.

Jed opened the door. He appeared more relaxed this evening. ''Hi. Lord, Emmy-M, I still can't believe you're really here.'' He tugged on a lock of her straight blond hair, much as he'd done when they were growing up.

''Gwyn said you asked about Frannie's personal effects. They're stored in my attic. I didn't know where else to put them.'' Draping an arm over her shoulder, he relieved her of the loaf of bread, which he tossed to Gwyn in passing. Then Jed guided Emmy up a winding flight of stairs. He led her into a large room at the top.

A music room, she saw, stopping in front of a wire stand. A violin case sat open on a velvet chair. Nearby stood a cello with sheet music spread around.

''You've branched out, I see.''

''Gwyn plays cello. She's quite good,'' he announced with pride.

Emmy would have asked for a private concert, except that Jed hustled her into the center of the room, where a wooden ladder already hung down from an opening in the ceiling.

''If Logan Fielder knew I'd kept Frannie's personal

effects, he'd be out here with a search warrant. To be honest, Emmy, I must have glanced through everything as Joleen helped me box it up. I swear these cartons haven't been opened since."

"Joleen? Does she still work as a nurse in Tyler?"

"She's retired."

"Losing Fran must have been horrible for her. They were so close."

"I rarely see her unless we accidentally run into each other. She's a hard person to read, Emmy. Distant— maybe that's the best word to describe her now."

"That doesn't sound like Joleen. I figured she'd take over for Fran. She came by most nights after work. Remember how she'd order us around like she had every right?"

"Here, let me give you a boost. That first step is a doozy. Um, if I had to define how Joleen has changed, I'd say she…folded up after Frannie disappeared. Like the lotus lily out on the lake does at night."

Emmy ducked under the eaves and waited for Jed. "I suppose everyone handles grief differently. Joleen stayed single, and Fran and us kids were her life. Or at least I think so as I look back. I wasn't very observant then. Kids are self-centered, aren't they?"

"Or tuned in to other interests. These two boxes contain everything that was in the desk. There's also one box of clothes and another of knickknacks." Jed stared down at the boxes as if he didn't want to be the first to touch them. "It's a pitiful amount to represent a person's entire life."

Emmy sighed. "I feel funny doing this. Like I'm poking my nose where it doesn't belong."

"Nonsense. You were her daughter. She had no other kin."

"Really? You and Will were a pair of frogs? Listen, Jed. None of us has a legal claim to any of this. She didn't—couldn't adopt me, I was told, because back then a woman without a husband wasn't an acceptable candidate."

"Technically you're correct. Joleen said Frannie didn't believe in wills. It seems her husband had one drawn up. In the end, nothing was left for Fran. It cost more to have the attorney handle the transaction than she actually got. She decided to put her money to better use—like take in needy kids."

Emmy sank to her knees and dragged the first box closer. "It's taken me some time to admit this, Jed, but I, for one am grateful she did what she did."

"Me, too." He swallowed hard when the first thing Emmy pulled from the box was a stack of certificates. Jed's old music awards.

Emmy handed them to him. He sifted through the parchments, saying nothing.

She glanced up to see why he'd fallen silent. Tears glistened in his eyes. Her stomach wrenched at the sight, and she wished she could snatch the certificates back. Last night Jed had talked some about how he'd struggled with the guilt attached to his and Fran's arguing over his music career. Not knowing what to say to ease his current pain, Emmy dug in the box and took out the next folder.

"Jed, look! Copies of your birth certificate and Will's. Plus, all of our report cards."

He came down on one knee to look over her shoulder. His voice was raspy when he spoke. "I remember she had to verify my age to enroll me in school. Will, too. Your birth certificate must be there somewhere. Check again."

"No." Emmy shook her head. "There's this note from

Social Services validating the date I was found, and my approximate age. I'd so hoped—'' She stopped midsentence.

"You haven't reached the bottom of the box."

"The rest is paid bills, receipts and old tax forms. Warranties on the appliances. Oh, here's a contract for the work she was having done on the porch."

Jed snatched it. "Hank left town without collecting pay for what he did. Ray Jennings thinks he went on a binge and ended up in a drunk tank somewhere."

"Without money?"

"It's Ray's theory, not mine. He said drunks can always find a bottle."

"Have you considered that maybe Belmonte demanded his money in advance? He could have flown into an alcoholic rage and killed her."

"Anything's possible," Jed mused, folding the contract. "I'll turn this over to my lawyer and see if he wants to use it to prod Fielder. The sheriff claims Hank was always unreliable. To me, his timing in this instance ought to be considered suspect."

"I agree." Emmy had opened the second box. It contained a small album filled with faded pictures of Frannie's wedding. Tucked into the back were Jed's, Will's and her school pictures and two packets of snapshots. "Would you look at us. What dweebs." Emmy hooted with laughter as she held up photos showing her with pigtails and gap teeth and Jed with an untamed cowlick. "Will must've thought it was cool or sexy to lower his eyelids and curl his lip. He's done that in every shot."

Jed touched the pictures reverently. "Shall we divvy them up?"

"Let's make copies—three sets of each. Of course,

we'll have to store Will's. Oh, Jed, don't you wonder where he is?''

"Yeah," he said gruffly. "But he knew damn well *I* wasn't going anywhere."

To sidestep what was obviously a touchy topic, Emmy closed the second box. She ripped the tape off the one Jed had said contained knickknacks. As it happened, the top item brought a stab straight to her heart. It was a music box. A sticker on the bottom said it played ''Greensleeves''—Fran's favorite song. A few bars tinkled the instant Emmy lifted the ceramic piece from its wrapping. A carousel horse twirled a half turn.

Emmy remembered mowing lawns and begging odd jobs in town for an entire year to earn the money to buy her mom this gift for Christmas. Their last, it turned out.

She fingered a bead of glue holding one of the horse's legs intact. That holiday, Will and Jed had both received footballs. They'd thrown them in the house even though Mom Fran forbade it. The trinket got broken before dinner was served. More upset than anyone had ever seen her, Fran banished the boys to their rooms until the culprit owned up to his misdeed.

Emmy couldn't eat, either. She sobbed into her pillow all afternoon. All the kids assumed Mom Fran would eventually give in. She remained firm. Emmy ended up sneaking food to the boys.

Jed touched the ornate horse. As if reading Emmy's mind, he murmured, "I know you got into trouble for smuggling Will and me cold turkey and dressing. But Frannie couldn't stand the thought of us going hungry, either. Did you know she saw you filling plates when she returned to the kitchen after doing the same?''

"I never knew. She didn't say a word to me."

"You know," he said, eyeing Emmy obliquely. "Neither Will nor I thought any of our throws came close to hitting the music box.''

"I knocked it off and broke it," Emmy blurted, her throat suddenly clogged with tears. "I was so mad at myself but too afraid to tell, because you guys ordered me not to touch your stupid footballs." Her eyes suddenly overflowed.

"Hot damn—truth at last. It's exactly what Will and I figured. You looked so guilty when you brought us those plates. But we weren't about to rat on you," Jed said, forgiveness etched in his smile. "Here, you have the music box. And don't let guilt keep you from enjoying it. Besides," he said, hauling in a deep breath. "Will and I did chip the living room lamp. We glued it ourselves. If Frannie knew, she never let on."

From below, Gwyn called out, "I have spinach salads dished up. I just drizzled hot bacon dressing over them. Are you guys planning to stay up there all night? If so, the greens are going to get very soggy."

Jed pulled out his handkerchief and gave it to Emmy to blot her eyes. "We're coming," he informed his wife.

Emmy stood and thanked him quietly. "I've cried more in two days than in all the years since I left Uncertain. I thought my tears had all dried up."

"I won't tell if you don't. Anyway, I read somewhere crying is the best catharsis. If anyone needs a release valve, Emmy-M, it's us."

CHAPTER FIVE

EMMY FELT wrung out when she arrived home, in spite of the fact that Gwyn had served a wonderfully relaxed meal on the patio. She'd artfully arranged multicolored ironstone bowls and wood-handled eating utensils on a glass-topped wrought-iron table. The chairs offered thick cushions a person could burrow into. Torchières edging the property reflected pathways through the lotus lilies on the lake. Frogs croaked up and down the scale, blending in peaceful harmony. While it made for a pleasant evening, Emmy hadn't been able to shake the tension shimmering inside her, brought on, no doubt, by delving into Mom Fran's possessions. Possessions that produced gut-wrenching memories, but nary a clue as to where Emmy should start searching for the person who'd brought her into this world.

Richard had once asked her if she didn't recall overhearing her foster mother talking to friends about her—some conversation in which she might have let slip some pertinent fact about Emmy's birth. And though Emmy had racked her brain, nothing stood out. Nothing except the story of a brooch, reportedly found pinned inside her baby blanket. A significantly large pearl nested in the hollow of an intricate twenty-four-carat gold tree whose branches were dotted with pricey emeralds, all set in a circle of gold.

The piece had simply disappeared from the house one

day. Frannie was positive she'd misplaced it, because she said only friends came to the house, so she'd always been reluctant to report it stolen. She'd told Emmy in later years that the house hadn't been broken into and nothing else was missing. That was how Mom Fran was—she found good in everyone. It was what made her murder so darned hard to swallow.

Fran was convinced the brooch would turn up someday when they least expected. Emmy had crossed her fingers that she'd find it tucked among her foster mom's belongings. If she closed her eyes, she could see the brooch as it had been described. Mom Fran had made up wonderful stories about how the lovely jeweled tree meant Emmy was extraspecial. She'd said it proved that Emmy's mother, probably a girl from a rich family, had loved her baby enough to provide for her.

When Emmy was older, Fran had explained that some families couldn't cope with the idea of illegitimacy. Which had certainly been true in the case of Jed's wealthy uncle. The old buzzard had disowned Jed's mother.

Emmy let the kitten, Egypt, curl up on her bed. The raspy purr was comforting. She drifted off to sleep, and dreamed of a day she'd be reunited with her parents, with family. It was a recurring dream.

She slept late, but was eventually forced to abandon her bed because Egypt persisted in batting her nose and licking her cheek. Yawning, she petted the cat, thinking she ought to get up anyway.

After feeding Egypt and playing with him until he wandered off to nap, Emmy dived into the task of putting away her remaining goods. She thought often of her scheduled meeting with Riley, but still refused to think of it as a date.

By afternoon, she'd unpacked the box that held her dart case. She'd played in a league off and on for twelve years. Often enough to have worn out five sets of darts. Her latest, top-of-the-line tungsten, were the best she'd ever owned. She spent a moment checking the steel tips and the composite shafts to make sure none had broken or vibrated loose. Finding all were ready for play, Emmy locked the case and set it by the front door.

Deciding on something to wear presented a problem. She wanted to look nice and admitted to herself that it was a question of pride—a womanly urge to show Riley Gray Wolf what he'd missed in letting her get away. In the end, a need for comfort won out. Throwing darts demanded freedom of motion. She ultimately settled on her best blue jeans and a yellow tank top that emphasized her tan. Then she worried her outfit might be too casual.

Even after taking time to wash her hair and apply pale-green eye shadow and a slick of natural lip gloss, Emmy was ready an hour early.

She sat down and picked up a new romance novel she'd bought to liven up a long, lonely evening. She became so absorbed, the next time she checked her watch she discovered she had only ten minutes before she was supposed to meet Riley at Crazy Jake's.

She tore out of the house in a panic, afraid Riley would look around the bar, see she wasn't there and leave. But as she backed down the long driveway, her jittery nerves subsided. If Riley didn't hold her in enough regard to give her fifteen minutes leeway, then to heck with him.

HE HAD WAITED.

Emmy's eyes were drawn to him the minute she stepped through the door. He stood at the back of the noisy, smoky bar, warming up with some practice throws.

He wore black dress slacks and a pale-blue shirt with long sleeves rolled just past his elbows. A suit jacket lay across the table of a nearby booth.

Emmy clutched the hem of her tank top and pulled it down over the two-inch gap between it and her blue jeans. Riley had obviously come straight from work. Why hadn't she realized he'd be dressed like a lawyer?

Then he turned to speak with a man who sat on the end bar stool. The guy had on a work-worn T-shirt, logger boots and a baseball cap set backward on his head. That was when Emmy realized a lock of coal dark hair had fallen rakishly across Riley's left eye. And his dress shirt was halfway open, exposing a bronzed chest dotted with sweat in spite of the lazy fans rotating overhead. Riley laughed at something his friend said. Emmy caught a brief flash of even white teeth as he raised a frosty beer bottle to his lips.

She saw him stop in the middle of swallowing. His dark steady eyes swept the entry; the moment he spotted her, his body relaxed. Riley held up a staying hand to his friend and started toward her at a trot.

"Hey, you had me worried there for a minute. I was afraid you'd forgotten. And I didn't have so much as a phone number for you."

"The phone company can't install a line to the bedroom until next week. They don't want to connect the existing jacks and give me a number before then. I wouldn't have thought there'd be a waiting list here." She shrugged and eased past him, walking toward the row of dartboards. "I'll bet you came early to practice, so you could get the drop on me," she teased, glancing at him over a shoulder that was bare except for the narrow strap of her tank top.

His grin vanished momentarily, then widened. "So the

pupil thinks she's ready to challenge the teacher, eh? Maybe you'd better take a closer look at the board, sugar babe.'' He blew on his fingers and brushed them over the left side of his chest. "This old man put two darts smack-dab in the bull's-eye." He wagged his bottle at Emmy, admiring the view of her backside as she marched up to check the placement of his darts. A row of male heads turned and the bar area grew quiet. When Emmy bent to inspect the bristles on the board, the move widened the strip of exposed flesh where her top again pulled away from her jeans.

She'd gone to examine the board because Riley's unexpected use of that private nickname had caused her stomach to tighten in a way she hadn't counted on. Maybe he used the endearment indiscriminately now, calling all women "sugar babe" in that gravelly, sexy tone of voice. If he did, she'd kill him.

Well, she'd pulverize him at darts, anyway.

Riley couldn't see her face to know what she was thinking as she studied the board so intently. But he noticed the stir her compact little backside created among his pals at the bar. Striding behind their stools, Riley smacked the heel of his palm against each man's head as he passed. "Mind your eyeballs," he growled. "The lady's with me tonight."

"Lucky dog," murmured a young cowboy in town from a nearby ranch.

"We can only hope," his neighbor said, "that she'll wise up when Gray here trounces her at darts. Think I'll stick around. Some enterprising dude should be ready and waiting to console her."

Riley ignored their banter. He'd bailed most of them out of tax jams at one time or another. The guys talked big, but they also respected him—not least because he'd won so much money from them playing darts. They were poking fun, and Riley knew it.

"You want a cola? Or you still drink sarsaparilla?" he asked Emmy when she'd finished her inspection of the board and paced off the throwing distance of seven feet six inches. She'd ended up beside him again and knelt to study the faint toe line someone had drawn on the traffic-worn floor.

"I thought I told you I'd grown up. I prefer a dark ale. Whatever Jake has on draft." Emmy flipped up the locks on her dart case. When he didn't immediately acknowledge her request, she glanced up.

Riley's eyes were trained on the left side of her tank top. Emmy realized a strap had slipped, allowing the material to sag. She'd lived with the quarter-size tattoo of a rainbow on her left breast for so many years she hardly noticed it anymore. But from the way Riley's eyes bugged, she could only surmise the women on his dating roster didn't come with any type of brand.

Discreetly tugging her shirt back into place, Emmy decided to let him make the first comment if he felt so inclined.

"Is that, uh, a transfer pattern? The kind that peels off?"

Her lips twitched in the briefest smile. "What's with you people? Gwyn asked if it was real. It hasn't peeled off in, oh, thirteen years. Look, Riley," she said, rising to her feet. "I once traveled with a circus. A roustabout put the tattooed lady up to daring me. They figured I was too chicken. Anyway, we were in a dinky town in Montana. No tattoo parlors there. The subject came up again in Seattle. Yes, I was scared. But by then I was determined to show them. So I went out and got this...."

A hint of some sentiment Emmy couldn't quite read flashed in Riley's eyes.

She heaved a sigh. "If you're going to lecture me, for heaven's sake do it, and then order my ale. I'm thirsty."

Riley ran an index finger up and down her narrow tank strap. "Where's your pot of gold?"

"What?" His question wasn't in the least what Emmy expected.

"Isn't there supposed to be a pot of gold at the end of every rainbow?" Riley barely managed to keep a straight face. Mostly because he yearned to trace the colorful arc that again peeked over the edge of Emmy's tank top. He couldn't remember when, if ever, anything had enticed him so powerfully.

She threw back her head and laughed, a rich sound that rolled the length of her throat. "I'm happy to see you still possess a sense of humor." Pirouetting out of his reach, she pretended to bat her eyes. "Give the man a kewpie doll for asking the sixty-four-dollar question. *Is* there a pot of gold at the end of every rainbow? That, my friend," she said with a flirtatious wink, "is for me to know and you to find out."

Riley pondered her answer a moment too long. He actually looked disconcerted as he turned to order Emmy's drink from the hovering bartender.

She stared at the rigid set of Riley's broad shoulders. Her laughter died away, replaced by a sense of yearning for years lost. For things that might have been had circumstances not torn them apart. Of course, if she'd stayed in Uncertain, she would never have become the type of woman who'd hitchhike to Florida, where she knocked around doing odd jobs until she fell in with a circus wintering in the sun. She'd likely have married Riley right out of high school, and maybe she wouldn't have been woman enough back then to hold his interest.

She accepted the beer he handed her with a simple "Thanks." After taking a sip, she set the mug on the table beside his suit coat. Without further talk, she removed a supply of darts from her case.

Riley, whose thoughts still lingered on whether or not her "pot of gold" remark had been some sort of challenge, whistled long and low, his mind jerked suddenly back to the game. "If you've graduated to tossing Black Widows, I may revise my earlier comment about the pupil not overtaking the teacher." He grabbed one of the slender shafts from Emmy's hand and ran a thumb over the trademark spider on a carefully weighted barrel. "Heck, this thing feels too light-weight to fly true. My nickel-silver's are heavy enough to shave the tail off these squirty things."

Emmy snatched back her dart. "How about if we say loser buys dinner?"

Riley brushed aside a perpetually stubborn lock of hair. "You're on. Hey, Paul," he called to the man wearing the backward baseball cap. "The lady has a hankering to part with some of her money. You gonna be around long enough to keep score for us?"

The man spun on his bar stool, eyeing Emmy with growing respect. "Aw, Riley, give the little gal a break. At least, tell her you haven't been whipped in over a year."

"Two," said Riley, hefting his first dart. "But who's counting?"

Emmy only smiled benignly. "Shall we play 301?" It was the most common game. Each player started with 301 points. A scorekeeper subtracted each player's thrown score from the opening figure of 301. The score doubled or tripled depending on where a dart landed on the ring. The first player to reach zero won. Unless his or her last throw broke zero, which meant backtracking to the previous score and trying again. Unless the opponent won on the next toss, something Riley apparently did with regularity.

"I'll be gentleman enough to let you take a few warm-up tosses," Riley said magnanimously.

"Uh-uh," Emmy responded. "I'll run 'em cold. By the way, where are you taking me to dinner?"

He smirked for the benefit of his line of friends at the bar, who'd all turned in their seats, gearing up for the promised show. "I'd intended to let you off easy for old times' sake and opt for burgers here. But you're entirely too cocky, Ms. Monday. How does a thick juicy steak at Bayou Jetty sound? They've gone highbrow since you left town. Be forewarned, it'll cost you some bucks."

"Are you going to talk all night, or shall we throw a round to see who starts?"

"Nah. Let's just do it. And by all means, ladies first." Riley stepped aside and made a sweeping gesture toward the toe line.

Emily blocked out the rumble of excited male voices at the bar and the clink of beer glasses. She brought her first dart straight back to shoulder level and fired it at the board. The second two followed in rapid succession.

Paul resettled his cap and tugged at one ear as he sent Riley an uneasy glance. "I need a minute to go check. From this angle it looks like she scored big."

Riley, who'd assumed a casual stance, legs crossed at the ankles and his hands loosely tucked into his pants pockets, threw back his head and groaned. "I think we both know what you'll find. The lady's a shark, and I walked into this deal with my eyes wide-open. At least

I can brag that I taught her the game—when she was knee-high to a grasshopper and still wearing braces and pigtails.''

''I never wore braces,'' Emmy said cheekily, inviting him to step up to the mark with the same exaggerated gesture he'd given her. ''Now let's see you shave the tail off one of my Black Widows.'' She batted her naturally long eyelashes, trying hard not to copy his smirk. Paul removed her darts and handed them back to her with a look of reverence.

The men at the bar guffawed and a few ribbed Riley unmercifully. But when he matched her score, laying his darts so close together the feathers actually shivered, the bystanders fell silent. The bartender might even have covered a few bets both for and against their favorite son.

The play went back and forth, with neither player giving ground. Riley threw the first dart that went wide. It counted as a double.

Tension wound tight in Emmy, the way it always did when she entered any competition. Especially competition with men. She'd learned long ago that males liked to win at any cost. She'd once had a foster brother who got her soundly spanked if she beat him at anything. She'd learned for a while to hold back, although holding back wasn't her nature.

And this was Riley. He'd taught her that winning was important, but not as important as loving the sport, win, lose or draw. In fact, Emmy thought she could feel his warm breath on her ear as he extolled her to relax and ''don't be so serious.'' It was her imagination, of course. Riley wasn't sixteen anymore. Emmy sincerely doubted any man went into the practice of law if he didn't get a thrill out of winning.

The thought was enough to make her falter. Two darts

in succession missed the board. A third might be on a line, but the others were definitely out. Way out.

"Are you okay?" Riley stepped in close to Emmy. He massaged the back of her neck as Paul walked to the board to make his unbiased assessment. "You don't have anything to prove to me, sugar babe," he said soothingly. "It's just a game."

Emmy gazed up, into his bottomless black eyes. She'd always felt she could lose herself in Riley's eyes. Nineteen years melted away. She was thirteen again, and just looking at his face made her ache inside. But now Emmy understood the source of that ache. She sucked in a long, shaky breath. "You're right. It's nothing but a game. Stack that against the two reasons I'm really here—well, not *here*, but in Uncertain—and the outcome of this match is trivial. Thanks, Riley," she said seriously, meaning every word, "for helping me clarify what's important and what isn't. It's your turn," she murmured, nudging him toward the line with a genuine smile.

Baffled by her remarks but turned inside out by her smile, Riley tripped over his feet getting to the line to collect his darts. Nerves caused his miscalculation—really a stupid error. Riley's three tries all dropped too early. He heard the collective groan go up from the crowd that had gathered.

Emmy traded places with him. She faced a choice here. Either do her darnedest to win the match, or purposely throw it to give Riley another chance. She did something a dart player should never do at this stage: she let her eyes meet her opponent's. Or maybe it was a good thing she broke the unwritten rule. Riley smiled encouragingly, no hint of jealousy in evidence. He went so far as to give her a thumbs-up. The tight coil in Emmy's stomach unfurled. Her darts landed precisely where she wanted them.

"She did it," Paul shouted, waving the score card. "Zero. She hit zero cleanly on a minimum number of throws."

A whoop went up from the people bunched behind the players, while a stunned silence seemed to grip the men seated at the bar.

Riley ignored everyone. He grabbed Emmy by the waist and swung her in a circle just as he'd done when she'd hit her very first bull's-eye.

Caught up in the moment, she laughed down into his face. Then she clasped his head between her hands and planted a huge kiss squarely on his lips.

The crowd really cheered then. Their scorekeeper, Paul, ordered a round for everyone. "Riley's buying." He had to shout to be heard.

Riley lost his grip on Emmy. She felt herself slide down his body and quickly braced herself to land on the floor. He'd obviously been more affected by Paul's too generous offer than moved by her kiss.

In truth, if Riley hadn't released Emmy when he did, he'd have embarrassed himself in front of guys who wouldn't let him forget it. He hadn't been struck by such unbridled passion since the day he met Lani Sky. That day he'd already been high from passing his bar exam. He'd driven to Oklahoma to tell his mom the good news. Lani happened to be at the house with his sister, Josey.

He'd done little over the previous five years at U.T. in Tyler except study, study and study more, and after that long experience of social and romantic deprivation, he'd been snared by what he saw as Lani's quiet charm. Oddly enough, it was the same day he'd run into Jed Louis, and

Jed had bluntly told him that he had to accept the fact that Emmy Monday was never coming back to Uncertain.

Yet, here she was, in his arms—kissing him. So different in some ways from the Emmy he remembered, and in other ways the same. Riley was oh-so-tempted to spirit her out of Jake's and see if she lived up to that sample kiss.

His cell phone rang. He turned away to listen. Alanna's sweet voice washed over him, instantly cooling his weak-kneed desire. The call reminded him that he had responsibilities beyond assuaging desires run amuck. He had a daughter. The child Lani had never wanted.

"What, Alanna? No. Remember, Daddy told you this morning Mrs. Yates is fixing you dinner? Yeah, I know you'd rather I was there to cook." Riley scraped the hair out of his eyes. "I...can't eat with you. I'm, uh, taking, an...um, client to dinner. I'll get home in time to tuck you into bed and kiss you good-night. I promise."

Emmy went about collecting her darts from the board. She felt Riley's angst as she quietly closed her dart case. She visualized Alanna holding the phone, imagined tears streaking her face. Even though it annoyed Emmy immensely to hear Riley describe her as a client, she'd suffered Alanna's type of disappointment so many times as a kid. She couldn't bear being the cause of the girl's unhappiness.

Emmy curled a hand over Riley's arm. "Let's skip going to Bayou Jetty. In fact, I bought two pounds of fresh shrimp this morning," she said spontaneously. "I planned to fry them up in that beer batter you used to like. Why don't you and Alanna come to my place for dinner? Suit yourself, of course. But I need to get home to feed my kitten, anyway."

Riley looked so relieved and yet torn, Emmy wished

she hadn't suggested dinner. She should've just let him off the hook and asked for a rain check, instead.

Pressing a hand over one ear to filter out the noise from the bar, he relayed Emmy's invitation to Alanna.

The smile and nod that followed was response enough for Emmy. She hefted her dart case, preparing to leave. "I'll go peel the shrimp."

"Wait." Riley closed his phone and fumbled it back into his pocket. "Let me settle up the bar bill Paul so kindly arranged for me. It'll take a minute to eat the requisite crow. Then I'll walk you to your car."

"Pickup. I drive a pickup. And I'm perfectly capable of getting there on my own."

"I know you are." He sounded moderately exasperated. "I'm angling for two seconds alone with you, okay? We won't get a word in edgewise over dinner. Or haven't you noticed my kid's a motormouth?"

Emmy set her empty mug on the bar. "Puts me in mind of me. You and Jed accused me of being the world's worst chatterbox." She waved off the denial she saw forming. "Go on, Riley. Clear your debts. If you trust me to touch your darts, I'll load your case."

"I trusted you to touch them when I taught you to play, didn't I?"

Emmy nodded, her memory returning to the innocent high spirits—and equally innocent attraction.

After Riley had settled his debts, it still took them ten minutes to make their way to the front door. Old-timers surged forward to congratulate Emmy on her game. A few even remembered her, which came as a shock. Especially when they offered condolences to her on Frannie's death.

Once she and Riley were finally outside in the fresh

air, he placed a proprietary hand on the small of her back as they crossed to the parking lot.

"During the game, Emmy, you said you'd come back to Uncertain for two reasons. Frannie's one. What's the other, might I ask?" At some long-buried level, Riley hoped Emmy would say it was him. That kiss told him she also felt the unfinished business between them. He should've been prepared for the reason she gave, but he wasn't.

"I want to find my birth mother. And my father, if possible."

"Why? For crying out loud!"

Her face paled. "I've been a nobody long enough."

Riley winced guiltily, realizing it was the description Ray Jennings had used earlier this week.

Emmy, lost in her own thoughts, missed his reaction. "It's time, Riley. Crucial pieces of my identity are locked in the past. I won't find them unless I can locate my birth family."

"If you ask me, I'd say you've grown up pretty well without any help from them. You can't relive the past, Emmy. Believe me, it'd be a huge mistake to try."

"You don't have a clue, Riley. You can trace your heritage back to when Caddo Lake was formed and this area was being settled. Anyway, it's not up for debate. I've decided to start a search, and that's that." Her jaw stubbornly set, Emmy yanked open the truck door.

He could say he knew all about the hell you created when you mixed past and present, but it was something he hated to discuss. "I'll say one more thing on the subject. Before you plunge into this, take a good look at what Tessa Lang's digging in the past has done to Jed."

"There's no comparison! And Jed did *not* kill Mom Fran."

"I know that." Riley's expression grew wary. "But who did?"

"Good grief, I have no idea. If I did, I wouldn't have waited nineteen years to tell someone. Are we going to go eat or stand here all night bickering?"

A smile reminiscent of the old Riley slid over his face. "Some things never change. Your mind was always on your next meal. I never understood how you could pack away so much food without gaining an ounce. If you haven't changed on that score, you're nothing like any woman I've ever taken out to eat."

"You aren't taking me out. I'm cooking, remember?"

"Yes, ma'am, and I owe you. Emmy," he said, turning serious again. "Are you sure you're up to Alanna's endless chatter?"

"That reminds me." Emmy sobered, too. "The other night at the market, you told me not to encourage Alanna's visits. She's eager to come over, and I enjoy having her. In fact, I picked up some children's books to read to her. But I don't want to go behind your back. If you truly object, I'll do what I can to discourage her visits. Everything short of being rude, that is."

"The other night, it occurred to me you might only be passing through Uncertain on your way elsewhere. That's why I may have seemed...negative. I know Alanna is lonely. Mrs. Yates is competent, but she's not—well, grandmotherly."

"Neither am I. By the way, how come Alanna isn't in preschool? She's sounding out words."

"Uncertain has no preschool. I'd have to drive her to Jefferson three days a week and pick her up midday. My schedule is unpredictable. I never know when I have to be in court, or extend a meeting with a client."

"It's not my business, but Mrs. Yates has a car. I should think she'd be happy to drive Alanna to school."

Riley laughed shortly. "It's easy to tell you aren't up on the way housekeepers operate. Their lists of *don'ts* is ten times longer than their list of *dos*."

"Boy, everywhere *I've* worked the employer set the rules."

"This town doesn't have an overabundance of nanny types."

"Mom Fran really was one in a million, wasn't she? I still can't believe someone mur-murdered her." Emmy choked up suddenly.

Riley curved a hand around the back of Emmy's neck and rubbed his thumb lightly under her chin. "There's no reshaping the past, Emmy. The best you can hope now is that Logan Fielder finds her killer."

"And that it's no one we know." Emmy shivered.

"Hey, lady. Those shrimp you promised aren't going to cook themselves. Plus, we've been standing here so long, these folks leaving the pub are beginning to speculate."

Emmy pulled away from Riley's soothing touch. "Give me half an hour to assemble the meal. If it's okay with you, I'd like to eat on the back porch. I've missed the lake sounds. As a kid, I could sit and listen to night noises for hours."

"I remember. Alanna likes them, too. She also likes helping in the kitchen. Would you be willing to let her set the table? It's one thing she does reasonably well. Just so I don't come empty-handed, I'll bring the wine. I think I have a Chardonnay."

"If you'd prefer we not drink in front of Alanna, I have iced tea and soda."

"Alanna knows I drink occasionally. I can hold my liquor, Emmy." He sounded defensive.

"I noticed your beer at Jake's was nonalcoholic. Jed and Will sneaked beer, but you never did. Will told me the deputies routinely stopped you and shook you down for signs of alcohol misuse, solely because you're Native American."

"They don't do that anymore," he said coolly.

"I didn't mean to offend you. But I..." She hesitated. "I read recently that alcohol is the biggest problem facing reservations. Hey," she said suddenly, "Cassie told me your mom lives in Oklahoma on the Caddo reservation. If life there's so bad, I'm sure you'd move her back here with you. In fact, why haven't you?" Emmy frowned slightly. "It seems to me that would solve the problem of Mrs. Yates. I can't picture a more perfect grandmother than your mom."

"Can't you? Then you've forgotten what my home was like. Mom and Josey never came into the twentieth century, to say nothing of the twenty-first."

"I loved your home, Riley. There was always a pot of some wonderful-smelling food on the stove. Neva and Josey know everything there is to know about making crafts. Between them, they have tons of talent. Has Josey taught Alanna to weave with lake reeds?"

"My daughter can be a doctor or a lawyer or...any other profession she chooses."

"Yes. Or she could throw beautiful pots or weave baskets, like your mom and Josey. What's gotten into you, Riley? It makes no sense to withhold such a rich heritage from your child."

"There's my point, Emmy. She's *my* child. To raise in the manner I see fit. Please leave my family out of future conversations with Alanna."

"But...Cassie said Josey lives in Marshall." Emmy waved a hand. "Twenty minutes away."

"We haven't spoken since Lani died. Lani and Josey—together, they... Well, never mind. Are we clear on the matter of my request?"

"Ye-es." Emmy drew the word in on a long breath. She didn't understand. She'd counted Josey among those nearest and dearest of all she'd lost. But there wasn't any sense in bucking Riley. The stony look on his face made her heart ache.

"I'll see you at the house. Relax, okay? I won't overstep my bounds. We have lots to talk about. That's something I really missed, Riley—our long talks. We could tell each other anything."

A beat or two went by before he finally inclined his head, offered a passable smile and carefully placed Emmy's dart case on the passenger seat of her pickup.

He didn't have to say things had changed between them. Emmy read the sad truth in his eyes right before he turned and walked away.

When she'd left home this afternoon, she'd held such high hopes for their evening. Unrealistic expectations— her biggest downfall according to a raft of social workers. Hadn't she learned by now?

She had. "But damn it all. For just one more night, I'm going to pretend Riley Gray Wolf is still the man of my dreams."

CHAPTER SIX

DINNER WENT a lot more smoothly than Emmy had expected, given the way she and Riley had parted. Alanna was so excited about eating at Emmy's, she livened the evening with her run-on patter. The child certainly didn't lack imagination.

When she'd shopped that day, Emmy had bought a catnip ball for Egypt. Alanna cleaned her plate as fast as she could in order to play with the cat.

Emmy and Riley finished their meal at leisure. Together, they cleared the table. Going to check on Alanna, they found her on the couch curled around Egypt. Girl and kitten were fast asleep.

"Now's when we need that wine," Riley said softly to Emmy. "We didn't have an opportunity at dinner to discuss old times. I'm sorry Alanna dominated the conversation. It was good of you to let her, Emmy. Some people would say she should be seen and not heard."

"I lived in a few homes like that," Emmy murmured. "I think it sends a message that a child has no value. Around Mom Fran's dinner table, we all jabbered at once and she never scolded us. I missed those times so much," she said with feeling.

"Jed mentioned you had it rough after Social Services took you away. Since the emissaries of the state pretended such concern about leaving you here under Jed's supervision, why on earth would they place you with no-madic circus performers?''

"Goodness! They didn't. The circus came much later. Actually, I was eighteen and still a seething mass of anger inside. Hitching cross-country was my way of rebelling against anybody representing authority. Circus folks are like a big family, though. It's not the hard-knock life you might think. Mostly, they're friendly people who love what they're doing. I give them credit for helping me through a bad period. With the attitude I had when I left Texas, I could've ended up in awful trouble.''

"I wish you'd come back to Uncertain then. Why didn't you?''

"Jed and I agree there's no point in flogging ourselves with should-haves,'' she said with finality. "If you're okay with letting Alanna sleep here, Riley, we'll have coffee on the porch. I started a pot earlier.''

"She's out like a light. Coffee sounds good. I take mine black.''

"I remember.'' Emmy hurried to the kitchen to turn on the coffeemaker, with Riley following her. A couple of minutes later it was ready, and she poured two mugs full. Handing one to Riley, she added four heaping teaspoons of sugar to hers.

"Holy cow, woman, it's a wonder you don't have diabetes,'' Riley exclaimed.

She glanced up sharply. "Does excessive sugar intake cause diabetes? Isn't it genetically passed along? How would I know if I had a tendency toward it?''

"I'm no doctor. Blood tests? You've had your blood sugar checked, haven't you?''

Shrugging, Emmy preceded him to the porch. "Isn't it a gorgeous night?'' She adeptly dropped the subject. "Although…last night I noticed how a full moon creates all sorts of creepy shadows down around the lake. It's the way moonlight filters through the Spanish moss on the cypress trees. They seem alive." Emmy stopped and blew on her coffee. "Gad. Before I read about Fran's murder, I never worried about shadows and stuff. But what if the person who killed her lives nearby?"

Riley set his cup on a wicker coffee table. He pressed his nose to the screen that closed out little more than the fireflies. Emmy sank down on one end of a matching wicker settee. Facing her again, he asked unexpectedly, "Will that contraption hold us both?"

"It feels sturdy. Sit beside me. It'll make me feel safer while you give me your theory on the murder."

Riley was far more interested in getting close to Emmy than he was in talking. The prospect of exploring the mystery of her rainbow tattoo enticed him more than speculating about an old murder. Or maybe it was just the full moon, confusing him. No doubt about it, though. That damned rainbow intrigued him.

Time and again, his gaze had locked on the flame-red arc as Emmy cooked and served dinner. He'd even found himself reciting the colors of the rainbow. *Red, orange, yellow, green, blue...*

He'd bitten his tongue more than once, straining to get a glimpse of indigo and violet, colors that never quite rose above the edge of Emmy's scooped neckline.

"Um, what did you say?" he asked, casually sliding his left arm over the back of the settee as he reached for his cup with his right hand.

"I said I have to go in and talk to Sheriff Fielder, and I'd rather take an attorney along. Can you recommend someone who's good but charges fairly?"

Riley's brow knotted above the steaming mug he held

to his lips. "Logan served you a subpoena?" He returned the mug to the coaster with a thump.

Emmy shook her head, her blond hair brushing her bare shoulders and Riley's arm. "Fielder and a deputy came by here the day I moved in. He asked me a bunch of questions about what I remembered from the day Mom Fran went away. He kept referring to a black notebook. I'm sure it's information he gathered back when she disappeared. Frankly, I have only the sketchiest recollection of what I might've told him then. It was a horribly confusing couple of days."

"That's all you need to say. Logan can ask anything he wants, but you don't have to answer diddly at an informal questioning. You don't even have to give another statement. As a matter of fact, you can say no to his invitation."

"You're kidding? He made it sound like an order."

"It's his job to revisit as many of the principals as possible now that he has a case. But technically, you don't have to cooperate unless he arrests you and charges you with something."

"Great. Like I want to go to jail. I prefer to cooperate, Riley. Sheriff Fielder is barking up the wrong tree trying to pin Fran's murder on Jed. If I can show the sheriff he's wrong and should look elsewhere, I'll gladly make ten trips to his office."

Riley's attention wandered again. His right index finger strayed to the upper curve of Emmy's tank top. Her skin felt so soft.... Although he did his best to listen intently to her staunch support of Jed, he was finding it more difficult by the second. "If you're sure you have no information implicating Jed in any way," he murmured, "I'll advise you, and sit in on your interview with Logan."

"You will?" Her eyes reflected her relief as Emmy leaned forward to set her cup beside Riley's. The move was so sudden and unexpected, Riley's finger slipped inside her tank top and grazed the tip of her breast.

She jerked upright, tensing against the sudden need that licked through her belly. An objection rose to her lips, but not because she wouldn't like to move in that direction. Emmy realized she wanted to go to bed with Riley Gray Wolf.

Emmy's gaze met his and she forgot why she'd ever imagined her feelings might be one-sided. His incredibly dark eyes were silvered by moonlight and heavy with desire. If she had any further doubt, the slow circling of Riley's finger on her breast disabused her completely. As did the wet tip of his tongue, suddenly cruising lightly over her tattoo.

Giving way to feelings—cravings growing tighter and hotter inside her—Emmy closed her eyes. Her head fell back against the settee cushion, giving Riley greater access to skin that begged for his attention.

And he didn't disappoint her. He kissed his way up her neck, along her jaw to her mouth, where he lingered long and sweetly before moving down the other side to give the same studied care to her right breast. His hair tickled her lips and her nose, the clean black strands soft against her face.

Suddenly feverish, Emmy worked Riley's shirt out from the waistband of his pants. Her hands roamed his warm skin, and needed more contact. This was *Riley,* her foggy brain kept reminding her. She'd made this same exploration a million times in her dreams. But dreams didn't compare to the real thing—to Riley in the sizzling flesh.

Swallowing a moan, he rucked both of their shirts

higher, then started peeling off Emmy's jeans. He'd never touched skin quite as smooth as Emmy's. No woman's scent had ever driven him quite as crazy as hers. She radiated the fragrance of honeysuckle....

"Emmy, Emmy, I want you. This is right. So absolutely right," he breathed in the damp crook of her neck. His hard, demanding erection strained against the fly of his pants as he pressed tight against her.

Unable to speak, she kneaded his chest, his tense and rigid shoulders. She finally managed a nod right before she pulled the knit shirt he'd changed into over his head. This wasn't how she'd envisioned their first time. Emmy had always imagined a huge bed with crisp, cool sheets, lit by the flicker of a hundred scented candles. *She'd take what she could get. Whatever he offered here and now.*

He'd already unbuckled and unzipped his pants and tossed the settee cushions onto the floor to better accommodate lovemaking. Propped above her on arms that labored to keep his heavier weight from crushing her, a heartbeat before he plunged into her, Riley growled, "Are you on any kind of birth control?"

"Yes." She pulled him toward her. "The pill," she said huskily. "For a menstrual thing." Suddenly, she stilled beneath him. "Oh, Riley, that won't protect—I mean, are you worried about anything else? I'm, uh, not promiscuous. Are you?"

"No. And all I'm worried about, sugar babe, is making this as good as it gets for both of us. We're at least ten years overdue." He lowered himself slowly until their lips met. Then he drove into her fast, stroking her with his thumb as she sheathed him tightly. His body shuddered violently as he withdrew and entered her again.

"Yes, oh, yes," she cried. Emmy closed her teeth over his earlobe to keep from shattering into a hundred thou-

sand bits. Stars in the sky outside went spinning past the
Milky Way. Or maybe it wasn't outside at all; maybe it
was happening inside her head. She'd always known
making love with Riley would be pure heaven.

Riley grabbed her hips to hold her still as he endeav-
ored to slow the rhythm that had taken on a life of its
own. His fingers brushed a small rough patch on her left
buttock. A birthmark? He stroked the spot again.

Suddenly, Emmy wrapped her legs around his waist.
Riley felt something inside him wind tighter and tighter.
He sought Emmy's mouth, his thoughts all jumbled to-
gether as mutual need fused them, body and soul.

Heat spread over Emmy's skin like a wildfire consum-
ing her. Inside, she felt like a volcano on the verge of
explosion. Then she did explode. She'd never experienced anything this cataclysmic, and she told Riley so in
halting joy.

"Same here," he gasped. He still gripped her hips
tightly because shock waves thundered through him,
leaving him too weak to do anything but fall limply
against her. Amazed, he realized he wanted her as much
now as he had before they'd started down the path of no
return. He continued to stroke her hip.

Emmy sighed contentedly and snuggled close to ward
off a chill breeze blowing from the lake. She stopped
pressing tiny kisses from Riley's navel to his collar bone,
made eye contact, then grinned mischievously. "So, I see
you've found the pot of gold."

Riley leaned his weight on one elbow. He stared down
at her, his expression puzzled.

She slapped his arm playfully and flopped over on her
stomach. Taking his free hand, she directed him to a spot
on her hip that would be hidden by panties or a bathing
suit. "Is there enough light for you to see? At Jake's,

you joked about a pot of gold at the end of my rainbow. Well, sir, you are one of the privileged few to learn the truth. After Seattle, I visited a second tattoo parlor in Portland, Oregon, where I had a final touch added to my rainbow. Just for the hell of it.''

Riley bent for a closer inspection. What he'd guessed to be a birthmark was really a thumb-print-size outline of a kettle with a handle. Yellow stuff spilling over the edge of the pot could pass for gold nuggets, he supposed.

He couldn't help himself; he swatted Emmy on the butt. Amid shared laughter, Riley gathered her into his arms and tumbled her into the cushions again for a steamy kiss. One that, in all probability, would have led to a second round of lovemaking, had he not heard a fretful voice calling from the other room. ''Daddy! Daddy? Where are you? I'm thirsty.''

Emmy, too, heard Alanna, and she sprang away from Riley. ''My God!'' Panting, she scrambled to find her scattered clothing. ''Alanna could have walked in on us at any time. What on earth were we *thinking*, Riley?''

''I'd say we pretty much acted out what we were thinking,'' he said, arching an eyebrow wryly. Then he called to his daughter in a calm voice. ''Hold on a minute, Alanna. Wait there. Daddy's getting your water.''

Emmy couldn't believe how easy and methodically Riley righted his clothes. She had one leg of her jeans inside out and was trying hopelessly to correct the problem and pull on her lacy underpants. Ultimately, she didn't manage to do either.

He took the tangle of clothing from her shaking hands, turned the leg, then dropped a kiss on Emmy's nose as he handed back the pants. ''I'll bring her some water. You probably ought to get hold of yourself before you put in an appearance, Emmy.''

She gaped after him, only freeing herself from the stupor when she heard a cupboard open and close and water running in the sink. As she hurriedly finished dressing, Emmy wondered how often Riley did this sort of thing—leave a hot session of making love to be a dad. He seemed so cool and collected while she was clumsy, and panicked, as well.

But she refused to allow the green-eyed monster to gain victory over her self-confidence. What happened between her and Riley had been brewing a long time and been put on hold due to no fault of their own. If she hadn't left Uncertain, they would've become lovers within half a dozen years. Before he went to college, anyway. However, that didn't mean either had a claim on the other now.

Checking to see that she had everything on and properly zipped and buttoned, Emmy went inside. She met Riley returning to the kitchen, an empty glass in one hand and a sleepy-eyed little girl cradled in his free arm.

Emmy took the glass. Avoiding his gaze, she turned and tucked the glass into the dishwasher.

"Alanna's asked to go home so she can sleep in her own bed," Riley said to Emmy's back. "I, uh, really hate to run off."

She twirled one hand negligently in the air, still not looking at him. "I didn't realize it was so late. You need to get up early for work tomorrow."

"Will you drop by my office in the morning and have Marge book you an appointment? Meanwhile, write down everything you remember about the last time you saw Frannie. We'll be better prepared for Fielder's questions. Oh, and catalogue the events that took place during the days after she disappeared."

"Two days. On the second, I was whisked away without warning."

"That's right," he said, sounding troubled. "Alanna, before you fall asleep on my shoulder, thank Emmy for dinner, please."

The girl lifted her head. "You cook good shrimp, Emmy. I had fun. Can I come over again tomorrow and play with Egypt?"

Emmy smiled. "If it's all right with your dad and Mrs. Yates, you can visit Egypt tomorrow afternoon. He naps a lot in the morning. He's more ready to chase his ball after lunch."

"Daddy, is it all right?" Alanna's words were muffled by a sleepy yawn.

"As long as you don't make a pest of yourself. Emmy, I'm counting on you to be the judge."

"We'll be fine. Will you inform Mrs. Yates? I'm not sure she'd take my word on anything." Emmy opened the front door and stepped back to give Riley room to pass.

Catching her eye, he mouthed silently, "I'll talk to you later."

Emmy blushed. She didn't know what they'd say in the aftermath—didn't know what there *was* to say. It had happened; that was all. They'd both had an old itch to scratch. And brother, had they scratched like pups with fleas. She was leery of trying to analyze what had happened. And reluctant to say she had regrets. Nor did she want to hear about any Riley might have. "I'll drop by your office in the morning and set up an appointment. Maybe I'll talk to you then."

"Dang, I hope you get your phone soon. Jeez, Emmy, I feel like crap leaving this way." Riley gestured helplessly, looking like he meant every word.

Emmy rubbed her arms. Because Alanna didn't act so sleepy now, Emmy mustered a smile for her benefit. "You're off the hook for helping with dishes this time. We, uh, had…old ground to cover tonight, Riley. But don't think I expect a repeat."

Riley glanced back more than once before he reached his property. He was bothered by Emmy's last speech. It sounded to Riley as though her carefully chosen words had placed tonight in the category of one-night stand. Unless she'd said it to divert the interest of his too curious daughter.

Emmy withdrew without a wave. That certainly didn't bode well. Damn, Riley wished he had the freedom to go back after he'd tucked Alanna into bed. But he was a father first. He'd never leave her alone in the house at night, not even for the few minutes it'd take to run next door. He'd have to try and corner Emmy when she came to his office to book an appointment. And he'd have to do it so Marge wouldn't read anything into his request for a private meeting with a new client. He groaned silently. Marge had eagle eyes where anything out of the ordinary was concerned.

He carried his daughter inside, resigned to the fact that he might have to wait a while before continuing where he and Emmy had left off.

EMMY SHOULD HAVE SLEPT like a hibernating bear since she no longer had a solid bone in her body. Except she was too keyed up. Making love with Riley was all she could think about.

She got out of bed once and tried to write the list he'd requested. She found herself sitting with chin in hand, daydreaming about the texture of Riley's hair and the warm, wonderful heat of his skin.

If she'd managed an hour of sleep before the sun streamed in the window and awakened her, she'd be surprised.

A shower helped only minimally. She needed to get out of the house, away from the sun-drenched, screened porch that was a constant reminder. On the spur of the moment, Emmy took the phone book Gwyn had left behind and looked up the address for the pottery in Marshall, where Josey worked. Emmy decided to pick up a box of fresh doughnuts and drop in on Josey during her coffee break.

The first thing Emmy saw when she drove in and parked in front of the factory was row after row of red clay flower pots in every size and shape imaginable. She slowly picked her way through the aisles shaded by wood-slat roofs, envisioning how Fran's house would look with pots of brightly blooming geraniums set along the front porch. Or was she foolish to spend her money decorating a place she might not stay in?

Possibly. But Emmy knew that by the time she left here, she'd definitely be poorer—and happier. Poorer still once she stopped at the nursery she'd passed on the highway.

A cashier at the pottery retail counter escorted Emmy to one of several picnic tables set in a shaded courtyard. The young woman said she'd find Josey and send her over. She asked for a name, which Emmy provided. "I haven't seen Josey in some time. I think she'll remember me, though." Emmy set her box of doughnuts on the table.

Josey did remember. She came charging out of one of the work barns, wiping clay-covered hands on a massive apron that flapped around her knees. When she got close enough to see Emmy's face, she let out a squeal of delight. "I thought my ears were playing tricks on me when Kim said who was here. Let me look at you.'' Tears gathered in dark eyes so like her brother's. ''I never thought we'd ever see you again, Emmy Monday. I want to hug you, but I'm a mess of green clay. Tell me you aren't just passing through. We have so much to talk about. Where have you been?''

''I'm here now, and I'm going to hug you regardless. Who cares about a little clay?'' Emmy flung her arms around Josey's sturdy shoulders and squeezed her for several seconds. ''I brought doughnuts,'' she said when they finally broke apart. ''Is there a place here we can buy coffee or sodas?''

''Both machines are over by the wall. Let me pay.'' Josey fumbled under her apron, and pulled mashed one-dollar bills from her pocket. ''If you'd get me an orange soda, I'll go wash up and be right back. Just promise you won't disappear again.''

''I won't.'' Emmy chuckled. ''For the record, it wasn't my plan to leave last time. And now there's no one with the power to order me away, thank goodness.''

''No husband?'' Josey picked up Emmy's left hand.

Emmy pulled back. ''Nary a one. What about you?''

Josey rolled her eyes. ''I've been dating the same guy for ten years. He and I are both master potters. We work opposite shifts.'' As if that explained why they hadn't married, Josey shaded her eyes and treated Emmy to a piercing look. ''How long have you been back? Have you seen Riley?''

Emmy nodded. ''Would you believe I rented Mom Fran's old house, so I'm living next door to him. A story in itself. Listen, go ahead and wash up. I'll get our drinks.'' Really Emmy needed a moment to figure out what and how much she'd tell Josey about her reunion with Riley. There'd been a time the two girls had shared the most intimate secrets. Emmy wasn't as willing now.

Josey returned in a flash. Emmy had just set two cans of soda next to the doughnut box when Josey sank down on one of the benches. "If you've talked to Riley, he's probably told you what a horrible sister I am."

"Yesterday, for the first time, he mentioned something vague about a problem. He just said you two hadn't spoken in a while."

"Five years," Josey replied darkly, pausing to choose a doughnut. She passed Emmy a napkin. "I should leave the story for him to tell. Maybe if he has to spell it out to someone, he'll see how bull-headed he's being."

"Wow, what happened? You idolized him." Emmy gazed at the crown of braids arranged atop Josey's head. She hadn't changed her style in all these years. Emmy, always a blonde, had envied Josey the straight black hair that swept her knees.

"You knew he got married?" When Emmy nodded, Josey went on. "I introduced them. We'd moved to Oklahoma. Lani Sky and I met at a Native craft fair. She lived on a neighboring reservation. I admired her beading. She made bracelets and necklaces using old techniques. To make a long story short, Riley had graduated from college with honors and passed the bar exam on his first try. The day he came to tell us, Lani was at the house, trying to talk my uncle into voting to ban non-Indian curriculum in the reservation school. Riley was riding high. Out of the blue, he invited Lani to go into Anadarko for dinner. It's not far from Binger, where Mama lives. Riley included me. I can't remember why I refused. Riley and Lani were opposites, so I never dreamed anything would come of his asking her out."

"Obviously they clicked," Emmy said lightly, not sure

after last night that she wanted the nitty-gritty details of Riley's romance.

Josey frowned. "She cast a spell on him. Or rather Lani's uncle did. He's a shaman."

Emmy stopped chewing her maple-frosted doughnut. She waited for Josey to say she was kidding. She didn't. In fact, she continued talking about Lani's practice of dabbling in the old lore. "Lani and her mother gave sessions in shape-shifting and soul retrieval. Her whole family believes the modern world threatens the communal way of life. They're entitled to their beliefs, but we're talking about Riley, who ever since Dad died, turned away from anything remotely Indian."

Emmy recognized the truth in Josey's statement. Looking back, she realized how hard Riley had tried to be exactly like Jed and Will and their friends.

Josey apparently didn't notice she'd momentarily lost Emmy. "Lani said once that her uncle held a quest retreat for the purpose of calling up someone versed in non-Native legalities. Someone capable of fighting for tribal rights. Lani's uncle said the spirits had sent Riley to them, and Lani believed him. All I can figure is that Riley didn't listen to what Lani was saying, and vice versa. She married Riley without really knowing him, then felt trapped when he insisted on practicing law in Uncertain."

"When they found themselves at odds, why didn't they divorce?"

"Two reasons. One, he was busy building his practice. Two, he served as chief contractor on the house he was having built. But to Lani, Riley had been sent by the spirits and she'd been chosen to open his eyes."

"The relationship sounds sad and hopelessly doomed."

"Yes. Riley woke up once Lani got pregnant. Up to then, he hadn't paid attention to how often she took the bus to Oklahoma. She didn't drive. Their house was done and he expected her to start taking an interest in making it a home."

"That's understandable. It's a beautiful place."

"Lani hated it. Remember, she preferred living in a remote hogan."

"Why deprive herself if she didn't have to?"

Josey lifted an eyebrow. "Not everyone is convinced our forefathers were deprived, Emmy. Many still believe the old way of life is better."

"I'm sorry, Josey. It's hard for me to comprehend. Anyway, knowing Riley, I'm guessing he saw the problem after his wife died, and now he's ridden with guilt."

"Oh, Emmy, if only it were that simple. Lani suffered more than the usual symptoms of pregnancy. Riley assumed she was under the care of Rico Santiago. He's a good, reputable M.D. When she was about six months along, Riley discovered that Lani had been relying on her uncle for care, and he hit the roof. By then, the signs were everywhere. Lani used chants and spells involving skulls, teeth, claws and feathers. She brewed wild grasses, beaded elaborate fetishes and hid them in cupboards and drawers. Riley stormed through the house, ripping up some and burning others."

"Oh, my. I see now why Riley got so upset when I asked him if you'd taught Alanna to weave. I'm afraid I don't understand, though, why he's so mad at you. You're family."

Josey crushed her soda can. "I'd already taken this job as a potter. It was a work day. A Friday. Lani phoned me quite early. She was close to her delivery date. Riley had apparently made her an appointment in Tyler for

Monday to see a woman OB. He thought maybe it embarrassed her to see Rico. Of course, that wasn't the problem. He and Lani had a huge fight over her uncle, who I guess insinuated the baby was cursed and would stay cursed until Riley returned to the fold. Lani begged me to take her home for the weekend. I can't swear she said it'd be okay with Riley if I drove, but she implied as much. I hadn't seen Mom in a month, so I agreed. Even asked for the day off. Lani didn't look well when I picked her up. I tried to talk her out of making the trip. To this day, I don't think Riley knows how hard I tried."

Emmy hated to rush Josey, but she sensed her friend might not otherwise finish the story. "So you went?"

"Yes. We'd no more than arrived at her family's hogan—it's miles from anywhere—when Lani started labor. Right off, I felt she was in too much pain. It seemed centered in her right side. Her uncle began to chant and shake his rattles. I pleaded with Lani's mother to let me take her to the tribal clinic. They ordered me to leave."

"Oh, Josey. How awful for you." Emmy curled her fingers around Josey's work-roughened hands. "Don't go on if telling me is too painful. I can guess. It wasn't just because of the labor, but partly a bad appendix. If it ruptured, it's a miracle Alanna lived."

"Exactly. And she might not have if Riley hadn't intervened. Lani's screams were so loud it scared me to death. I drove to my mom's. I didn't know what else to do. She phoned Riley at work and luckily caught him. Lucky for Alanna, anyway. He pitched a royal fit and ended up intimidating the tribal police. He ordered a private ambulance to collect Lani and deliver her to the county hospital. In doing that, he touched off a huge tribal ruckus. Jed flew him to Oklahoma. But it was too late. Lani died in the ambulance on the way to the hospital. The crew delivered the baby. By the time Riley got there, Alanna was in infant ICU at a nontribal hospital.''

"I still don't understand why he won't speak to you, Josey. It's clear to me that without your intervention, he wouldn't have Alanna.''

She shrugged. "Or he might have saved Lani if I hadn't taken her to Oklahoma." She shook her head sadly. "Her uncle claimed his rituals could have pulled Lani's sickness out. Riley had to appear before the tribal council to explain why he sent Lani to a non-Indian hospital. In the end all that saved his neck was the fact that he's Indian himself. For all the good it does him. He was so angry, he ordered our council to strike his name from the Caddo rolls. He literally denounced his birthright, so Mother and I are supposed to consider him a nonperson. He has every right to refuse to see me. We're no longer connected.''

"Nonsense! I can't believe Neva would disown her son.''

"I've caught her mailing him an occasional letter. I haven't contacted him. I can't.''

"Crossing a name off some stupid list doesn't change the fact you're brother and sister.''

Josey dipped her chin in a guilty fashion. "Riley chooses not to be in our family.''

Emmy didn't know what to say. She realized Josey might have taken her silence for censure when she jumped up and tossed her crushed can in a trash receptacle. "I have to get back to work. I'm over my allotted break.''

"So soon?" Emmy glanced at her watch. "At least give me your address and phone number. You know where I'm living. I'll have a phone later this week.''

"If you're taking up with Riley again, it's better you

stay away from me." Josey started walking off. "He'll never forgive me."

"Wait." Emmy scrambled off the bench. "We're friends, Josey. No one tells me who I can and can't see."

Josey didn't slow down. If anything, she sped up. Emmy felt powerless to stop her. She stood there vacillating until a group of potters emerged from another building and entered the courtyard. They cast Emmy odd looks. She disposed of her empty soda can and left the nearly full box of doughnuts for them to deal with as they saw fit.

The problem between Riley and his sister appeared to be one of pigheadedness on both sides. Emmy bought her flower pots and drove off, pondering what, if anything, she could do to help mend the rift. She, who'd give anything to have just one blood relative, couldn't imagine cutting herself off from family for any reason. Riley was not an uncaring man. Emmy didn't understand how he could deliberately keep his daughter from seeing her aunt and grandmother.

She swung by the nursery, then drove straight to her place, where she dropped off the pots, potting soil and flats of geraniums and petunias. Her next stop was Riley's office. She was hard-pressed to say why she found it so difficult a task. Yet she paced in front of the building for a few minutes before she took a deep breath and climbed the stairs to a second-floor office that had his name and title etched in the door's frosted glass.

A gray-haired woman seated at the only desk in the room glanced up when Emmy shut the door too hard, making the panel rattle "Sorry," she said meekly. "I guess I don't know my own strength."

The woman smiled. "You'd be Emmy Monday."

It flustered Emmy to have Riley's assistant identify her

by name. "Um, yes. Is my being an outsider that obvious?"

"The whole town's abuzz about how you beat the champ yesterday at darts. You're nothing like I expected. No muscles. I admit I watch too much TV, but I pictured Xena, queen of the women warriors."

Emmy blushed to the tips of her hair. "I don't know whether to be flattered or not."

"Be flattered. Say, you phoned here asking questions about Riley's fees. I knew I'd recognize your voice if I ever heard it again. He mentioned you two are old friends. Does he know the exact nature of the legal advice you're after?"

"Yes. Last night he told me to make an appointment. I've brought the diary he asked me to prepare. Once he looks it over, he's going with me to see the sheriff." Emmy pulled a folded paper from her purse. "This is everything I remember that happened at the time Fran Granger disappeared."

"I wasn't referring to the criminal matter. Is Riley aware you want him to dig around in your past to search for your birth parents, Ms. Monday?"

Riley charged out of his office in time to hear Marge's question. He waited for Emmy to correct her. The longer the silence dragged on, the more unsure he became. He gave a short laugh. "I know Marge has a reputation for being infallible, Emmy, but it's okay to tell her she's wrong, that all I'm handling is your interview with Logan."

Emmy cleared her throat. "I need someone with a computer who has access to the state's legal records. I do want to hire you to help me mount a background search."

"It's out of the question," he said explosively. "I guess I didn't make myself clear. Today is all that's important. Today, and the future. Forget the hell about any stupid search, Emmy.''

"I can't," she cried.

Riley's face closed. Spinning on his shiny Italian loafers, he headed into his office and attempted to shut her out.

Emmy blocked his retreat with a stiff arm. "Don't confuse me with your former wife, Riley. I saw Josey today. She told me what happened." Storming in after him, she slammed the door to his private office. "I have no desire to *live* in the past. I only want to know whose blood runs in my veins.''

"What does it matter? You are who you are. A self-made woman.''

"Who *is* that woman, Riley? Can you promise no evil lurks inside me?''

He grabbed her and pulled her toward him. And fused their mouths on an anguished groan.

She wanted to respond, but she didn't. When he released her and warily stepped aside, she whispered brokenly. "Who were you kissing, Riley? The daughter of a lunatic? Of a drugged-out whore? It matters to me, dammit. And if you care anything about me, it should matter to you.''

He said nothing, merely waved her away.

"Fine. With or without your help, I intend to find Emerald Monday's roots.'' With each step Emmy took in retreat, she prayed Riley would relent and stop her.

He let her go into the reception area and he let her leave the office. She didn't look back until she was unlocking her pickup. She saw him staring down at her through the window, hands clasped behind his back as if he were afraid something would drive him to reach out to her. His face remained set in an unreadable mask. A stubborn, unreadable mask.

CHAPTER SEVEN

EMMY DIDN'T WANT to go directly home. She wasn't up to dealing with Alanna, not while she was so upset with Riley. Especially not while her lips still burned from his last kiss. A puzzling kiss, to say the least. He and she had reached the same type of stalemate that existed between him and his sister. If Josey hadn't been able to forge a truce with Riley in five years, how could Emmy ever hope to succeed?

She didn't doubt that Riley was physically drawn to her. But a purely physical relationship was a long way from what Emmy wanted with him. It surprised her to find she still wanted what they'd so briefly shared nineteen years ago. Sizzle and spark, but also a bond of friendship and respect. Minds that met on issues that counted.

Emmy wasn't sure what possessed her to drive down the road past the spot where, according to Gwyn and Jed, archaeologist Tessa Lang had unearthed Fran's bones. Her thoughts were consumed by how she'd left things with Riley. She emerged from those thoughts to suddenly find herself parked in front of a dirt path roped off with yellow crime-scene tape.

Emmy climbed dazedly from her pickup, hearing only the trill of mockingbirds and the whisper of wind through loblolly pines. There was nothing particularly spooky about the place. Off to her right, a gentle slope led to the lake. One of the wood duck habitats, she remembered. An inlet warmed by heavily foliaged oak and elm. White cranes swooped overhead, on their noisy way to feed at lily pads. On the lake, yellow cypress, grayed with webs of Spanish moss rose high above low-growing scrub brush, protecting the habitat along the bank from human intrusion.

Emmy skirted the first police barrier and followed a line of tape strung between stakes, apparently leading to the burial site. In spite of fighting a gloomy chill, Emmy continued on doggedly. Perhaps seeing the place itself would provide a sense of why her foster mom might have come to this isolated location—or why she'd been taken here. There were no homes here. Most of those she'd cleaned were summer places dotting the opposite shore. So why here? Why, why, why?

Emmy wished she'd been gifted with clairvoyance. Or more to the point, she wished she could turn back the clock and revise everything that had happened that fateful day. She tripped over a clod of dirt and realized she was walking in furrows—deep tire tracks made by a heavy machine. An earthmover? The tracks were intersected and crisscrossed with smaller tire marks and the waffle-prints of boots.

Rounding a bend, Emmy let her steps slow. Spread out before her lay the actual dig. Equipment and tools were still strewn about, as if any day the archaeological crew would return to work. Tall clumps of native grasses were still flattened. Some had been bulldozed. Several gaping holes gouged the dark, loamy soil.

Emmy's stomach started to roll as she surveyed the depressions. Her discomfort probably came from know-ing that one pit had contained Mom Fran's skeletal remains. She covered her mouth to keep from gagging, but did it anyway.

What had she hoped to prove by coming here?

That was easy. Since the day she'd read the news story, Emmy had felt unstrung. As though a portion of her life had stalled in her thirteenth year. The tangled, knotted threads all led back to Uncertain. What she needed in order to get on with her life was *closure*. It might be a pop-psychology commonplace; it was also a very real need.

Confused by a scene she'd hoped would cleanly sever old ties, Emmy ducked under and stepped over low strips of yellow tape to head back to her pickup.

A white Bronco, bearing a flashing light bar, wheeled off the main road and bounced and jounced over already deep tire ruts, headed in her direction. Emmy's heart slammed violently in her chest. She jumped behind a tree.

Almost before the vehicle came to a halt, the deputy who'd accompanied Sheriff Fielder to Emmy's rented house sprang out. He might have tipped his hat courteously, but he eyed Emmy with distrust as she peered around the tree trunk.

"Ma'am. Sheriff Fielder sent me to check on a tip he received that someone was trespassing on a marked crime scene." The deputy used his hat to jab toward three spots. "There are signs posted out at the main road and all along this path. Plus, the tape itself says Keep Out Under Penalty of Law. I'm afraid I'll have to take you in, ma'am."

"Ta-take m-me in?" Emmy faltered. "Why? I've done nothing. Touched nothing. Who phoned you? I haven't seen another soul." She gazed around and across the lake, feeling her skin crawl. Had someone spied on her?

"The sheriff's sources are confidential, ma'am. If you'd like to lock your vehicle, I'll stick an official tag on it for safekeeping. You'll be riding over to the jail with me."

"This is absurd. I've done nothing." Emmy repeated a useless defense.

The young deputy resettled the big, western-style hat on his head. He then hooked both thumbs over a wide, leather belt weighted down with the intimidating tools of his trade. Handcuffs, pistol, cell phone and pepper spray.

Emmy licked her lips with a nervous tongue. In a rational moment that surfaced through another angry protest she was about to make, she decided to give it up and save her breath. Her interview with Logan Fielder was overdue. She'd blown her chance to have Riley's help at the debriefing, but she was going to end this…this threat, nonetheless. Squaring her shoulders, she swept past the man whose name tag read Deputy Masters. "My pickup is already locked. I'm ready to go any time you are, Deputy." She marched around the Bronco and reached for the front passenger door handle.

"In the back, ma'am. Behind the screen. And I'll take your purse just in case you're carrying a weapon."

"Oh, good grief! I'm not even carrying a lipstick. My Louisiana driver's license, a packet of tissues and a small amount of cash is all. But suit yourself," she muttered, tossing him the handbag. However, if Emmy had thought her stomach was jumpy before, her nervousness increased once Masters closed her inside the Bronco like a common criminal. She felt even worse when she happened to notice that it was impossible to open the back doors from within the vehicle. Though she was innocent of any wrongdoing, she felt like a prisoner, already judged and convicted.

RILEY'S ASSISTANT tapped on the door to his private office. She poked her gray head inside without waiting for his invitation to enter.

"What is it?" he asked shortly, glancing up with a scowl. He should have been preparing for an upcoming court case, in which he was scheduled to represent a local landowner against two scavengers caught logging the man's stand of loblolly pine. The timber rustlers claimed they'd accidentally wandered onto his client's acreage. It was true the accused had authorization to log a much smaller piece of property in the vicinity, but it was a stretch of the imagination to think they'd lost their way as badly as they alleged—right onto his client's land.

Riley wanted to win this case in the worst way. Heisting virgin timber from the land of absentee owners or from longtime residents who owned unconnected tracts had become an increasing problem over the last few years, due to a shortage of aged trees. So how come his mind hadn't been on his case since Emmy's midmorning visit? In fact, as Marge interrupted him, Riley discovered he'd once again been covering a legal pad with Emmy's name and initials. He hastily tore off the page and thrust it into the desk drawer where he'd put his previous doodles.

"Sorry to bother you, Riley," Marge said as she walked toward him. "I received a call from Cheryl Ott, at the jail. Kyle Masters just brought in your friend. Cheryl's not sure of the charge. She thinks it's a trespassing infraction. A technicality."

Riley half rose from his desk and automatically reached for the suit jacket he'd hung over the back of his chair. "So Logan's really going to charge Jed Louis? Get Dexter Thorndyke on the phone. Jed and Gwyn have probably contacted him, but tell him I'm available for any legwork he may need locally. And as usual, he and Jed are welcome to make use of the conference room here if they need it.''

"Excuse me, I'm not talking about Jed. It's Emmy Monday Kyle hauled in."

"What?'' The word exploded from Riley's lips. He paused with his jacket half on, pinioning his arms behind him.

Marge looked worried. "Bart Jones is due here for an appointment in fifteen minutes. Shall I tell him you're tied up with an emergency and try to reschedule him for later in the week? It's Bart's usual complaint about the Varner kids using his fence posts to practice calf-roping. I already tried telling him you wouldn't bring a suit against Dale Varner. After all, Dale replaced Bart's rickety old posts with spanking new ones, same as he's always done.''

Riley broke into her tale of the two old neighboring ranchers' ongoing feud. "Has Emmy phoned here asking me to provide counsel?'' His breath caught as he waited for Marge's response, hoping to hear she'd asked for him—that Emmy wanted him. Ever since he'd acted like such an ass and let her storm out, Riley had been trying to come up with some workable way to make amends.

Marge was shaking her head. "No one's called but Cheryl.'' She gave him a stern look. "Since when do you need an invitation to lend a hand to an old friend?''

Having employed Marge for six years, Riley was well acquainted with every facet of her meddling. Sometimes he let her get away with it, and sometimes he didn't. Never had he hedged as much as he did now.

"Ah, hell,'' he exclaimed without elaborating. Riley finished shrugging into his jacket, threw a fresh legal pad into his soft-sided briefcase and zipped it closed. Then he patted his pockets, checking to see if he had an adequate supply of pens.

As he rounded his desk, Marge tried awfully hard not to look smug. She hid her satisfaction even as she stopped him long enough to fuss with straightening his collar. Marge assumed her most professional tone. "For whatever reason Logan dispatched Kyle to fetch her, he'll undoubtedly get around to questioning Emmy about Fran Granger's disappearance. Here. These are the notes Ms. Monday drew up, the ones she said you'd asked her to compile. A diary of events the day Fran went missing, I think Emmy called them." Marge shoved folded papers into a side compartment of Riley's briefcase.

He laughed and felt the tension leave his shoulders. "You know, Marge, Emmy might well toss me out of Logan's office on my butt. Don't nag, woman. I'm going. I probably owe her an apology for the way things ended this morning."

"No probably about it. You acted like a first-class jerk."

"Thank you very much for your unbiased analysis." Riley stopped around his suddenly chagrined secretary to open the door. "Oh, I see you've suddenly remembered who signs your paycheck."

"I spend more hours at this office working for you than I do at home. The day comes when I can't speak my mind, you won't have to fire me, Riley. I'll quit."

"You don't even know Emmy Monday. Why champion her cause?"

"Well…my cousin Laura had an illegitimate child. My aunt and uncle forced her to give the baby away without so much as seeing it, or knowing if she'd had a boy or a girl. Not all birth mothers walk off and never think of their babies again. Some, like poor Laura, feel terrible guilt and shame about giving the baby up. She suffered for years. My sister and I wish the child had searched for her before Laura flipped out and had to be committed for trying to steal someone else's baby."

"I'm sorry about your cousin's plight, Marge, but Emmy wasn't *given* up for adoption. She was abandoned at Monday Trade Days. Thousands of people roam those stalls. She might have been picked up by a nutcase. Or a pervert. Whoever left her didn't know or care. And Emmy was dead wrong to think I give a damn about who her parents might be. People should be valued for who they are, not how they came into the world."

"Emmy was right on one point. You *have* mixed her situation up with Lani's. Your wife didn't delve into the past to discover her ancestry, or because she wanted to be more than a case number on a state social service roll. Lani knew who she was—a pivotal member of a larger spiritual movement. The only unanswered question in her mind was why we couldn't all see that her lifestyle was perfect. Therein lies the problem. Like many people with uncompromising beliefs, she lacked tolerance. Therein also lies the difference between Emmy's quest and Lani's."

Riley ripped open the door without a word.

"You aren't going to want to hear this, either. Everyone who knows and cares about you has kept quiet on the subject of Lani for too long. You haven't told your daughter anything about her mother, have you? If you aren't careful, one day Alanna will be in Emmy Monday's shoes. You'd better ask yourself how you'll handle her questions when she starts kindergarten and some wiseacre kid breaks the news that storks don't deliver babies."

"I've never told Alanna anything that stupid," Riley

objected. He was almost out the door and stopped cold. "She knows her mother died."

"She doesn't know she has aunts, uncles and two grandmothers." Marge's voice dropped to a gentle rebuke. "I've been to your home, Riley. Alanna's room has every conceivable material thing a child could ever want—except a single picture of her mother. In fact, the house is stripped clean of Lani's photos. She did exist, Riley."

"Call Logan. Tell him if he asks Emmy so much as one question before I get there, I'll cry foul play from here to the county seat." Riley didn't exactly rock the building's foundation slamming the door, but the glass shuddered. And his hands were shaking, he discovered, when he tried to unlock his car door.

Dammit, he felt ganged up on. First Emmy, then Marge. Only...Marge was right. He came to the realization slowly, after he'd cooled down and managed to open his car door and climb inside. His experience with Lani was why he'd refused Emmy's request. Bad memories, barely held in abeyance, affected everything he did.

The other day, Emmy had asked him why Alanna wasn't in preschool. The bald-faced truth—he hadn't been ready to field questions about his daughter's mother. It was never enough to say a parent died. People wanted to know when and how. And kids *would* ask, Riley knew. He'd been young when his dad died in 'Nam. That might be another reason he'd hated the circumstances surrounding Lani's death. Both deaths were senseless. Both had died for a pointless cause.

Jeez, Marge packed a wallop like a sledgehammer when she took a notion to work a guy over.

"Well, hell," he growled, backing out of his parking space. "I'd have saved both of us a lot of grief if I'd just said I've already decided I don't want Emmy walking out of my life again."

Thing was, Riley couldn't quite reconcile the reservations he still had about the search Emmy wanted done. But searches sometimes took years, didn't they? Whipping into the parking lot next to the jail, it dawned on him that maybe he could, in good conscience, promise to nose around for Emmy. Poll a few colleagues who had experience locating lost relatives. It wouldn't hurt to compile their feedback and hand it over to her. With luck, considering how things had progressed between him and Emmy the other night, he might buy enough time to convince her she'd be better off canceling what would surely end up a disappointing wild-goose chase.

Riley thought he had a plausible-sounding plan put together by the time he strode into Logan Fielder's waiting room and saw Kyle Masters in the process of dipping Emmy's fingers in fingerprint ink. It was a messy, antiquated method not used in more modern jails.

"Kyle, what in Sam Hill are you doing? Stop. Now!" Riley flung his briefcase into a chair.

"Riley!" Emmy's eyes widened almost as much as Kyle's did.

The men engaged in a staring match. "Did this jerk mention you had the right to phone your attorney, Emmy?" Riley demanded.

"Yes, he did. I told him I don't have a lawyer."

Riley jammed one hand in his pocket, let his head drop to his chest and massaged the back of his neck with the hand that was free. "What the hell am I, cat food?"

"You refused my request."

"I didn't." Riley glared at the deputy. "Call and ask Marge. Ms. Monday retained me yesterday. I want to know why you brought her in. What's the charge?"

"Uh, trespassing, and unlawful entry of a marked crime scene, I guess."

"You guess?" Riley turned to Emmy for verification.

She hunched both shoulders. "I followed a row of tape to the excavation site where Mom Fran was found. I didn't touch anything at the site, I swear."

A woman quietly reading a magazine in the waiting area outside the sheriff's private office jumped up and pushed her way into the circle. "There's not a lot left for anybody to touch." Sounding peeved, she flipped a gold-red braid over her shoulder. "I'm Tessa Lang," she said, introducing herself to Emmy. "I heard Deputy Masters tell the clerk that you're Emerald Monday. I'm the one who discovered Frannie Granger's remains. I know what she was to you. Please let me say how sorry I am, Ms. Monday."

"Call me Emmy. You don't look like my image of an archaeologist, Ms. Lang."

"Tessa, please. Hello, Riley." She slanted him an oblique smile. "Last time I saw you was at Gwyn's wedding. Where have you been keeping yourself?"

"I've been winding down a high-profile case. Why are you hanging out here?" He grinned. "Crazy Jake's is a lot more fun."

Emmy gazed from Tessa to Riley and back. She wondered what Riley's relationship with the attractive archaeologist was or had been. It brought home to her, like nothing else had, the gap between her and Riley. Tessa Lang would not only appeal to a man like him because of her beauty, but also as a fellow professional. Jed's wife and this woman were both gorgeous, congenial and they had interesting careers.

Emmy reflected on her own erratic work history. While never boring, most of her jobs were dead-end. She emerged from a cloud of dismay to hear Tessa's reply to Riley's question. "The jail's become my home away from home. I check every few days, hoping Sheriff Fielder will lift the ban on my digging. I'm at risk of losing my grant. I wish to heaven I'd never found those bones."

Riley and Kyle Masters both nodded sympathetically. Turning to Emmy, Riley said, "Tessa's grant time is ticking away and Logan left her to twiddle her thumbs."

Tessa sighed. "I had such high hopes. I researched a full year to find this site. It's my dig from start to finish. I need a comprehensive report of results to complete my doctoral dissertation. So far, everything's gone wrong."

"That's too bad," Emmy murmured. She didn't know squat about what it took to write a thesis, but she wanted Tessa Lang to finish her doctorate so she'd get out of Dodge, so to speak. At least, Emmy wanted her far away from Riley. She doubted that outside of the one Caddo Lake site, Uncertain, Texas represented a huge drawing card for archaeologists. Emmy assumed they preferred moldy jungles and Egyptian tombs.

Fielder poked his head out of his office. "What's all the ruckus out here? Kyle, are you through processing Ms. Monday? Oh, *you're* here," he barked, scowling at Tessa Lang. "If I've told you once, I've told you a passel of times—nobody's disturbing that site until I'm done with this investigation."

"Grids have to be carefully maintained and the soil has to be sifted and brushed properly. Just let my crew do your search. I promise we'll turn over every bit of evidence that doesn't belong to the Caddo Indians."

Fielder shook his shaggy head. "It seems you have your agenda and I have mine. The law says my active murder investigation takes precedence over whatever

your twitty bunch of college kids wants to prove. Someone murdered Frannie Granger within my jurisdiction. I
aim to find out who. So stay the hell out of my way, Ms.
Lang. I said I'd notify you when you can resume digging,
and I will. Until then, beat it.''

Tessa clenched her fists. She marched out after a quick
wave to the others.

Fielder swung round, leveling a glower at Riley. ''Today must be my day to have half the folks in town telling
me how I oughta do my job. I see you're champing at
the bit to add your ten cents' worth, Gray.''

A harsh smile slashed Riley's lips. ''What I have to
say is worth a whole lot more than ten cents, Logan.
Tessa Lang has a point. Who better to hunt for evidence
in and around a grave than a team trained to locate and
preserve buried artifacts?''

Logan grunted.

''You were mad before you lit into Tessa. Who else
has been rattling your cage?''

''Ray Jennings.'' Fielder stiff-armed his office door
open. ''Get out here, Ray. You and the rest of the town
council are so all-fired intent on jailing someone for Frannie's murder. Come on out here and tell Riley what you
witnessed. Ms. Monday's got herself a lawyer, so we
need to do this all legal-like.''

Ray Jennings took his time putting in an appearance.
He walked out straightening a burgundy silk tie that perfectly contrasted his pearl-gray suit. ''I only reported
what any concerned citizen would, Logan. As I already
explained twice, I was headed down Piney Loop Road,
going home for lunch. I recognized Ms. Monday's pickup
parked off the road, right next to where you roped off
the Caddo Lake shortcut with yellow tape. Riley'll tell
you I know her truck—we saw her drive away in it the

day she came to my bank. Anyway, as soon as I noticed it, I turned around and drove straight back to town. How was I to know the girl had willfully trespassed? For all I knew, the same person who'd done in Frannie Granger had—well, you know.'' He fluttered a hand toward Emmy.

"I ain't saying you did wrong, Ray.'' Fielder paced around the banker. "Let me get this straight, because from your earlier babbling, I assumed you saw Emmy Monday actually poking around the grave.''

"I didn't poke anything,'' Emmy protested.

"Hush,'' Logan and Riley ordered in unison.

Jennings cleared his throat. He smoothed a thumb and finger over his mustache. "Did I say I saw her? I thought all I verified was that it was her vehicle. Maybe Kyle said she'd been poking into the grave when he radioed in.''

Now it was the deputy's turn to stutter. "I—I mighta used poking in the generic sense. You know, Sheriff, like…when I caught Leon Hamilton *poking* around Mrs. Baker's henhouse where he didn't belong. That didn't mean I saw Leon steal chickens.''

Logan Fielder blew out an exasperated breath. "What in tarnation do Leon or Mrs. Baker's chickens have to do with this case? Did you or did you not catch Ms. Monday contaminating our crime scene?''

"Well, she'd been in there,'' Masters insisted. "'Cause she stepped back across the tape just as I drove onto the site.''

Riley propped his hip on a desk. "So you searched her because you had probable cause to think she'd stolen something from the scene?''

"I didn't search her.'' The young deputy's face flamed poppy-red.

"Ah. I see. You're telling us there's no tangible evidence that Ms. Monday did anything more than stand and look at the landscape, just as she described in her statement."

Having obtained a copy of Emmy's original statement from the recording clerk on the way in, Riley pulled it out of his briefcase and scanned the text again.

The other three men in the room glanced at each other, all of them ultimately lowering their eyes to avoid Riley's stare.

"In the absence of physical evidence, it seems to me all you have is a case of my client's word against Kyle's."

The deputy hunched his shoulders unhappily, while Fielder allowed as how Riley might be correct in his assumption.

"Good." Riley broke into a grin. "Then I guess none of you will object if Emmy goes to the ladies' room to wash off that fingerprint ink."

Three disgruntled men stared after Riley, who escorted Emmy to the door and pointed her down a brightly lit hallway. He rejoined the men in time to hear Ray demanding of Fielder, "You're letting the girl walk, Logan? If she's not up to something shady, why was she nosing around out there?"

"Last I heard Uncertain's still part of a free country, Ray," Riley said in mild tones. "Fran was the closest thing Emmy had to a mom. The property belongs to her foster brother. Maybe Logan should ask why you're pressing to have her locked up. If you've got proof Emmy's involved in the murder, cough it up."

"I told you my only interest is as a concerned citizen. Well, also as a member of the town council. Last night at our meeting, Mayor Babcock pointed out how focused the whole town is on this murder. It'll hurt our upcoming tourist trade. Logan needs to arrest and convict someone, so our town can get back on track. Unsolved murders attract the tabloids. Reporters have already booked into Alligator Bayou B-and-B. We don't want Uncertain making those kinds of headlines.''

Riley crossed his arms. ''Ray, did you ever think how much worse our publicity will be if we go on record as a town that badgers innocent women or tosses them indiscriminately in the slammer?''

The sheriff squinted at both of them. ''That's a fact. So, Ray, next time you bring me an eyewitness complaint, first make sure you're dealing with the real McCoy.''

Ray drew himself up and buttoned his suit jacket over his slight paunch. ''I missed lunch with Catherine to perform a civic duty. You've got no call to lecture me, Logan. Anyway, you said you were planning to question the Monday girl.''

''So I am,'' agreed Fielder as they watched the banker leave in a righteous huff. ''We can do it now, Riley, which would suit me. Or book it for later this week.'' Logan went into his office for a moment and returned with a calendar. ''I've never met a lawyer yet who didn't stall for all the time he could get.''

''There's where you're wrong, Logan. Emmy talked to me yesterday. You'll be happy to know she wants to cooperate fully, even after I advised her that she didn't have to talk to you without a subpoena. As soon as she's back from the ladies' room, we can sit down and have a friendly chat.''

''You're all heart, Gray. I assume you've coached her on what not to say.''

Riley smiled secretively. He hadn't, of course. But there was no sense letting his opponent know that.

"What next?" Emmy asked Riley. She sensed the lingering tension, even though the banker, the sheriff and his deputy had all disappeared.

"Are you up to answering some questions now?" Riley slid his hand down Emmy's back, settling a warm palm at her waist. "Remember, you can still beg off."

"I'm cleared of the trespassing charge?"

"It wasn't really a charge. So, the answer is yes."

She cocked her head to one side. "Thank you, Riley. Have you really decided to represent me?"

"Say the word, and I'll go tell Logan we're ready."

"Okay. But I'm a little nervous."

Riley smiled into her eyes. "Relax. Do you want to recheck the diary you left with Marge? I have the copy in my briefcase."

"I'm okay on those points. It's whatever else he might toss at me...." Emmy let her sentence hang.

"Just shake your head if he throws you a curve. I'll suggest he skip that question and go on."

"Won't that make me look evasive or guilty?"

"Questioning a witness is all a game, sugar babe. You're allowed to pick up your chips and cash out at any time."

"I know you said that before. By the way, thanks for changing your mind. I know I made you really angry this morning."

Riley guided her toward Logan's office. He stopped outside the closed door. "Marge gave me what-for after we heard Logan had you brought in today. I guess you could say that you and Marge are pretty convincing. I've rethought things. When we finish here, I'll go back to the office and put out feelers to colleagues who've done birth parent searches. I can't promise you'll find your family, Emmy, but I'll get what you need to start the process.''

"You will? Riley, I don't know what to say." Tears sparkled in her green eyes. "I feel a hundred-percent better already.''

"Now don't get too excited," he warned, knocking harder than he'd intended on Logan Fielder's door.

Emmy rose on her tiptoes and aimed a kiss at Riley's cheek just as Fielder opened the door. It wouldn't have been so bad, except that Riley turned into the kiss and met Emmy's lips head-on. They both felt the sparks ignite.

"Ahem." The craggy old lawman shifted uneasily. "Ray said I should be alert to hanky panky if I'm dealing with Frannie's bunch of mavericks. Riley, I'll be on the lookout for conflicts of interest in this case. And let me remind you—we're conducting a murder investigation, not playing post office out behind the boy's gym."

Emmy blushed to her earlobes, but Riley only chuckled. "Since kissing in public isn't a crime, Logan, confine your questions and remarks to the case. And hurry it up. I'm taking my client to lunch at Catfish Corner."

"You are?" Emmy wheeled in surprise. "We can't." She shook her head. "I promised Alanna she could come over this afternoon and play with my kitten. I won't disappoint her."

Warmth and pleasure burst in Riley's chest. "Tell you what. Marge owes me big-time for—well, she just does. We'll make it an early dinner instead. I'll phone her when we're done here and ask if she'll take Alanna out for pizza."

Fielder opened the door wider. "If it's not too much trouble? I mean, if I'm not interrupting your social schedules, could we get on with this interview?"

Sharing a guilty glance, Emmy and Riley crossed the threshold together. "Yes, sir," Emmy murmured at the same time Riley seated her and said, "No problem, Logan. Our social calendar is set, so go ahead. Ask away."

"Nothing's set, Riley," Emmy said out of the side of her mouth. "I promised Alanna. Kids suffer too many broken promises. Besides, there's Egypt to consider."

"Alanna and Marge can feed the kitten. Jed gave me a key to Frannie's house in case of any emergency."

"You have a key to my house?"

"Yes. What? Do you think I'd walk in unannounced?"

"I want that key, Riley. And I'm not reneging on my promise to Alanna."

Riley's face fell. "Damn, but you're one stubborn female. How's this? We take Alanna out for pizza tonight, and you and I go to Catfish Corner tomorrow night."

Emmy ended up agreeing. Deep down, she wanted to patch things up with Riley. She tried telling herself it was because after years of wondering—imagining all sorts of things about her birth mother—she was ready to learn the truth. Her soaring heart knew better. Riley had always been her anchor. He might not want to be, but he still was.

CHAPTER EIGHT

"I'M PROUD of you, Emmy," Riley told her as they left Logan's office, after initialing for receipts of her truck, which Kyle Masters and a second deputy had brought in. "You stood up well under the heat he blew your way. He did his best to try to rattle you."

"I told the truth as I remember it. But it's harder looking back than I imagined," she said, sounding distant and shaken. "You and Jed stayed here. The sheriff treats you like adults. He acts as if Will and I remained kids. Oh, I hope Will survived. Fielder hasn't tried to locate him. Don't you wonder why?"

Riley clamped a broad hand around her neck and gently massaged the tight muscles. "For one thing, there's the size of Logan's workforce. Just two deputies, and one of those is part-time. While I wouldn't exactly say our sheriff is fumbling around in the dark, neither do I believe he has the best tools available for investigating a murder. Especially one that's almost twenty years old."

"I know Jed didn't…couldn't have done it. Sheriff Fielder will never find the culprit if he doesn't widen his investigation."

"You don't think Will—?"

"Certainly not." Emmy glanced up at Riley with eyes that flashed ominously.

He dropped his hand. "The state relocated you. Jed stayed and took his lumps. Will flew the coop. You heard

Logan. He interviewed a credible witness who saw Will hitch a ride with a trucker headed toward Dallas. The guy said Will acted furtive. Nervous.''

"How can you even *think* Will might have killed Mom Fran? You were friends.''

"I wish I could swear that was true.'' Riley thrust a hand through his hair. "Will McClain was a loner. He always held back something of himself.''

"Like *you'd* have been so trusting if you'd lived his life? Over the years I've met my share of no-good double-dealers. Will was solid gold where it counts.''

"Maybe I've been a lawyer too long, Emmy. The truth is, good people can do bad things. I wish I could see everyone the way you do.''

"It comes from navigating the system. To survive, a kid has to learn to read who's trustworthy and who'll let you down.''

"So if none of the people closest to Frannie Granger offed her, who did?''

Emmy looked startled. "That's twice you've hinted I might know.''

"Sorry, that was a rhetorical question. One that everyone in town has been asking since Tessa made her grisly discovery.''

"You seem to know her pretty well.''

"Tessa?'' Riley stuck his hands in his pockets. "She interviewed me when she first came to town, hoping I'd have family history to document her theory about the placement of the Caddo burial mounds.'' A muscle in Riley's jaw flexed. "It goes without saying that I wasn't as helpful as she'd have liked.''

"You must not have treated her too shabbily. She acted quite happy to see you.''

"Whoa! You're totally wrong if you think anything's

going on between Tessa Lang and me. Is that what you're implying?"

Emmy hiked up one shoulder. "I didn't see a wedding ring on her finger."

"What's that supposed to mean? You think I hit on every single woman I meet?"

"Do you?" Emmy fixed curious eyes on Riley. "I'm operating on old data here. If memory serves, you cut a wide swath through our town."

A splash of red stained his high cheekbones. "As did Jed and Will, and a dozen other guys I can name. We were normal horny adolescent boys. Give me credit for having developed discretion along with maturity."

It was clear from the expression flitting across Emmy's face that she was remembering his lack of control last night, when they'd made love on the floor of her porch. "I really need to get home," she said in a strained voice.

"Emmy, wait." Running after her, he caught her as she reached her pickup. "I can't explain. What's between us confuses me. Rationally, I can say you're the best part of a turbulent past. Hell, this isn't coming out right," he exclaimed with a frustrated sigh as Emmy tugged the door out of his hands. The driver's window was down so he continued talking when she climbed inside the cab. "I never made any secret about wanting to change my life. You may believe I'm the same, but I'm not."

"You only think you've changed, Riley. You're from a strong, proud family with a lifetime of values you can't just slough off. My history is nonexistent."

"You're comparing peaches and prunes. You were coming into your own at thirteen. You were tough, funny and completely honest. *You,* sugar babe, not your ancestors. What you're missing hasn't affected the woman you are."

"Oh, Riley. You still don't get it. I lost my history when my birth mother set me adrift. I want pieces of it back. I'm not a complete idiot, though. I'm not looking for someone to mother me. It's facts I want, facts about my origins."

Riley curled his hands over the top of Emmy's lowered window. He seemed troubled. "I said I'd ask some of my colleagues."

"I know. Any information will help. I can tell I'm not really getting through to you, but I *am* going forward with a search, Riley. If you find that thought repugnant, then we have to end everything other than a purely professional relationship right here."

"You don't mean that."

"I do." Her voice wavered, but her eyes met his and remained firm.

"I think you're making a mistake, but I'll start those inquiries for you. Meanwhile, I'll do some soul-searching. By tonight, I'll either be ready to assist you or I'll provide you with a referral."

Emmy clamped her top lip between her teeth and nodded. The lines were clearly drawn, and she felt like crying. It wasn't fair that he'd expect her to give up either their relationship or her pursuit of a past.

Since when is life fair? nagged an insistent voice in her ear as she drove away. She'd actually reconciled herself to losing him by the time she turned down her lane and saw his daughter pacing beside the fence.

"I thought you weren't ever coming back," Alanna cried, running up to the truck when Emmy had parked.

She heard real fear underlying Alanna's statement. Emmy reminded herself that this child had experienced a series of nannies coming and going all her life.

"I didn't mean to worry you. I'm home now, and

Egypt needs feeding. Go and ask Mrs. Yates if it's okay for you to give me a hand. I'll wait right here so she can look out the window and see me.''

Alanna took off at a dead run. Her black hair streamed out behind her as she dodged among the trees. *Oh, to have her vitality.* Emmy smiled to herself, half wondering what it would be like to spend all day, every day, with a child, keep up with that boundless energy. The idea rather appealed, and it gave her pause. Was that why she'd developed this urge to find her roots? To prove once and for all that she wasn't damaged goods? At some very basic level, did she crave her own children?

Emmy decided she'd need more time to consider that. She put the question aside as Mrs. Yates stepped out on Riley's porch and acknowledged her presence with her usual unsmiling expression.

Alanna immediately reappeared at the fence. Emmy helped her climb over. ''Don't ever do this unless someone is around to help you,'' Emmy cautioned. ''We wouldn't want you to fall, would we?''

The girl shook her head. ''Mrs. Yates said my daddy called. He's taking you and me for pizza tonight.'' She rubbed her stomach, her eyes alight with excitement. ''Pizza's my favorite food. Is today your birthday, Emmy?''

Emmy turned from sliding the key into her door lock. ''No.'' Technically, though, she wasn't sure. Talk of birthdays always caused Emmy consternation. Since the day she'd overhead Mom Fran say to her first-grade teacher, ''We're not positive this is Emerald's birthday, but the state authorized us to use March 12th.''

Even though later Mom Fran had assured Emmy that the date they'd settled on had to be within mere days of the actual date of her birth, she'd never felt very enthusiastic about celebrating.

Alanna's answer dragged Emmy back from the brink of old hurts. "When me'n Daddy go out for pizza, it's my birthday. Otherwise a man in a truck brings it to us."

"Well, it's not my birthday. If it's not yours or your dad's, we'll just have to consider this an extraspecial treat."

"'kay. I'm glad it's not your birthday, 'cause I don't have a present for you."

Emmy smiled at the child's easy acceptance. Alanna skipped ahead and scooped up the kitten. "Look, Egypt ate all his kibble while you were gone. Miss Gwyn always gives her cat milk. Can I put some in a clean bowl?"

"Sounds good. I'll get a bowl. But if you're planning to get the milk out of the fridge after handling the cat, you'll need to wash your hands."

"Oh, bother." The girl sounded so adult as she set the kitten down and pulled a chair over to the sink, Emmy giggled and felt her earlier cares fall away.

Woman and child were snuggled side by side on the couch, reading one of the books Emmy had taken out of the library when Riley drove in a few hours later and tooted his horn.

"Daddy's home," Alanna announced as she scrambled up. "Don't put the book away, Emmy. I'm going to ask him if we can finish the story before we go for pizza."

Emmy had been about to say they could finish another day. She wasn't fast enough. Alanna had banged out the front screen door and begun cajoling her dad at the top of her lungs.

Emmy was still sitting there, her thumb marking the page, when Riley and his daughter walked in, holding hands. They presented a picture that had played repeatedly inside Emmy's head. Sometimes the child she envisioned with Riley was a boy, sometimes a girl. Sometimes both. Emmy's stomach pitched and her heart tripped faster.

Transferring the smile he'd donned for Alanna to Emmy, Riley greeted her in a voice as warm and thick as honeyed whiskey. "That has to be some story to beat out pizza." He swung Alanna aloft, then plopped her down next to Emmy. His smile faltered as his eyes strayed to the title: *Are You My Mother?*

"We don't have this book, Daddy. A baby bird lost his mama. He thinks the Snort is her." Alanna bounced on the cushion, presenting twin dimples. "Isn't that silly?"

"Um, yes, completely. Kids' books are designed to make you laugh, Alanna. They aren't real."

"I know. The Snort is like one of those digger machines you showed me when somebody built that house across the lake. Emmy said a machine can't be a bird's mama. I 'spect he'll find her," she said wistfully. "But I can't go for pizza till I know if he does."

Riley wore a much cooler expression. One that told Emmy he wasn't pleased with her choice of story. All he said, however, was "I'll leave you ladies to your book while I go home and grab a shower."

Emmy drew Alanna close. She'd be darned if she'd let Riley make her feel guilty. It was a delightful story. She'd left her copy behind at Mom Fran's with the majority of her childhood things. For a few years, she'd slept with this book under her pillow. At the age of five or six, Emmy had prayed nightly for her real mother to walk in through the door. Of course, her mom was a vision of loveliness. Blond and green-eyed. In Emmy's dream, she smelled of the sweet jasmine soap Fran let Emmy use on special occasions.

"Emmy?" Alanna snuggled closer. "Does this story make you sad?"

"What? Oh, no. I was just thinking how much I loved this book when I was your age. I couldn't read, but I had all my books memorized."

"What's mem-mem-rized?"

"It's when someone's read a particular story out loud so many times you know it by heart."

Alanna pressed her head against Emmy's shoulder. "Mrs. Yates doesn't like books. All she does is watch soaps on TV. Mostly," she said with a sigh, "Daddy's too busy. I'm not s'posed to bug you, he said. But I'd sure like if we could do this every day."

Blinking rapidly to hold back tears, Emmy cleared her throat several times before she was able to read on. When she had kids, by gosh, she'd make time to read to them and they'd go to the local library. It was a crying shame that so many adults were too busy to enjoy simple things with their kids. Although Emmy remembered that Fran was sometimes too tired when she came home after a hard day's work. On those nights, she'd asked Jed to read to Emmy. He'd done so without complaint. Emmy hadn't thought of those cherished moments in a long while.

She gripped the book so tightly, Alanna had difficulty turning the pages. Emmy wished she'd remembered to convey *that* Jed Louis to the sheriff. She wanted Fielder to see the Jed she carried in her heart. The serious boy who took on the chores of a man at an early age. And Will—he'd been around the block by the time he came to live with them. Tough as he was on the outside, he'd willingly skipped lunch and given Emmy his money whenever she'd accidentally left hers on the kitchen counter. No one else knew that Will had spent a whole evening reading a silly pamphlet on how to French braid; all the girls in junior high wore their hair that way and he was determined Emmy wasn't going to cry herself to sleep over being different.

Alanna and Emmy were closing the book as Riley returned. He must have seen something in their dreamy expressions because he didn't comment further on the book. He tickled Alanna and hoisted her up to ride piggyback to the car. And he held the door open for Emmy, whispering his thanks for making Alanna happy as he tucked her inside. He might have had differences of opinion with his deceased wife, as Josey indicated, but it was clear to Emmy that Riley loved his child unconditionally.

At the pizza parlor, they'd placed their orders and taken a table before Riley brought up the subject of Emmy's search. Alanna had flitted to another table to watch some kids playing a Pokémon game.

"I touched base with a former college classmate this afternoon, Emmy. His name is Duncan Fisher. He claims to have a computer program that'll let you locate anyone. According to Duncan, the program has everything we need. I guess it lets you access public records and provides other investigative tricks. He referred to it as an Internet underground. He told me where to order it, and they're overnighting me a copy. I had Marge make you an appointment for tomorrow at four. If that's good for you, we can walk through the program together. If four isn't convenient, stop by and have Marge reschedule."

"I'm supposed to get my phone line tomorrow. They said a.m., but you know how that goes. If they haven't shown up by three, I'll ask Mrs. Yates to call you."

"Sure. I don't know how you've managed this long

without a phone. I'd be like a pinwheel in the wind without access in every room."

"It's not easy, but I've gotten along without one before. But I've discovered that businesses look with suspicion on a person who has no telephone. To them, you're automatically a deadbeat."

"I suppose you're right. To me being without one is a damned inconvenience. We didn't have a phone when I was growing up, though. Money didn't stretch that far."

"And did you consider yourself deprived?"

A distant, uncomfortable emotion crept into his eyes. "Deprivation was a given to some people in this town. But some people called it other things. Growing up Indian came with a lot of labels."

Emmy automatically reached out to grip his hands. "I loved your family. I must not have paid any attention. I thought you were popular in school. Who—who called you names?"

Instead of answering, Riley stared over Emmy's shoulder and muttered an invective. She turned to see a sultry blonde homing in on Riley. Emmy felt a jolt at seeing and recognizing Amanda Jennings. In appearance, she'd changed remarkably little.

"I declare, Riley Gray." Amanda's affected drawl was too syrupy. "I didn't believe Daddy when he said you'd compromised a career you've worked so hard to build by taking up with a little nobody. I see it's true."

Alanna had run back to the table in time to hear Amanda Jennings take a jab at Emmy. The child flew to Emmy's defense, stamping a foot as she faced Amanda. "My Emmy is somebody. You're *bad* to say she's not."

Riley tightened his hold on Emmy's hands. "Alanna, sit down and apologize for that outburst." Lifting contemptuous eyes to Amanda, he said, "The same goes for your rude behavior."

The child mumbled her apology first. Amanda tossed her head. Eventually, she said something too low for anyone to really distinguish.

Emmy hid a smile, but she was oh-so-tempted to thumb her nose and say, *Neiner, neiner, now who looks like a big fat weiner?* Of course, she didn't. Amanda wasn't addressing her. She never had. She'd always had a way of looking through Emmy, of acknowledging people around her with the express purpose of making her feel lower than dirt. That was in the old days. Emmy had since learned that a person could only make you feel unworthy if you allowed it to happen.

Leaning back, she ran her gaze slowly over the old schoolmate who still thought she could trade on her family name. At the casino, when Emmy dealt cards, she'd perfected a bored, disinterested air. She donned it now, achieving the desired effect. Amanda barely concealed her blatant dislike.

"Daddy's only thinking about your professional reputation, Riley. You should hear what people at Crazy Jake's are saying. Positively everyone's laughing because you let her beat you at darts. And really, she has that tacky tattoo."

Emmy tried to jerk free of Riley's clamp on her fingers. She ought to have anticipated that kind of back-stabbing, given small-town attitudes. It wasn't fair that Riley should take the brunt of it. She felt even guiltier since he revealed how he'd struggled to overcome childhood slights—no doubt from kids in Amanda's circle.

"Get lost, Amanda. Our pizza's ready." He stood, casting an ominous shadow over their uninvited guest. "By the way, I didn't *let* Emmy win. She's that good."

Amanda tarried only long enough to telegraph Emmy a withering glance. Her flouncing exit in the short, oscillating skirt and three-inch-high sandals was worthy of an Academy Award.

"Riley, you shouldn't have provoked her. What if she runs to Ray and he spreads the word in the business community and ruins your practice?"

"Ray has no hold over me. He tried to talk Hamish Abrams out of selling me his law practice. Hamish told him where to get off. He carried the contract so I wouldn't have to borrow at the bank. Jennings isn't nearly as influential in town as he and his family like to pretend. Amanda parrots Ray's opinions. He had the nerve to refer to you as a nobody that day you and I met at the bank. It was laughable, him warning me off that way. Especially as he's had a low opinion of me for years. Hey, that's the second time they've called our number. I'd better grab our order before they give it away."

Another comment sat on the tip of Emmy's tongue. She swallowed it the moment she noticed Alanna's worried features. "It's all right, hon." Emmy pulled Alanna onto her lap. "That woman can't hurt your daddy. She's just a big old Snort. Remember how snorts shake the ground and make a lot of noise? Nobody pays attention because all they really do is spin their wheels."

"I 'member. She didn't look like a Snort. I don't like her, Emmy."

Cuddling the child cheek to cheek, Emmy swayed back and forth. "Here comes your daddy with the pizza. The man behind him has our drinks. Let's forget Miss Amanda and enjoy our special night."

"'kay."

Riley returned in time to hear his daughter sniffle. He

flagged an inquiring eyebrow at Emmy. She answered with a brief shake of her head.

As the evening wore on, Emmy did her best to sustain the conversation. But Amanda had succeeded in what no doubt was her goal—to cast a pall over their outing.

After they'd eaten all anyone wanted, Riley attempted to interest Alanna in some of the kiddie video games so he could talk seriously with Emmy; his attempt failed. Once they were all buckled back into his car, Riley returned to the subject of Emmy's search. "We may need a while to figure out that program. I'm new to this, Emmy. Not only that, I can't imagine finding someone who's succeeded so long in not being found."

"That's just it. What if my mother is open to being contacted? I've heard there's a registry. It's funny. Until I read about Fran—the finality of it—I'd been reluctant to launch a search. It seemed somehow disloyal to Mom Fran. Suddenly I'm thinking, what if my real mom's tried to find me? Does that make sense?"

"None of it makes sense to me, Emmy. Your mother deserted you. Is a woman who does something so abominable worth finding?"

From the back seat, Alanna chimed in. "Have you lost your mama, Emmy? Me, too," she said in a voice rife with feeling. "Maybe you and me could go on a 'venture like the baby bird. He found his mother. I bet if we went together, we could find ours."

"Alanna, you can't find your mother." Riley shot Emmy a smoldering glance all but accusing her of wreaking trouble.

Quite frankly, Emmy didn't know what to say. Riley had brought up the subject. Did he think Alanna couldn't hear? Still, she felt a measure of guilt that prompted her to remind the child, as Riley had earlier, that the story they'd read wasn't real. "It's make-believe," she told Alanna earnestly.

"Right. Emmy and I were discussing business. You know Daddy helps people with legal problems. Emmy needs me to locate some old records. Records are files, like I keep in my office cabinet."

"Oh." Alanna picked up the stuffed animal she'd brought along on the ride and popped her thumb into her mouth.

It was the first time Emmy had seen the child suck her thumb. She studied Riley out of the corner of an eye. He seemed bothered by the turn of events but didn't remark on the thumb sucking.

Alanna had fallen asleep by the time they reached home. "I'll wait here until you get inside your house, Emmy." He avoided her eyes, although his expression seemed placid enough.

"I've been finding my way home for a lot of years, Riley. I don't need anyone to hold my hand."

He drummed his fingers on the steering wheel. "You never could hide your feelings, Emmy. You've got something you're dying to say. So say it."

She clenched her hands in her lap. Facing him, she lowered her voice. "It's not my business, Riley, but it sounded to me as if Alanna's unsure about what happened to her mother. Take it from someone who understands how she feels—it's a mistake not to be honest with her."

"You're right, it's none of your business." Riley's eyes had turned cold.

"If I, a virtual stranger in town, have already learned the details, some kid in school is going to spill the beans just for the hell of it. I didn't realize Mom Fran wasn't my real mom until I started school. It cost the kid who told me a black eye. For a while after that, I didn't believe anything Fran told me. The only way you can control how the news affects Alanna is to be honest with her.'' She glanced into the back seat to make sure the girl under discussion was still sleeping.

"I explained that her mom died. Beyond that...I can't...won't risk having her ask to see Lani's family. They blame me for Lani's death. What would I do if they convinced her of that absurdity?''

"It's human nature for her to be curious. The more open you are with her, the less likely she'll be upset by random questions.''

"Marge said almost the same thing to me today. Alanna has increased her inquisitiveness about her mother since Jed and Gwyn's wedding. Apparently Gwyn pointed out jokingly to someone that having babies came after a couple got married. Miss Big Ears overheard.''

"I'm surprised some little friend in the neighborhood hasn't introduced the subject of mommies, daddies and babies.''

"There are no neighbor kids.''

"Surely you have married friends you socialize with who have children.''

"Not really. Jed has none yet. Rico and Layla have kids, but being the town's only doctor, he's even busier than me. And the guys I meet at Crazy Jake's, we share a beer and play darts. It's nowhere we'd bring the family.''

"No wonder Alanna's so lonely. Kids need playmates.''

"I take her to the park when I can. There are other children on the gym sets. The last two years we've attended the county fair. She joins tons of kids her age on the kiddie rides. You saw her cavorting around with those girls at the pizza parlor. She's not repressed.''

''No, but little girls need a best friend, like I had Josey. If for no other reason than to trade secrets.''

He mumbled something noncommittal, and Emmy decided to expand on her remarks. ''From the time I was in first grade, your sister and I were best buds. I thought you knew. We'd play for hours, beading friendship bracelets, weaving pot holders for Christmas gifts. Josey taught me how to make clay. I have wonderful memories of those days.''

Riley fell silent again. ''Uh...well, it's getting late,'' he said. ''I need to put Alanna in the tub and then it's off to bed.''

''While we're on the subject,'' Emmy said. ''There are worse things in life, Riley, than having a talented, gifted aunt who could teach Alanna crafts she could do during the hours she spends alone.''

''Dammit, Emmy,'' he whispered fiercely, ''you always did push the bounds of friendship.'' Riley caught her as she turned to open the car door, and slid her back across the seat, welding their lips together as if kissing her hard would make her forget their clash of opinions.

Emmy wanted to tell him diversions wouldn't work. Unfortunately, kissing Riley had the effect of emptying her mind. She braced against him for only a second or two, then she gave in with a sigh and flowed into his arms. Being together like this had a way of wiping out any opposition they might have. She shouldn't be seduced off course by a few kisses, Emmy tried telling herself. No other man had ever made her forget her principles the way Riley did. Call it chemistry or karma— whatever—Riley had the power to turn her functioning brain to slush.

By the time they came up for air, shared sweet good-byes and Emmy stumbled across the yard to her house, she'd forgotten why she and Riley had disagreed—if, in fact, they had. Her sights were set on seeing him again tomorrow. At his office. She sure hoped the telephone man came when he was supposed to.

EMMY GOT HER WISH. The phone truck arrived before noon. The house had an old-style jack in the kitchen; it took the installer no time at all to update it and add a phone in the bedroom. He was gone by one o'clock. His truck had no sooner left than her phone rang. She snatched it up, assuming it would be Riley. It was Gwyn.

"Where have you been keeping yourself? I'll have you know I had to bribe the phone company for your number. Just kidding."

"Sorry. I've been working through my list of to-dos."

"We heard Logan Fielder grilled you, Emmy. Jed asked me to call and make sure you were okay. He's off looking at property all day."

"Fielder wanted me to substantiate things I'd said the first time he checked into Fran's disappearance. I was grateful that Riley sat in, but I can't say I felt like I'd been grilled. I guess you also heard about the trouble I stirred up by visiting the site where Tessa Lang found the…bones." Her voice thinned markedly.

Gwyn sighed. "Even though the land technically belongs to Jed, and Tessa had permits to excavate, the area is off-limits since it's a crime scene."

"I should've known better than to cross their tape. I'm lucky Riley made a point of saying that Deputy Masters didn't search me at the site to see if I'd taken anything. Of course I hadn't touched a thing."

"I'd hoped the investigation had turned away from Frannie's foster family."

Emmy wished she could reassure Gwyn. "Fielder doesn't seem in any rush to look elsewhere. I asked about the handyman who'd been working on Fran's porch. The sheriff said Belmonte was prone to go off on benders."

"For nineteen years? I know the man didn't have a permanent address and he drifted from town to town. But Jed remembers this Belmonte character was always hanging around."

"Don't worry, Gwyn. Jed is innocent. Fielder isn't going to find the proof he needs to charge Jed because it simply doesn't exist."

"Oh, am I glad you came back, Emmy. I know Jed didn't kill anyone. I also know half the town thinks I was crazy to marry him under this cloud of suspicion."

"They need to get a life. Some people in this town are too quick to follow the lead of officious toads like Ray Jennings. Did you also hear he's the one who turned me in? He claimed he thought I might've been kidnapped from my truck."

"Gee, most people would've figured you'd gone for a walk."

"Ray Jennings thinks his family owns the town. They poke their noses in everything. Say, before I forget—I did ask Riley to help me search for my birth mother. At first he said no. Later he changed his mind. A friend of his recommended a computer program that'll help us start. I was about to call Riley to firm up our appointment."

"Then I'll let you go. Good luck, Emmy. If Jed or I can be of any assistance, you know where to find us. Even so, don't be a stranger. We're out with our stock a lot, but we'd love it if you followed us around just to chat.''

"Thanks, Gwyn. I'm sure there'll be some difficult times during this search. Talking generally helps. Plus, you have a friend who already went through this.''

"Come by any time you want.''

"I will.'' Emmy hung up, and when she got a dial tone, called Riley. Marge put her right through to his office.

"Hey,'' he said, a smile in his voice wafting over the wire. "I guess this means your phone's working. The program arrived. I'm still free at four. Mrs. Yates agreed to stay late and feed Alanna. I owe you a dinner, don't forget. I thought the Lake House instead of Catfish Corner.''

"Okay, but I don't know if I'll even be able to eat. I'm so nervous, it feels like I'm about to launch into a completely new phase of my life.''

"I ran through part of the program. Just to make sure it works on my computer. Don't get your hopes up too high, Emmy. It seems to me a person needs a certain amount of information to get results using these methods.''

Emmy tried not to let his predictions dampen her enthusiasm. "Well, maybe the information's been there all along and I haven't recognized it.''

"Yeah, maybe,'' he said without much conviction. "Sorry, I gotta go. Marge buzzed to say I have a client waiting. See you soon.''

CHAPTER NINE

BY THE TIME Emmy parked outside Riley's office building, a late-spring storm had moved in to obliterate the sun. The air smelled damp. Gusts of wind kicked up a discarded cigarette packet, tumbled it along the asphalt, rattling it against the curb. Emmy stepped on it as she ran for cover. She fought a losing battle in her mad dash, keeping her hair out of her eyes and her skirt at a decorous level.

A carful of teenage boys rounded the corner. All but the driver leaned out the open windows to deliver wolf whistles. Ignoring the boys' youthful hijinks, Emmy slipped into the building out of the determined wind. She'd been foolish to wear a full-skirted sundress. But she didn't own many dresses, and she wanted to look nice since Riley had invited her to dinner.

She tripped lightly up the stairs and ran full-tilt into Marge as the older woman exited Riley's office.

"Oh, good, you got here before I left." Marge shooed Emmy toward the closed door. "The boss hasn't outright asked after you, but every five minutes since about ten to four, he's stuck his head out of his office to check the reception area. My, don't you look pretty on this blustery afternoon." Marge wound down, moving back a few feet to appraise Emmy's outfit.

"We're going to the Lake House after Riley shows me the search program."

"I wonder if you know what a huge step this is for him," Marge murmured.

"And me." Emmy twisted the shoulder strap of her purse. "I've thought about instituting a search for so many years, but always got scared, for one reason or another."

"Then I'll keep my fingers crossed that it goes like clockwork."

The door behind them flew inward. Riley peered into the hall. "I heard voices. Why are you two lurking out here? Marge? Weren't you worried about being late to a town council meeting?"

"Mm-hm." Marge glanced between the two people whose nervous actions announced their edginess about the upcoming meeting. "Maybe I ought to stay and chaperon. Or is *referee* a more apt term?"

The barb hit its mark with Riley. He reached past Marge and snagged Emmy's arm. "I think I can be civilized. I know I've been acting like I am afraid this computer program will crack some window in time and suck Emmy right out of my hands. It's really no more than a simple database of references."

Emmy saw that Riley did seem extratense. But he looked as good as ever. Today, the white shirt he wore rolled up past his forearms appeared rumpled, held in place only by a cool pair of suspenders. Until this moment, Emmy had never considered suspenders sexy. Or maybe it was because Riley wore them without a tie and his shirt was unbuttoned at the throat, exposing an inviting amount of smooth, bronzed flesh. A combination that made her palms sweat.

"In case you decide to follow up on any leads," Marge was saying as she clattered down the stairs to pause on the first landing, ''I marked out afternoons on your calendar all next week, boss.''

Riley seemed to freeze in the doorway.

Emmy backed him into his office after a wave to Marge. Shutting the outer door decisively, she smiled. ''Let's see what the program recommends first, shall we? I'm sure there'll be things I can do on my own without disrupting your schedule. Gwyn said her friend's search took over a year. I'll be bankrupt if I spend all my money up front to retain you. By the way, how much do I owe for the program?''

''Nothing.'' Riley checked to make sure the main door was locked before he ushered Emmy into his private office. ''Emmy, there's something I want to get straight before we start. I'm doing this as a favor. The subject of money is closed. However, I'm going to try one last time to talk you out of continuing.''

Worry lined his face as he relieved her of her purse and dropped it on a love seat in one corner of his office. Placing two fingers on her lips to stay her response, he turned her to face a large oval mirror. Stepping to the side, he tilted her chin, giving her a complete view of herself. Of him, too, but he clearly wanted her to study her own reflection. ''Take a good, long look, Emmy. No matter how you've changed your hairstyle, the color is unique. It reminds me of old-fashioned vanilla ice cream. You have a distinctive widow's peak, and darker eyebrows with a little arch. Most people's eyes are made up of several colors. Call yours grass-green, emerald-green or plain green. The green is unmistakably pure.''

Emmy fidgeted under Riley's scrutiny. ''Your point is?''

''I knew you to the age of thirteen. Outside of slimming down and shooting up, you look essentially the same. Chances are, there are strong genes running in your family. Except for a short hiatus, I've lived here forever. I have clients in all the neighboring towns. I attended college less than seventy miles away. It's a hell of a thing for a guy to admit, but I'll say it flat out—yours is an image I've carried with me for three-fourths of my life, Emmy. You think that if I'd seen a younger version of you, or an older one, I wouldn't have made the connection?''

Emmy felt pressure behind her eyelids. Riley was saying he didn't think she'd find her roots in or around Uncertain. She refused to consider what that implied. It suggested someone, her mother presumably, had traveled a distance to First Monday Trade Days for the express purpose of dumping an unwanted baby. Emmy started to shiver. She couldn't help it.

Riley saw, and he drew her into his arms. ''I'm not trying to hurt you. Lord, sugar babe, I just want you to be happy as the person you are.'' He kissed her shimmering eyes closed. Gathering her tight, he tried coaxing her to relax with kisses. He didn't ease his onslaught until he felt her grow limp against his chest.

A cold emptiness that had opened in Emmy's stomach began to slowly warm. She felt herself sliding toward weightlessness—toward the same combustible flashpoint she'd hit the night Riley made love to her on her back porch. Shameless though it might be, given her reasons for being in his office tonight, she welcomed the prospect of their making love again.

She'd imagined these kinds of stolen moments so many times. Vivid dreams had her and Riley doing it in some pretty inventive places. At the beach under a moonlit surf, in an airplane set on autopilot, on the back of a galloping horse. A law office actually seemed tame. Although the rattle of the wind as it buffeted undraped windows added a dimension of excitement.

Emmy slid her hands up Riley's chest, easily divesting him of his sexy suspenders before returning to clasp either side of his strong neck. Not giving him a chance to catch his breath, Emmy kicked off her sandals and circled his lean hips with bare, unsteady legs.

Riley fell backward over his wastebasket. He took Emmy with him, though fortunately his fall was stopped by the edge of his cherry wood desk. He felt it crease his back pockets. A lightning desire to possess this woman slammed like a hot meteor into his stomach. "Emmy, Emmy, Emmy!" He repeated her name over and over while each rained kisses on the other.

Riley's desperate need hammered and pulsed through every part of his anatomy. In mere seconds he had Emmy's short sundress scooped up around her waist—out of his way. The scorching fire at her center locked onto him like a heat-seeking missile.

She sighed—an incoherent sob. Or maybe a plea for deliverance.

"Oh, Emmy, baby. Making love to you has been on my mind since that night at your place. Only," he said, pulling back with a great deal of effort, "I don't want you accusing me of setting out to distract you from your mission."

"What mission?" Emmy bit Riley's lower lip sharply. Her hands moved from his face to the button at the waistband of his slacks. The backs of her fingers brushed the erection ready and waiting behind a straining zipper. Maybe at this moment she did need validation that her background didn't matter to Riley. So what?

Riley required no other invitation. He easily flipped their positions, ending with Emmy's shapely bottom on the desk. And though he still tried to kiss her, he lost no time shucking tangled suspenders, followed by his loafers and suit pants.

At the same time, she worked to unbutton his shirt, which wasn't easy as the straps to her sundress kept slipping over her shoulders to bind her arms.

Riley realized the bodice of her sundress hid the quarter-size rainbow he'd begun to think of as *his* at odd and inopportune moments. Like in the middle of serious meetings, or yesterday when he stood before a fully robed, humorless judge. Only when he held her like this did the troubled years roll away....

Ignoring the winking cursor on his computer monitor, he swept file folders, blotter and keyboard aside, his hands shaking as he watched her unzip her dress and slither daintily out of it. She was wearing the smallest scrap of red lace underpants he'd ever had the good fortune to see up close and personal. "Something I always knew about you, Emmy Monday," he growled as he stripped away the last barrier, "was that given a few years, you'd torture a guy out of his ever-loving mind."

Her accepting, womanly laughter sent warm prickles along his spine as Emmy lay back on his desk and welcomed him fully into the saddle of her thighs. Pale thighs that glowed like fresh cream against his darker skin. Riley didn't know if he'd ever be able to do a lick of work at this desk again—at least not without remembering and longing to repeat this moment. From now on his secret weapon to pass the time in boring meetings would be to run his fingers over the exact spot where Emmy's pot of gold had left its indelible mark.

As if reading his mind, she said as much.

Riley marveled that they could be so uninhibited. *Especially him.* From the first, his and Lani's coupling had been in bed. In the dark. Brief. The word *duty* intruded seconds before his control shattered, and he and Emmy floated together somewhere above the satiny wood desk. Duty would never be a word he'd attach to making love with Emmy. More like spontaneous combustion, he thought, smiling all over.

Except for the hum of the computer and their combined breathing, the room was silent; the normal downtown sounds had faded. Even the wind had died down. It struck Riley that what he'd experienced in his marriage couldn't compare to the joy he felt when Emmy tickled him and whispered in his ear quite graphic suggestions as to where and how they might try this next.

The *next* surprised them both.

It occurred when Emmy tugged Riley with her into his closet-size shower after they'd finally untangled from atop his desk.

"Emmy," he protested faintly. "You said we didn't dare show up at a restaurant until we'd showered and made ourselves presentable."

Rising up on tiptoes, Emmy grinned and pushed Riley beneath the spray. She kissed away his resistance while behind his back she adjusted the nozzle to a fine, warm spray. "This saves time," she murmured against his lips. "Don't think you've dissuaded me from having a look at the computer program."

Riley paused in spreading soap over her breasts. His thumb idly traced the colorful arc of her rainbow. "We're going to go back out there and sit, fully dressed, side by side at my desk?" He had the oddest look on his face.

"You'd rather sit there naked?" she asked mischievously, taking her sweet time soaping from his belly to the point where his most private part sprang erect again. "I suppose we could," she mused, stretching the length of him to nibble his ear. "I guess you didn't happen to glance into the next building—the one with an office that looks directly into yours? I'm afraid you mooned the cleaning lady. If we went out as we are now and turned on the lights so we could see the computer, I expect she'd die of heart failure."

Riley tensed. He reared back from licking the rivulets of water trapped along Emmy's collar bone. "You're kidding! Someone saw us? Tell me you're joking." He gave her a little shake.

"God's honest truth. Well, look at it this way," she said, grasping his neck to lift herself high enough to settle over his erection again. "The side she saw of you won't be identifiable as yours." Emmy's delighted laughter filled the cubicle, mingling with steam that rose from their connected bodies. Riley braced his hands against the back wall and gritted his teeth to keep from exploding too soon. He'd always suspected life with Emmy would never be boring. He'd just never dreamed how truly daring it could be.

Forty minutes later, they were clean, dry and dressed, seated next to each other in front of the computer.

Riley didn't know when he'd last felt so totally loose and happy. Still, every so often he couldn't resist snatching a quick peek over his shoulder at the cleaning lady who seemed to be spending an unusual length of time dusting the office furniture across the alley. Thank goodness he didn't recognize her. Not that he'd change what had happened between him and Emmy, but he'd hate it if people in town spread rumors about her. And they would, if word leaked out. In small towns, men could get away with having their dalliances. Their partners were chewed to pieces in the gossip mill.

Emmy jabbed him with a sharp elbow. "Earth to Riley. I've read the instructions twice. They sound pretty simple. Skip past the first section and go on to section two.''

"Why?" Riley scrolled past even as he asked.

"It deals with locating someone who's served in the military. Oh, stop a minute. Back up. There. An address." She pulled over a legal pad Riley had given her and copied the data from the screen. "Jed and I think Will may have joined the military. He mentioned it once or twice. Maybe Jed could draft a letter explaining our situation and we'll be able to trace Will."

"What if Will doesn't want to be found?"

"Why wouldn't he? I think he'll at least want to hear what's happened to Mom Fran."

"They were close." Riley wished he felt easier about all this proposed digging into people's private lives. He wasn't a religious man, but he'd always had a strong belief in predestination. A belief that everything happened in a particular order for a predetermined reason. What Emmy was proposing tampered with that order. But what could he do? Sitting here, seeing her eyes bright with hope as she filled her legal pad with notes—he already knew he was helpless to refuse her anything. Mentally giving in, Riley edged his chair closer and curved an arm around her. They sat for some time in silence as he worked the mouse with his left hand, moving the cursor down frame by frame. The fingers of his right hand brushed idly over the soft flesh of her upper arm, as he read the program's checklist aloud.

There were a few ideas that made sense, like creating a search journal so as not to keep covering old ground. A lot of the advice had to do with adoptees, such as retrieving a copy of the final adoption decree. Stuff like that. Of course there were practical suggestions like checking phone books, old newspaper articles, county and state records in and around the area where the searcher lived—for information on marriages and divorces. Except it wouldn't work with Emmy, because you needed a name and Emmy's name was totally made up.

Unless maybe it *wasn't* made up.

"These hints are pretty sensible. Visit hospitals and churches in the area where the baby—in this case, you—was abandoned. And revisit people who lived there at the time. Old-timers who might know more than they let on to social workers. Oh, this, too. Check college and high-school year books in the years preceding your birth—looking for similarities in faces."

Emmy nodded. She had several pages filled with neatly penned notes by the time she sat up straight and flexed her cramped fingers. "This last part seems logical. I've taken a lot of notes, but now I need time to really digest them. To decide whether or not I should pursue any of these ideas."

Glancing at his watch, Riley was surprised to find that more than an hour had passed. He hadn't expected to be drawn in. "Let's shut down. Here's a folder for your notes. We've got barely thirty minutes to get to the Lake House or risk losing our reservation. We'll need to hurry."

"Are we taking separate vehicles?"

"I don't mind swinging past here afterward to pick up your truck. That way I'll be able to follow you home."

Emmy's eyes twinkled. "That sounds promising." She laughed as Riley's arms got stuck in his suit jacket sleeves. "Oh, dear. I suppose you're thinking I'm insatiable."

"Are you joking? I'm wondering how fast I can eat."

"We could skip dinner," she said nonchalantly. She

slipped the folder under one arm and smiled as she ran a hand up his chest. "Call me shameless if you want."

He curled her fingers in his. It broke the connection and cooled the heat her touch had created. "I shouldn't be surprised, and I should be flattered...."

"But? I hear a but coming, Riley. What? Am I being too forward? Did I read more into our encounters than is there? Tell me, please. I feel like we've lost half a lifetime together. If you don't feel the same, all you have to do is say so."

"Do I act like a man who needs hog-tying? If you want to know the truth, I've thought of little else since that first night but how soon I could get you alone again."

"Then I don't understand." Emmy shook her head as Riley turned off the office lights and they crossed the dark reception area.

"I don't understand either. Unless it's that I catch myself thinking about you as if you were still thirteen."

"Thirteen-year-old girls who reside in Uncertain don't proposition lovers," she said lightly, clattering down the stairs ahead of him.

"In my experience," he said dryly, "neither do the thirty-year-olds I've dated. Granted, there haven't been that many, but..."

Something about the way he kept hesitating poked a warning finger at Emmy. "Because I'm not acting like a shrinking violet, I guess you think I do this sort of thing all the time."

He jabbed the key into the door of his convertible without saying a word. He didn't have to. When he held the door open for Emmy to slip inside, she saw the questions swimming in the depths of his guarded eyes. Disappointment clutched at her stomach. Or maybe it was simply hunger, after all. Riley hadn't grown up in the system, where girls were fresh prey and the ones who were strong enough not to fall learned plenty of techniques to survive. She hadn't let the system steal her self-respect.

"I tend to forget that the pill allows a woman freedom. Our pace is slower here."

"Grow up, Riley," she snapped. "I knew before I went on the pill that I'm responsible for me. I decided a long time ago that I'd never bring a child into this world—not until I can guarantee what's in the poor kid's background. Doesn't mean I can't enjoy sex. I'm sorry if that rocks your sensibility. Fact is fact."

Riley turned on the car's lights. His exit from the parking lot was anything but smooth. "You're saying you never intend to have children? What if your search doesn't produce answers, Emmy?"

"Then I won't have kids. Anyway, at my age it's more likely that I'll marry someone who already has a family. Regardless, for the record, I don't sleep around."

"Did I accuse you?"

"Not in words, but it was on your mind."

"No. It's just that I want more than sex from you, Emmy." A heaviness settled in Riley's chest. He took a hand off the wheel and rubbed his sternum, but the heaviness remained. Perhaps because his daughter loomed in his thoughts. He'd never intended Alanna to be an only child. He wanted more kids. Yet here was the woman he couldn't seem to keep his hands off matter-of-factly stating that the subject wasn't negotiable.

"It's not a decision I made on the spur of the moment, Riley. Put yourself in my shoes. Kids ask questions about their family trees. If Alanna asked you to write in her grandparents and great-grandparents, you could do that.

Her tree would have branches. Mine has none. It's a straight stick."

Riley would rather not be having this discussion. It was more or less what Marge had said to him the other day. Considering the way Riley had cut himself off from both sides of the family, he'd be the only branch on Alanna's tree. "I think you're blowing this family tree thing out of proportion. What kid would propose such a topic? Family trees aren't common in casual conversation."

"It's a hot topic in school. My first-grade teacher cut out brown trees. We glued them on construction paper and took them home to have our parents help us add branches. In Grade Four, we made albums for Mother's Day. We were supposed to draw pictures of our moms, their parents and possibly one generation back if we knew our great-grandparents. I was smarter by then. I drew Mom Fran and got her to tell me about her side of the family. But in first grade, I sobbed my heart out. I was the only kid in class without a tree on the board on parent-teacher night."

Something inside Riley shifted. He couldn't stand the thought of anything or anyone hurting Emmy. And hadn't he set his own daughter up for the same pitfalls? "I had no idea ancestry was such a big deal in school," he muttered. "You always seemed remarkably...self-composed."

"You do what you have to do." She shrugged. "But it's far from satisfying to say *What you see is what you get.*"

"Marge has been after me because I don't have any pictures of Lani in the house. I didn't tell her, but I never had a picture of my wife. We were married at her home in a traditional Indian ceremony. That should've been my first clue about things to come, but I thought Lani agreed to it to please her family. If I hadn't filed papers at the courthouse, our marriage wouldn't even have been legal."

"If you two were so different, Riley, why in heaven's name did you get married? No, don't answer that if you don't want to. I'm sure you loved her."

"That's one of us who's sure." Riley gazed at Emmy with troubled eyes. "I often think if I'd loved her the way I should have, I would've made concessions for her. Instead, I uprooted her from everything and arrogantly expected her to shed those old teachings once we left Oklahoma and came here."

"It's always a mistake to think someone will change."

Riley heard a sad warning in Emmy's statement. He chose not to delve beneath the surface. Besides, they'd arrived at the restaurant with only moments to spare. "Whew, we just made it," he exclaimed, hitting the button to raise the top to his convertible. The wind had picked up again and rain clouds drifted over a hazy moon.

Emmy set her purse and folder on the console and turned the lever to lock the top in place. "I've always pictured you in a car like this, Riley. Bright-red, though, instead of blue. You were saving money for a red convertible the summer before I left."

"Yeah, well, that money moved the family to Oklahoma. The next amount I earned bought an old clunker to drive back and forth to college. This car's pure self-indulgence. As for blue rather than red—that's probably a belated stab at maturity." Grinning, Riley came around the rear of the car to assist Emmy. "You have an uncanny memory. With everything that's happened to you, I wouldn't have thought you'd remember a sixteen-year-old kid's fanciful dream."

Leaning back inside the car to retrieve her purse, Emmy wasn't quite sure how she should answer Riley. Would he want to hear how for years he'd remained a symbol of hope to a girl who had lost all else? The way Josey talked, he'd been a symbol of sorts for Lani, too. Knowing Riley as she did, Emmy was pretty sure he still carried a boatload of guilt for letting Lani down.

"Bring the folder with you." Riley's voice rumbled near Emmy's ear.

"What?" She straightened, relieved that their more personal discussion seemed to be over.

"The folder. I said to bring it. We should have time after we order to take a look at what you've written and maybe set down some ideas on how to proceed."

"Are you sure? You've made your feelings on the subject of my search pretty clear. I don't want to ruin dinner." She grabbed the folder anyway, before he locked the car. She'd take any help he was willing to give.

Riley reached around Emmy and opened the door to the restaurant. He didn't answer her until after he'd given his name to the hostess. "If I've hesitated to help, Emmy," he said, feeling his way, "it's because I never understood your reasons. I'm still not convinced we'll find anything to reconcile you to your loss. I just know I want to be around to hold you if everything falls apart. And I want to see your eyes light up if we're successful. I can't put it any plainer."

Emmy touched his face. She was sorry the hostess chose that moment to pick up two menus and call to them. Emmy was forced to wait until they were seated to thank Riley for his support. Even then, she couldn't find words to express her gratitude.

He shrugged, and in the next sentence denied it was personal. "Lawyers are generally good at solving puzzles. In going over the program, I saw that what you have is a giant jigsaw. Sometimes you're too close to the picture to find the right pieces. An outsider can often step back and better analyze. You'll let emotions get involved. Are you ready to order?'' He smiled at her over top of his menu. ''I see our waitress headed this way.''

Emmy had barely glanced at the menu. ''Ever since I left Shreveport, I've been dying for scampi,'' she said. ''But only if you eat something loaded with garlic, too. At least I hope you're planning to kiss me good-night.'' Emmy hadn't realized how close their table was to one seating eight well-dressed women. Women who fell silent just as Emmy made her announcement.

Eight pair of eyes studied the couple curiously before the waitress cut off their view. Emmy had set her purse and folder on the edge of the table. The waitress accidentally nudged it and sent the whole stack spinning. As Emmy grabbed for the folder, her purse popped open and among other things, her lipstick and a package of tampons spilled out onto the trail of yellow legal paper.

The incident touched off a babble of voices. Two women nearest Emmy bent to help her. A chic blonde paused, skirting around the damning box. *Or was she scanning the pages?* Emmy bumped heads with Riley as she reached to snatch up the pages from the stranger's hand. But the woman apparently knew Riley, as did several others, judging by the number who greeted him by name.

All of them gave Emmy a bold once-over. ''Thanks,'' she mumbled, far too embarrassed by the episode to supply her name.

Fortunately, the waitress had been returning change to their neighbors. She completed her task and stood between the tables while the ladies gathered their purses and jackets. It wasn't until they'd gone that the waitress asked for their orders. Involved in straightening her notes, Emmy let Riley do the honors.

"Is everything there?" he asked when the waitress had walked away.

"I think so. Talk about embarrassing you. I'm sorry, Riley, I hate looking like such a klutz around your clients."

"You think I care? Only one is a client. Lauren Stevens. She inherited a piece of property here last year. I helped her unscramble the will. Dana Bartlett sat next to her. Dana's married to Neil. He's Jed's age. The Bartletts own the funeral home, remember?"

"I do. Neil was red-haired and really chubby. He married the prissy blonde? Wow."

"Dana has dark hair. She's short and flighty. Blonde? The one sitting directly behind you? That was Catherine Jennings." Riley chuckled, reading Emmy's shocked expression.

"I can't believe I didn't recognize Amanda's mom."

"Probably because she's the one who looked down her nose at you."

"Actually, I thought she was reading my notes. Obviously not. She wouldn't lower herself to do anything so crass. Tell me, does my blunder get any worse?"

"Besides Catherine, the most influential woman at the table was Valerie Farr. Her husband, Dwight, is an architect who bid on revamping the former men's club on the east side of the lake. Old man Pettygrove left it to the town. A group led by Catherine's husband plans to push through a vote at tonight's council meeting to make the club grounds into a park and public boat launch."

"I suppose that's commendable, isn't it? I mean, I

would've expected Ray Jennings to try some under-handed deal to sell to developers.''

"His bank still wins. To build a park, the town has to float bonds. Huge bonds…''

"Oh. Those women seemed to be celebrating, so I guess they're not worried the proposal will be defeated.''

"Frankly, I doubt it matters one way or the other. Let's forget them and talk about a strategy for beginning your search.''

"I've already decided on step one. I'm going to start right here in town. The program suggests interviewing people who knew me as an infant. That would be Mom Fran's best friend, Joleen Berber. Reverend Briggs, the pastor at our church. And the people she cleaned houses for, if they're still around. The Parkers, the Hartfields, Noreen Baxter and…Catherine and Ray Jennings,'' she said after a brief hesitation.

"That's a good start. Reverend Briggs was transferred to a church outside of Canton a few years back. Maybe we can combine a visit to him with a turn around Trade Days. Just to see if anyone who still exhibits there remembers a baby being found in one of the permanent stalls.''

"We?'' Emmy folded her hands on top of a new list she'd started. "You're going with me to visit these people, Riley?''

He reached across the table and clasped her hands. "Granted, Frannie died a long time ago. But Logan has officially declared it murder. I'm not suggesting that digging in your past is in any way connected. However, if the person who killed her stuck around town, he or she might not like what you're doing. If you know what I mean.''

Emmy was afraid she did. And she'd rather Riley had kept that worry to himself.

CHAPTER TEN

REPLETE FROM finishing off two piping hot platters of scampi, Emmy and Riley discussed leaving her truck parked at his office. But they decided to follow their original plan, and he fell in behind her until they separated at the lanes leading to their respective houses. Riley had intended to hop the fence and join Emmy for coffee—and maybe more. Intentions that came to an abrupt halt when Mrs. Yates stepped to the edge of his porch and called to him.

"What is it?" Emmy asked in an undertone, juggling her house keys from hand to hand. "Is Alanna ill?"

"I'll see." Riley jogged over to his housekeeper. He quickly returned to Emmy, an apology already on his lips. "An IRS hearing for one of my clients has been advanced to tomorrow morning. The guy's a nervous wreck and has been calling all evening. I need to phone him and then I have to hunker down in my den and prepare for the case."

"Is that all? I was afraid something had happened to Alanna. Why didn't Mrs. Yates notify you on your cell phone?"

"She called my answering service and then talked to Marge, who forbade her to disturb me. Mrs. Yates is put out. She hates being bothered during her favorite TV shows, and my client called repeatedly."

"Alanna said Mrs. Yates...ignores her during soaps,

too. Riley, shouldn't your sitter's number-one objective be to entertain Alanna when you're gone?''

''The woman doesn't drink on the job or have male friends to the house. Believe me, Emmy, I've dealt with those situations. Sure, I'd like her to be warmer. But in a town of this size it's tough to find reliable domestic help.''

''I feel guilty for having taken you away from Alanna this evening.''

''Don't. Until she was two, I worked at home. She was three before I left her for any length of time in the evening. I see Mrs. Yates heading for her car. I need to go inside, Emmy. I'd ask you in for coffee, but…''

''I know.'' She bobbed her head. ''You have a case to prepare. That's okay. I want to go over these notes.'' She tapped the manila folder she had tucked under her arm. ''I think I'll write out a list of questions to ask each person I plan to interview. The same set of questions won't do for everyone on my list.''

''I should be back in my office by one tomorrow. I'll ask Marge to pick us up a couple of deli sandwiches when she goes to lunch. That way we won't waste time stopping somewhere. We'll see Joleen first, then work through Fran's clients. Save Reverend Briggs for last. Depending on how late it is, we may see him the following day. I have to be home at five-thirty on the dot—I promised Mrs. Yates. She has an appointment.''

''I appreciate you working me into your busy schedule, Riley. I know I said I'd handle the interviews alone. But as the time draws nearer, I'm getting more and more nervous.''

''I only have one added question for you, Emmy, and then I have to go. There's no need to answer now, but please give this serious thought. If you find something horrible, can you walk away and simply accept that you needed to search, regardless of the outcome?'' He backed away slowly, feeling bad for quashing her growing excitement. But far better that she start out grounded in reality.

He paused beneath the spreading limbs of the big live oak tree, watching her until she finally lowered her head and hurried into her house. When he'd heard her close the door and saw a light pop on, he loosened his tie, removed his jacket and meandered up the steps to his porch. His first act once inside was to check on Alanna. She'd kicked off her covers. He straightened them and smoothed back the silky hair that lay in a tangle around her small face. He considered what Emmy said about Mrs. Yates's lack of compassion. She kept the house polished. Alanna's toys sat on their shelves like rows of attentive soldiers.

But would his daughter be better off amid the type of clutter he'd grown up with, as Emmy had suggested the day they argued about his split with Josey and his mother?

His mother was a good woman. Riley honestly didn't know how he'd let his relationship with her deteriorate to the point it had. After Lani's death, she'd tried to be supportive. He'd been bitter. Bone-deep bitter. At the time, he couldn't imagine ever wanting to visit the reservation again.

He might go now, though. With Emmy. She'd pricked his conscience. Some part of him really didn't want his daughter, twenty years from now, being angry with him—maybe even rejecting him—because he'd kept her from a family that might have loved her. *Would* love her. He knew, without doubt, that his mom and sister would love Alanna to pieces. The estrangement was entirely his fault. He'd cut off everyone and turned into a regular SOB where family was concerned. That included sending back his mom's letters unopened until she'd finally stopped writing to him.

Riley brooded over his past actions long after he should've started work on his client's case.

EMMY SAT IN Riley's office reception area, nervously spinning a full cup of coffee on a glass coaster while she awaited his return from court. He'd phoned thirty minutes ago to say he was on his way. Emmy had convinced Marge to let her make the deli run. Even then, preferring to wait for Riley, she was left to twiddle her thumbs and watch Marge devour her sandwich.

Riley burst into his office, shedding a wet topcoat and shaking droplets of water out of his hair. "Brr. We've picked a fine day to go on our little Easter egg hunt," he said, tossing the dripping coat over a metal coat tree. "The storm that's been teasing us all week has finally hit with a vengeance."

"You'll probably find more people at home because of it," Marge advised, peering over the top edge of her half glasses. She tossed her deli wrap in the wastebasket.

"I agree," Emmy said. "The women Mom Fran cleaned houses for played tennis or golf on sunny days. I had imagined they'd be old by now, until you pointed out Catherine Jennings last night. I started thinking she must have been really young when she had Amanda. My—my—birth mother could be Catherine's age."

"Emmy." Riley's voice held caution and something more. Anguish?

"You think it's getting my hopes up to speculate on the age of the woman who gave birth to me? Look, Riley, if you're going to examine every word I say throughout this search, then I'd better do this on my own."

Marge glared at her boss. "I'm going out to buy stamps before I'm forced to hurt you, Riley Gray."

"All right, you two, I know when I'm outgunned." He went into the conference room and came back with his corned beef sandwich and Emmy's smoked turkey. As he unwrapped his, he said, "The guy who recommended the program called me today. He said he's only been successful in one out of four searches. He's not very optimistic about our chances because we have so little to go on, Emmy. Hell, I don't know why I agreed to get involved." Riley took a big bite and mumbled, "I don't want this causing you even more pain, dammit."

"That's sweet of you, Riley." Emmy waited until Marge banged out of the office to hug him. "But you don't have to worry. I've had years to deal with the pain. What I'm suffering from now is curiosity. Who were my parents? What's their nationality? What did they look like? What interests did they have? Were they predisposed to any degenerative illnesses?" She waved her sandwich at him. "Should I worry about food allergies?"

Riley skimmed a finger down her cheek. "Last night, I promised that was my final question. I'm in this with you, Emmy. For better or worse."

She swallowed a lump. "You sound as if we're embarking on a lifetime commitment instead of heading out to talk to a few people I used to know."

Riley debated venturing onto ground better left unplowed. He fought the urge and won. "I'm starved. Let's finish eating, then we'll don our Sherlock Holmes hats and set off on our Huckleberry Finn adventure."

"Talk about opposites. Hey, speaking of Huck Finn," Emmy said, washing a bite down with a slug of sweetened coffee. "I circled by Beaumarais on my way here, to give Jed that military address for maybe locating Will. Gwyn jumped right on it. Said she'd write a letter today."

"That would be quite the reunion if old Will rode back into town on a white charger."

"Why do you say that? You think he might have become a cowboy or something?"

Riley grinned. "More like Zorro. Don't you remember how Will used to clown around slashing his initials through the air? And despite the unfairness he experienced all his life, he was definitely a believer in justice. I can see Fielder coming unglued. I never sit down with him that he doesn't make me feel like I'm still the town's worst juvenile delinquent."

Emmy broke another piece off her smoked turkey sandwich. "You, Will and Rico all vied for that title. There's the Halloween you painted a big, fluorescent *U* on every vehicle in the city yard. Fielder had just been elected sheriff and he'd taken delivery of the town's first brand-new police car, if I recall."

Riley threw his sandwich wrapper away and opened a bottle of water. "You should've heard him last year when he found out that Will and I, with Jed's reluctant help, were the ones who heisted those fifteen cases of beer." He grinned. "We removed them from a car belonging to a couple of thieves—who took 'em from the Legion Hall. That was the summer before our junior year."

"You didn't! Fifteen cases? I'm surprised you all weren't sick as dogs."

"We didn't drink it. A patrol car pulled in behind us right after we loaded it all into the trunk of Jed's old beater. Scared the heck out of us. That car didn't do more than forty miles an hour. All we could think about was getting rid of the evidence.''

''You dumped it?''

''Nope. We lost our deputy tail, and Will directed us to Santiago's.''

''Oh? Does Rico's family still serve wonderful Mexican food right out of their home kitchen? My mouth is watering just thinking about it.''

''Santiago's has grown. We'll have to go there one evening. Getting back to my story—one of the cousins was getting married that weekend. Will had the clever idea of letting them have the beer for their reception. I didn't go to the wedding, but Will said later they all partied till the cows came home.''

''You guys! Don't tell me any more. And to think I used to idolize you.''

''Yeah. Those were the good old days. If kids tried stunts like that today, you'd hear the hue and cry from here to the state penitentiary. Nobody looks on simple mischief anymore as juvenile pranks. Now they call it by harsher names—like vandalism.''

''Hey, when Alanna's a teen, she might be hanging out with guys just like you and Jed.''

Riley blotted his mouth on his napkin. ''Don't say that. I doubt there's anything scarier to a single dad than the thought of facing his daughter's dating years.''

Emmy folded her sandwich wrap into a neat square before she dumped it in the wastebasket. She didn't know why her turkey sandwich suddenly felt like lead in her stomach or why she found it hard to breathe. ''I guess I assumed you'd remarry long before Alanna goes to her first school dance.''

''It's possible. I'd really like her not to be an only child.''

Emmy grabbed her coat, then rummaged in the umbrella holder and found her brightly patterned umbrella. "If you're ready, we may as well take off. We're on my dime."

"I said I was doing this as a favor, Emmy."

"I had Marge draw up a contract. I decided it'd be better to keep this search strictly business, Riley. I don't want the town gossips to say I'm sleeping with you in payment for the help you're giving me."

"They wouldn't. We're not." He looked confused, then hurt. "As you wish, Emmy," he muttered, shrugging back into his still damp top coat. "My car might be more comfortable, but your pickup probably uses less gas. It's your choice, since Marge will undoubtedly bill you for transportation costs."

Emmy loitered at the threshold. "Uh, she and I agreed on a flat hourly fee. And I'd rather you drove. You know the area better. How about if I put the gas on my credit card? That should work."

Seizing the end of her umbrella, Riley spun her around. "Dammit, Emmy. What happened between last night and today to change you so drastically? Last night we parted as friends and lovers. Today we're client and attorney."

Color flooded her cheeks. She drew in a deep breath and let it out in ragged spurts. "At the risk of sounding schizophrenic, let me say I *feel* like two people. The me who's here, and a woman running in the background like…like some kind of shadow. Call it crazy, but I have to separate the two, until one way or another, this chase comes to an end. Please, Riley. You belong to the best part of my life. Riley Gray Wolf does. Not the lawyer Riley Gray. In a way, *you're* two people, too. Oh, shoot. I'm not making sense. You probably think I should be committed."

"Oddly enough," he said, kissing her on the forehead. "You make perfect sense." He grasped her hand and brought it to his chest. "You've shown me I can't continue to live my life as though I'm in the spin cycle of a washer. I can't change the past, but now it's patently clear that ignoring my background hasn't made me like Jed or Will."

"And now?"

He looked rueful. "The jury's still out in my case. But in yours… I want to go on record here. How I feel about you will not change, regardless of what we uncover. Because you're important to me, Emmy. I love you just the way you are."

"Oh, Riley. I hope with all my heart that what you've said will always be true."

Stooping, he kissed her again. "Let's go. The sooner we find answers, the better."

The rain had slackened before they parked in front of Joleen Berber's small yellow house. The siding was peeling badly. Her once-showplace flower beds had gone to weeds. Windows Emmy remembered as having bright, cheery curtains were now covered in foil, possibly to cut heat and cooling bills. "The place looks dark," she murmured. "Do you want to wait here while I go see if she's home?"

"Marge said she's something of a recluse. An oddball, generally speaking." Riley turned off the engine and pocketed the keys. "I'll come with you."

Emmy stopped with one foot out of the car. "You mean she might not remember me?"

"It's possible."

The gate creaked. It needed oiling. Emmy's knock was more tentative than she'd planned. She repeated it twice before they heard shuffling feet, and the door cracked open a few inches, releasing an odor of stale cigarette smoke. "Joleen. I'm—"

Emmy glimpsed a stark expression of fear a split second before the woman stumbled backward and fell against the wall. Emmy made a helpless gesture, and Riley shoved at the door, but Joleen was no lightweight and her stout legs blocked him for a few minutes.

Once they pushed their way inside, Emmy reached for the woman's plump hand. She chafed it while Riley pulled out his cell phone to dial 911. Protesting, Joleen struggled to sit up straight before his call went through. He disconnected.

"Joleen, it's Emmy Monday. I lived with Frannie Granger. I'm sorry, I should've phoned before we came. I didn't mean to give you a start."

"Emerald? Oh, I thought you were— Never mind. What do you want? Frannie's gone. Murdered." The word exploded out, her entire bulk shuddering.

"I know." Emmy watched with sad eyes as Riley expended a lot of effort to help the once-spry nurse to her feet. "You were Mom Fran's best friend. I'm sure the news devastated you."

Joleen shook off Riley's help. She twisted a lank gray braid back into the knot from which it had fallen and readjusted the pin. Shifting, she clutched the neck of the robe she still wore, though it was afternoon. She started to close the door, moving them out. Emmy raised one hand.

"Go away," Joleen told them. "Talking won't bring Frannie back. She's gone." Joleen's lips remained a thin slash in a sallow face.

"And I'm so sorry," Emmy said. "But since Sheriff Fielder's asking questions anyway, I'd hoped something from that time might provide a lead to who I really am."

"You said you're Emmy." The faded eyes darted from side to side as the woman pulled a packet of cigarettes from her pocket and extracted one with a shaking hand.

"I am." Emmy didn't want to lose patience, but it was difficult. "May we come in and ask you a few questions? This is Riley Gray. He's an old friend of Jed and Will's, Mom Fran's other foster kids. You remember them, don't you?"

"Talking won't bring Frannie back," Joleen said again. She lit the cigarette and exhaled fast.

"I agree. I know you found me at First Monday Trade Days. I want very much to locate my birth parents, Joleen. Anything you remember may be the information I need."

Joleen muttered darkly. She was surprisingly strong and succeeded in shoving them out onto the wet stoop. "Frannie loved you. She gave you a good home," Joleen said harshly around a bobbing cigarette. "No good will come of disturbing the dead. Before you know it, folks'll be saying she wasn't a good mother, and she was."

"This isn't about Mom Fran. I loved her, too," Emmy said, tears sticking to her lashes. "Please, try to understand. I need to know who—why someone discarded me. I'm interested in any memories you have. No detail is too small."

For a moment Joleen's face softened. "You were in a basket under a table in the last row of antique booths at First Monday Trade Days. You looked so pretty. Like a life-size baby doll. Your dress was yellow as a buttercup, and you were wrapped in a pale-green blanket. The woman whose booth it was had gone to grab a bite to eat. She had no idea where you'd come from. No idea at all."

"That's hard to believe," Riley said.

"I was there," Joleen snapped. "Do you want to hear what I have to say or not?"

"Oh, yes, please." Emmy shot Riley a warning look.

"Well, then...Frannie, my good friend, had lost her husband. She was deep in grief. Frannie needed to be *needed* again to get back on track. I notified Social Services. I knew Fran had applied for foster care and been approved. I talked them into turning you over to her. The agency's probes turned up blank, so they left you with Frannie. It's been thirty years, so any trail would be stone-cold by now."

"Thirty-two years," Emmy said absently. "Did Social Services phone the police? Did they check the hospitals to see if any single mother had given birth around then? Is the date on my unofficial birth certificate accurate?"

"I can't help you." Joleen was more forceful this time. "You look like a nice girl. And smart. My advice is to let the dead stay dead." She flipped the cigarette through a crack in the screen.

Emmy blinked, her nose mere inches from the door Joleen slammed shut.

Riley let a moment pass before he slipped his arm around Emmy's waist and gently urged her off the rain-slick porch. "Come on, Emmy. I warned you Marge said she'd gone around the bend."

"Has she, or is she hiding something? She seemed lucid enough when she described how I looked the day she found me."

"What would she be hiding, sugar babe?" He said it softly. Brokenly.

Heaving a sigh, Emmy let Riley bear her weight as she matched her steps with his out to the car. "I let myself believe that Joleen would have all the answers. You told me not to pin my hopes on these interviews, but I'm afraid I got carried away.''

"Are you all right to push on?" he asked after joining her in the car.

"I'm fine. Heavens," she said around a little laugh, "we're only beginning. I'm in this for the long haul, Riley."

He didn't say anything. Not even as he watched her grow more despondent after each stop. The women for whom Frannie had cleaned were more willing to talk than Joleen. None, however, had anything to add.

Catherine Jennings, the last on their list of former clients, invited them into her parlor, a cold room that reeked of old money. Riley and Emmy sat side by side on a white damask sofa. Their elegantly turned out hostess rang a silver bell—like a queen, requesting her maid to serve coffee.

Magically, a mousy-looking woman appeared wheeling a silver coffee service on an ornate serving cart. Catherine poured three dainty china cups full of strong brew. She listened politely to Emmy's questions, but remained aloof. "I never involve myself in the private lives of my employees. All I can really tell you is that Frannie Granger did her job well. She wasn't a gossip like so many domestics. She was honest. If Frannie found so much as a penny under the couch cushions, she left it on the table. You would appreciate that trait if, like us, you'd had sticky-fingered help. We've had an entire set of silverware vanish. In the past, Amanda's been...well, careless with leaving money and jewelry lying around. We're insured, of course, but I'd never tolerate keeping a thief in my employ.''

Emmy made no comment. Riley, who had his own horror stories about housekeepers and sitters, commiserated with Catherine briefly. As nothing else came to light, they thanked her for the coffee and her time, and left.

"We worked through that list quickly." Riley glanced at his watch. "You want to call it a day, or forge on to Canton?"

"Do you think there'll be anyone hanging around the flea-market grounds today? It's next Monday the market opens, right?"

"Yes, but I think it takes days to set up. Although I'll be first to admit the chances of finding any exhibitors who were there thirty years ago are slim to none. We could see if Canton has a newspaper, and if so check their archives."

"Are throwaway babies newsworthy?"

Riley hooked his arm around Emmy's neck and pulled her toward him. "There you go, sounding bitter again. Stop, or I'm going to be sorry I agreed to see this thing through."

"I know we've just begun. But it's already discouraging."

"Keep taking good notes. In a few cases I've worked, I missed a detail the first time around. Next time, though, the very clue I missed popped out at me."

"We've learned zip," she said in a despairing voice. "Nada. Absolutely nothing."

"Not exactly true," he pointed out. "Did you know you'd been found wearing a yellow dress and wrapped in a green blanket?"

"I vaguely remember having a blanket fitting that description for one of my first dolls. Fran loved buying me dolls. You know, Riley—I found something Catherine said interesting. The part about them losing jewelry and silver. An expensive brooch, reportedly pinned to my baby blanket, disappeared from our house. Catherine blamed her hired help, but Fran didn't have any. Do you think it's possible someone in Uncertain was or is a jewel thief? Am I making any sense?''

"Gotcha. If the thief fences through a pawn shop, there'd be a record. See, that's a possible lead. I wonder if other residents have had robberies?''

"I meant to ask Joleen about the brooch. Hardly a day went by that she didn't stop at the house. She often ate supper with us before going home to change out of her uniform. It's how I remember her, all dressed in crisp white. She looked...so...old, today.''

"Where did she work? Not at a hospital in Canton?''

"No. In Tyler. She took care of people who had terminal cancer. I remember Fran saying she didn't know how Joleen could stand working year after year with people who almost always died. You know Fran nursed her husband until his death. He had lung cancer.''

"If Joleen was assigned to the oncology ward, it shoots my theory that she might've met the woman who delivered you. Why couldn't she have worked in obstetrics? But that would've been too easy.''

"Nothing about my case is easy. I didn't think it would be. Then again, I'd hoped some magical answer would leap out and hit me between the eyes.''

"Maybe Reverend Briggs will be your savior.''

"Are you always this optimistic, Riley?''

He wrinkled his nose. "Rarely. Among colleagues, I'm known as the voice of gloom and doom. I tend to look for the storm clouds that ruin sunny days. My feeling is, if you prepare for the darkest hour, you're better equipped to meet whatever comes.''

"Well, today the storm has passed.'' And indeed, the sun had come out and dried up the puddles when they finally found the rectory where Reverend Briggs lived. The humidity curled Emmy's hair into ringlets.

"I recognize you, my dear," the pastor said the minute Emmy introduced herself. "Mrs. Granger used to pull a wool cap over your head on the way to church, no matter what the weather, so when you arrived at Sunday school your head was a mass of golden curls. Pure angel she said you were."

"Hardly, Reverend." Emmy hid a smile.

"I was so sorry to hear how that good, good woman came to such a bad end. But ours is not to question God's will."

"I didn't actually come to discuss my foster mother, Pastor Briggs. I've decided to try to locate my birth parents, or my birth mother at least. I'm hoping you might know something—anything that might provide me with a clue."

He invited them to walk in his rose garden. Emmy and Riley dutifully followed the old man's measured steps. He stopped every so often to sniff one of the fragrant buds. They stopped, too, and waited. Emmy tried to be patient, but she fidgeted.

"I do my best thinking out here," Briggs explained when they reached one end of the garden and had circled back. "Not long after Mr. Granger passed on, Frannie applied for a foster care license. You were truly a gift from heaven for the poor, dear soul. Have you spoken with Joleen Berber? She found you when you were just a bit of a thing. I think that's how it went. Oh, it was such a long time ago. My memory isn't what it used to be."

Emmy traced her finger around a rose. "We visited Joleen earlier today. She isn't really herself anymore."

"No. She took the disappearance of her dearest friend very hard. Her decline started when no trace was found.

I was transferred from the church in Uncertain a while ago, but Joleen had already stopped attending services. She would be your best source, I believe.''

"So you can't help Emmy? Did you ever see a brooch that was supposedly found with the baby?" Riley asked. "It later disappeared."

"There were rumors to that effect, but Mrs. Granger never confirmed or denied their accuracy to me. She wasn't a complainer, Lord love her."

Emmy's face fell. "Mom Fran used to draw me pictures of the brooch. We drew together a lot if I was sick and had to miss school. I didn't save the drawings."

The reverend smiled indulgently. "Perhaps the brooch was a figment of her imagination."

"I remember her description vividly. I'm sure she wouldn't have fabricated it. Why would she?"

"I don't know, child. People make up fantasies for all kinds of reasons. Was Ms. Berber able to tell you about the brooch?"

"I forgot to bring it up. I'll talk with her again." Emmy asked a few more questions and carefully logged the old minister's responses on her legal pad. He didn't recall hearing any gossip about illegitimate pregnancies among the town's young women around the time of Emmy's birth.

"Things of that nature have a way of slipping out. Gossip has wings in small towns. Pregnancies and marital infidelities are extremely difficult to conceal. If I were the sort to pass on tales, I could name at least five prominent men who were cheating on their wives back then. But I believe in silence. No good ever comes of divulging the private concerns of others."

Riley cleared his throat. "We wouldn't be interested in that type of information unless one of the assignations resulted in an unplanned pregnancy. And since you say with authority that no young women were spirited out of Uncertain for roughly nine months, I guess that concludes our business, Reverend.''

''As Emerald was found nearer this parish than my old one, I'll be glad to have a look at records here. They're catalogued by sacrament and then by date. Sometimes unwed mothers have a pressing need to have their babies baptized—even those given up for adoption.''

''Oh, would you?'' Emmy clasped his deeply veined hands. She pulled away long enough to write the probable date of her birth and her phone number on a piece of paper, which she passed to him. ''I'll gladly follow up on any leads you find. And, Reverend Briggs, I'll be discreet.''

''I'm sure you will. Have you written to the Texas birth registry to request a list of babies born within four or five days on either side of your birth date? They won't necessarily show if a mother's married or not, but in a town of this size, how many births could there be in a year? Twenty? Fifty? Since people tend to remain in this area, it shouldn't be hard to discover if the baby girl grew up and is still living here. Or, I heard of one adoptee who traced clothing tags to find out who'd purchased the items she wore to her adoptive home.''

''Today is our first day at this,'' Riley informed him. ''Thanks so much for your time and advice. Here's my business card. Emmy lives next door, so I can get a message to her if you can't reach her at her number.''

''I wish you both luck,'' said the old man. He watched them walk to their car and waved a palsied hand as they pulled out.

''I hope he doesn't kick the bucket before he has a chance to read through those files,'' Riley muttered.

"You are a pessimist." Emmy folded up in laughter. It was the first time she'd allowed herself to laugh all day. "But you have to admit he couldn't have been nicer."

"I agree, and so far he's been the most helpful." Riley looked at her. "Want to go by the Trade Days stalls?"

"I think I'd rather wait and come back on a day they're open for business. Reverend Briggs gave me a good tip. Not about the clothing tags, because those are long gone. But I still have the basket I was found in. It was made locally. Maybe tomorrow we can drive to the factory. I don't know why I didn't think of that before. Just think, if they kept records of individual purchases, it might be a simple matter of locating the purchaser."

"Sounds good. So, we're headed home?"

"Yes. This should give you an extra hour to spend with Alanna. The weather's clearing up nicely. You two could go for a boat ride around the lake."

"Hey, great idea. Want to join us? I'll barbecue hot dogs when we get back."

"I hate to horn in on you and Alanna. She needs one-on-one time with her dad."

"What if I leave it up to her? If she wants me to herself, fine. If she'd like your company, I'll send her over to extend the invitation."

"And you won't put the question to her like a lawyer? I mean, you'll give her an honest opportunity to say yes or no?"

Riley clapped his hand over his heart. "You wound me, sugar babe. What kind of lawyers do you know, anyway?"

"Shysters. Is there another kind?" She batted her eyes prettily, and he punched her arm hard enough to make her hit him back, the way she used to when they were kids. Also like a kid, she said, "Ouch, you bully." It served to ease the day's tensions, and they reminisced during the drive home. Both were relaxed when they reached the house, only to find Alanna sitting on the top porch step in tears. Gwyn Louis sat next to her, punching buttons on her cell telephone.

She rose when the car rolled in. Gwyn met Riley and Emmy with a look of profound relief as they exploded from opposite sides of the car.

"What's up? Where's Mrs. Yates?" Riley knelt and scooped up his daughter, who threw her arms around him and sobbed into his neck.

"That woman," Gwyn snapped, "telephoned me at a quarter to five. She's accepted a new job with a state senator who's at his summer home on Lake Sam Rayburn. Apparently she had the interview several days ago, and he got back to her this afternoon, asking her to start work tomorrow morning. She left the minute I arrived. I was just trying to raise you on your cell."

"What? She did *what?*" Sputtering, Riley squeezed Alanna too hard. He couldn't seem to comprehend everything Gwyn was saying.

Alanna stiffened in his arms. "Mrs. Yates said her new job pays more, Daddy. And she won't have to take care of any kids. I can't stay alone, and you hafta go to work. What'll I do?" Tears poured from already reddened eyes.

"I'd help out until you can find a replacement," Gwyn offered. "But tomorrow I'm supervising a cheetah on set at a studio in Austin. I may be there overnight."

"I'm free as a bird," Emmy chimed in. "It's no problem, Riley. I have nothing on my agenda, except in the afternoon you and I were going to the basket company. Alanna can come along. Or not. We can always go another day."

"Daddy," Alanna squealed. "Can I stay with Emmy?

Oh, please say yes. I could play with Egypt, and Emmy can read me books.''

"Are you sure about this, Emmy?'' Riley asked, sounding unsure. "What a debacle. I can't believe any responsible adult would walk out on a job without giving notice. I've got half a mind to call the senator and tell him what kind of person he hired. On second thought, he's welcome to her.''

"I'm fine with watching Alanna, honest. She and I will get along famously, won't we, hon?''

"Yep. We sure will.''

"Well, thank goodness that crisis is averted.'' Gwyn pocketed her cell phone and headed for her Rover. "I'll call you when I get back to town. Maybe the five of us can have a barbecue over the weekend. Riley, would you call Jed tomorrow if you get a chance? Fielder gave him more flak today. Thorny said the sheriff's employing subtle harassment techniques—annoying but not actionable. He told Jed to not let it get to him. You know it did.''

"I'll call him tomorrow from the office, Gwyn. I wonder what Logan has on his mind. Did he mention finding new evidence?''

"I didn't ask because Jed's so angry. Fielder's wearing blinders when it comes to this case.''

"Fix him a double margarita when you get home. And tell him I agree with Thorny. Logan has nothing, so he's replowing old ground, hoping to stir something up.''

"I hope that's all it is. Well, bye, guys. Emmy, when I get home we'll meet for coffee. I want to hear what all you've found in the search for your birth mom.''

Emmy didn't want to admit they'd found virtually nothing. Besides, maybe their luck would change at the basket company. She made the okay sign with her fingers and waved Gwyn off with a smile.

CHAPTER ELEVEN

"Do YOU STILL want to take our boat around the lake and picnic afterward?" Riley asked Emmy out of Alanna's hearing when Gwyn had gone.

"Not if you need to call around to find out what Fielder's up to. Alanna can come home with me and help assemble taco salads for when you're done."

"Tell you what. I'll go change and put out a couple of telephone feelers. You and Alanna fix salads and store them for when we get back. Let's meet at the boat ramp in, oh, twenty minutes? That gives us time for a little ride around the lake before dark. I hope it'll give my sources time to do some digging, as well."

"Sounds good to me. Does that meet with your approval, Miss Alanna?" Emmy nudged the child who'd returned in time to hear the final plans.

"Uh-huh. And I know where Daddy keeps the life jackets. We all have to wear them," she informed Emmy importantly.

"I'm afraid I don't have a life jacket." Emmy cast a worried glance toward Riley.

"Can she wear the one you bought Miss Blair?" Alanna tipped her head to study Emmy intently. "Miss Blair's bigger...on...top," the child said, reaching up to pat Emmy's chest. "You can tie the life jacket tighter for Emmy, can't you, Daddy?"

Emmy found herself blushing. "Who's Blair?" she

blurted, although it was the last thing she wanted to ask
about. *Not true.* She wanted to know in the worst way,
since Riley was acting downright uncomfortable. He
seemed ready to clap his hand over Alanna's mouth.

"I'll show you," Alanna was saying. "Daddy thinks
she's pretty, but I don't like her." The child wriggled
down out of Riley's arms and hit the ground running.
"I've got a picture of Miss Blair with Daddy at the Fish
Ball," Alanna called over her shoulder as she bounded
up the porch steps, clearly on a mission.

"The Anglers' Ball," Riley corrected in a loud voice.
"And I don't think Emmy cares about seeing pictures of
a local charity event."

"Oh, but I do," Emmy murmured.

Alanna didn't hear her dad. The screen door banged
shut on her heels.

Emmy tucked her tongue into her cheek. She let Riley
sputter and fume, digging himself in deeper.

"Blair Dunning is a fellow attorney. Well, not a *fellow*
fellow. Another lawyer. The assistant county D.A. We,
uh, are professional colleagues."

"Of course. I imagine you buy life vests for your male
colleagues, too." Emmy reeled out the line and left the
bait dangling as Alanna ran pell-mell toward them, a couple of snapshots flapping in her hand.

Riley groaned and rolled his eyes. "It's not the way it
appears, Emmy. Marge gave her the damn pictures."

Alanna skidded to a stop, her sneakers touching
Emmy's sandals. Without ceremony, she thrust the photos into Emmy's hands.

The woman draped all over Riley in the first shot could
indeed be classed as pretty. Tall, blond, sleek in a low-
cut black dress. A life vest bought for the woman falling

out of that dress was unlikely to fit her own size 32B—no matter how tightly it was fastened.

Emmy cleared her throat a few times. "Nice event. I guess you're a member of the country club now. Do you remember when we'd sneak up from the lake, joking about what those fancy-dancy folks would do if we crashed one of their parties?" She framed the second print with her fingers, blocking out the statuesque blonde, focusing instead on how sexy Riley looked wearing a tailored tux. Emmy had occasionally envisioned him in one over the years, especially when she dealt cards to high rollers. She'd even passed an evening wondering what she'd do if Riley walked up to her table. Of course, in her daydreams he'd always been alone.

She quietly handed the photographs back to Alanna, although she'd give anything to ask the little girl why she didn't like the beautiful, coolly chic Blair Dunning.

"The club isn't such a big deal, Emmy. I'll take you there anytime. I guarantee you still won't like the stuffy atmosphere. To answer your question, whenever I go, I look over the lake and wonder if there are high school kids hiding in the bushes making grandiose plans the way we used to."

"Listen," Emmy said abruptly. "It's probably too late to go boating this evening. I didn't think about needing a life vest, but I'll see about picking one up at the Tackle Shop. We can go another time."

Alanna shoved the pictures into her dad's pocket. "I want to go *now,* and I want Emmy." Her lower lip protruded as she flung her arms around Emmy's slender waist.

Riley hadn't lived in a household full of women his entire life without gaining some insight into their sudden, changeable moods. He decided to ignore Emmy's refusal.

"I didn't buy the vest *for* Blair. In fact, I bought two to have on hand for guests. They're made to fit men or women and they're easily adjusted." He wagged his watch at Emmy. "We've lost five minutes of our twenty, ladies. You've only got fifteen left to make your salad."

"We'd better hurry, huh?" Alanna tugged Emmy toward the fence.

"Sure." Emmy sighed. "The lettuce is already chopped and the meat's cooked. I'll slice onions and tomatoes and you can toss stuff together, Alanna."

"So it's settled?" Riley called.

By way of answer, Emmy and Alanna broke into a run. They giggled, both enjoying the moment. Emmy tied a too big apron around Alanna. Watching the girl as she scrambled up on a chair brought an unexpected rush to Emmy, spinning her back to her own childhood. She'd stood on a chair in this very kitchen as Fran patiently taught her how to cook. The table had changed and the appliances, but the four walls had not. If only they could talk, Emmy thought, absently massaging an aching chest.

The three of them met at the dock. Alanna and Emmy had one minute of their fifteen to spare. It seemed to Emmy that Riley spent an inordinate length of time adjusting her life jacket. His fingers brushed the tips of her breasts, causing heat to pool in the pit of her stomach. He was doing it on purpose and with a straight face, the rat.

I'll get you, she mouthed behind Alanna's back.

"Promises, promises," he murmured, tickling her ear as he reached around her, deliberately pulling her close to make the final adjustment.

Blair, the sexy D.A., was forgotten in the heat of the moment. Emmy's blood didn't cool until they were well into the center of the lake—and then only because of a westerly wind rippling through the lacy Spanish moss.

She settled back to enjoy the ride, liking the way the breeze billowed Riley's half-buttoned shirt above his life belt, and the way his hand on the tiller let the afternoon sun play on his muscles. "This boat's a big improvement over the one you borrowed the last time you took me for a ride on Caddo Lake. Which, by the way, is also the last boat I've been in."

"No kidding. None of your circus pals in Florida had boats?"

"Circus players barely make enough to eat. They don't own bass boats or have memberships in ritzy country clubs."

Alanna squealed, and pointed to a family of ducks swimming between the lily pads. She saved Riley from having to defend a social status he'd worked hard to earn.

A moment later, a pair of egrets swooped down and landed one-legged on the knee of a century-old cypress. Emmy made up a story about the lake for Alanna as Riley slowed to let a replica of an old paddle-wheel steamboat chug past.

He pulled into the bigger craft's wake. Emmy and Alanna waved to the bevy of tourists who hung over the steamer's railing. "We'll tail him through Mossy Brake and circle back when he swings into Jackfish Alley. I love motoring through the alley," Riley said, "but Alanna thinks it's creepy."

"So did Blair. She threw a hissy fit. You said so, huh, Daddy?"

Riley controlled a grin. "Blair, uh, did prefer land over water."

Emmy gazed into the gloomy arch, where the steamboat churned up brackish water. "As kids, we used to pole through Jackfish Alley on homemade rafts. It's a wonder half of us didn't drown or get lost back in the bayous. I loved pretending I was a girl pirate," she admitted. "Will and Jed and I had a contest every year to see who could find the first Yonqupin blossom," she told Alanna.

"I can't come down to the lake by myself. Daddy said there's still alligators. And sometimes they come out to sit in the sun."

"There *are* gators," he said, "although most have disappeared into the inner corridors that were set aside as a wildlife sanctuary. I remember what we did as kids, but think differently now that I'm a parent. So, there's still no going to the lake unless you're with an adult, young lady."

"That's a good rule, Alanna." Emmy pointed to some giant, umbrellalike blue-green lotus leaves. "Look! Soon those will sprout stems of bright-yellow blossoms the Caddo Indians called Yonqupins. See how different they are from the other water lily pads? You know," she added, "Mom Fran said when she was a girl, there was a time this lake lost all its water. Right where we're boating was all mud flats." Emmy straightened and frowned at Riley. "I just remembered something. Fran said area residents dug mussels in the flats. Some had pearls inside. Caddo pearls. Tiffany's in New York bought the larger ones, but local wealthy oilmen or timber barons had pearls set for their wives and daughters." Emmy spoke with rising excitement. "What's significant, Riley, is that Mom Fran said it was a Caddo pearl in my brooch."

"That is important, I should think. I wonder if local jewelers have records of pieces they crafted. Could you draw the one that was found with you?"

"Not accurately because I never saw it. All I have in

my head is a pattern Mom Fran sketched. A gem-studded tree inside a gold circlet. I can't—oh!'' Her eyes grew wide as a sudden memory flashed through her mind. ''One day, not long before her disappearance, Mom Fran sat me down and cautioned me not to mention the brooch to anyone at school. I'd completely forgotten that.''

''Did she say why you weren't to say anything?''

Emmy shrugged. ''No. And I can't recall asking.'' She stiffened. ''Do you think she might have discovered that someone we knew stole the brooch? Oh, Riley. What if the day she disappeared she accosted the thief? What if it was the thief who murdered her? What if it was someone in my class?''

Riley pulled a wry face. ''That would be the height of speculation, Emmy. Who? Most of those kids except you, Jed, Will, Rico, Josey and me came from wealthy families. And if Fran *had* proof, wouldn't she have gone straight to Sheriff Fielder? She wasn't a reckless sort. Not only that, you were little, you said, when it went missing.''

''You're right. Darn it, though, I wish I'd been more inquisitive back then.''

''Look at everything you've dredged up during a simple turn around the lake. I wish we had more time. But we're losing the light. Given the tangle of duckweed, spatterdock and golden club among the lilies and lotus, I don't care to navigate these waters after dark.''

Alanna crept from her seat in the center of the boat to cuddle up to Emmy. ''Miss Gwyn said you're trying to find your mama. What about your daddy? You've got a daddy like I do, right?''

Emmy darted a helpless glance at Riley.

''Alanna, honey, Emmy's situation is kind of complicated. She was separated from her mom and dad when she was a baby. The woman who owned the house where Emmy's staying, the one right next to us—well, she gave Emmy a home.''

Alanna stared at her father with wondering eyes. ''But—but—Mrs. Yates told somebody on the phone that you were helping Emmy find her mama.''

''Who? Who did she tell? Why?''

''I dunno. I wasn't s'posed to be listening.'' Alanna hung her head contritely.

''I'm not mad at you, Alanna. I *am* helping Emmy…sort of. I guess it's no secret,'' Riley added as he guided the boat into the dock, jumped out and lashed it to the metal cleats jutting out from the wood.

Alanna tracked his every move. As did Emmy, who sat still while he hoisted his daughter out to straddle his hip. He extended his free hand to Emmy and kept it wrapped tightly in his, even after she'd stepped onto the dock.

''Alanna, I can read your mind. I want you to listen to me. Your mother isn't lost. She died when you were born. I've explained that. Emmy's case is different. The woman who gave birth to her may be out there somewhere.''

''I know my mama's in heaven. You said she's up there with the moon and the stars. So did Miss Marge. I'm glad you're helping Emmy. 'Cause it's sad and lonesome not havin' a mama of your own.''

Riley gaped, then kissed Alanna's little nose. He felt Emmy squeeze his hand and wrap her free fingers around his wrist. ''Alanna, I've been wrong not to talk about your mother more. I have a mom, too. She's your grandmother. Lately I've been thinking of asking Emmy to go with us to Oklahoma to visit Grandmother Gray, uh, Gray Wolf,'' he muttered, aiming a guilty glance at Emmy.

Her eyes filled with tears. "I'd love to go," she finally managed. "How about Friday—tomorrow. We could leave after we visit the basket company."

"So soon? Well, uh…s-sure," Riley stuttered. "Although, didn't Gwyn mention getting together for a barbecue this weekend?"

Emmy batted Riley's shoulder. "No plea bargaining, counselor. It's time."

Riley's sigh spelled his resignation. "I'll phone my uncle in the morning. He's another person I owe amends."

"And Josey? Will you include Josey?"

"You're asking for a lot, Emmy. I'll think about it. Josey meddled where she had no business."

"Unintentionally, Riley. She's been sorry every day since."

"I said I'd think about it. For God's sake, Emmy. That's the best I can do."

"All right." She gave in with a shrug. "Hey, is anybody hungry? Last one to my kitchen sets the table." Shaking Riley's hand loose, Emmy slipped out of her life jacket and tossed it to him, then took off running.

Alanna scrambled out of his arms and did the same with her life vest. He watched the two join hands and dart across the lawn—and silently blessed Emmy for giving him time to collect his scattered emotions.

Emmy and Alanna loped along, hair streaming in the wind. One very blond and one dark, both beautiful in the fading sun's glow. Riley jammed his hands in his pockets and followed at a leisurely pace. He figured that old saying about confession being good for the soul must be true; he didn't know when he'd felt half as content.

As girlish and womanly laughter mingled and drifted back to him, he was struck by a sudden sense of family. *His* family. Alanna—and Emmy.

The two disappeared inside Emmy's house. Riley quickened his pace, breaking into a jog, suddenly overwhelmed by disorienting feelings—a sense of déjà vu.

Though his heart banged unnaturally in his chest, he walked in on a perfectly benign scene. Alanna jiggled a string tied with bright spools for the kitten to chase. In the kitchen, Emmy had her head inside the refrigerator.

"You lost," they both sang out.

"No," Riley said. In three short strides, he'd grasped Emmy around the waist and spun her to face him. "I won," he growled, stealing a fast kiss. "I get to have dinner with the two prettiest women in the universe."

Flushed, Emmy ducked from his hold. "The moon's not out yet, or I'd say you were suffering from moon madness. I know what it is, Alanna," she called. "Your dad thinks flattery will save him from setting the table."

The girl appeared in the archway. "What's flattery?"

"Your dad says we're the prettiest women in the universe. It's nicer to call that flattery than to say he lied."

"Oh. Well, we are pretty."

"See." Grinning, Riley walked Emmy backward to the counter. He deliberately pressed his weight against her as he reached over her head to take down salad plates.

This time Emmy didn't push him away. She let herself enjoy the lingering scent of his aftershave, and the comforting feel of his solid strength. All too soon he stepped away to set the table and left her with vague yearnings.

It was clear that he'd been teasing. Her feelings were too serious. Way too serious, considering the amount of old baggage they each carried.

VERY LIKELY the combination of a stressful afternoon, the lake outing and chasing a frisky kitten around the house explained Alanna's falling asleep over her meal. Emmy caught her seconds before she tumbled from her chair. "Poor kid. If you've finished eating, Riley, go ahead and take her home to bed. Oh, does she sleep late or is she an early riser? Will you bring her here in the morning? Or should I go over to your place?"

"Come home with us tonight."

Emmy turned and searched Riley's eyes, expecting him still to be teasing as he bent to relieve her of Alanna's dead weight. What she saw was blatant desire, barely contained behind Riley's thickly lashed eyes.

Heat licked along her bare arms. He could make her want him with a mere glance. But she resisted it.

"I care too much for Alanna's feelings to let her find me in your bed, Riley."

"What do you mean? The kid's crazy about you."

"Believe me, her feelings would change if she discovered us sleeping together. You heard what she thought of you buying Blair a life jacket. Alanna may have never known her real mom, but she views the women you date as a threat. She doesn't want a stepmother."

"Blair's not stepmother material. Never has been."

"Neither am I, Riley."

"You are, too. I watched the way you and Alanna interact. You're natural together. It came to me how good we'd be as a family."

Emmy's heart sank. She put her fingers over Riley's lips to keep him from muddling on with a backhanded marriage proposal that stemmed from all the wrong reasons. "Let's wait and see how Alanna likes me as a sitter. I told you, Riley, I can't...won't make commitment to anyone until I learn about myself. Who I really am."

"Dammit, Emmy. I don't care about any of that. I love

you—the whole package. Lord knows we all have flaws.''

"That's just it," she cried, her eyes brimming with tears. "You know the origin of your flaws. You have a history. I love you and Alanna too much to come to you with less than the truth about myself. Except I don't know the truth yet, and maybe never will.''

Her eyes, awash in tears, reflected such agony, Riley could do nothing but turn away. "Then we won't quit until we find the truth," he said harshly. "Beginning tomorrow. I'll have Marge cancel all my appointments. We'll work on this problem until we find your birth mother or we run out of leads.''

"No. I won't be responsible for ruining your practice. We'll do this part-time. Alanna and I will find things to keep us busy all morning. When you complete what's on your calendar, come pick us up and we'll go to the basket factory. Or I can drive us to your office.''

"Not unless you ride to work with me in the morning. You left your truck parked on the street outside my building.''

"Then we'd better go in with you. I'd hate to be stuck without transportation. What if something happened to Alanna?''

"You're right. I planned to go in early, though. Can you be ready by seven?''

"No problem.'' She trailed him to the door. After he'd stepped out on the porch, she rose on tiptoes and kissed him full on the mouth. "I do love you, Riley.''

His eyes tracked her as she sank back on her heels, seemingly reluctant to break the connection. No less reluctant than he was...

"I just want you to know I've never said that to any other man. I'm miserly with my I love yous.''

Riley groaned and bent to kiss her again. Emmy was too fast and slipped behind the screen. Then the door itself closed. He felt like kicking it down and snatching Emmy up, along with Alanna, to take both of them home. Where they both belonged.

Slowly the wind blowing off the lake cooled his impatience. Walking home, he knew that he'd have to redouble his efforts to dig out the answers that would make Emmy feel whole. For the first time, Riley realized this wasn't so much about his loving her and accepting her but about loving her enough to support her search one hundred percent. Until now he'd been *going along* to humor her. Suddenly, he wanted Emmy to succeed because what he wanted most in the world was for her to be happy.

FRIDAY, EARLY, they met at the appointed time. Alanna, though still sleepy, was in good spirits and not cranky as Emmy feared she might be. They didn't go with Riley up to his office, but climbed in Emmy's pickup, heading to the grocery store. "To get pancake mix for breakfast," she informed Riley when he stated that his cupboards were full.

She did her best to keep a straight face, but Riley knew what they were up to. Alanna, never able to keep anything secret, had told him she and Emmy planned to bake him peanut-butter cookies. The news had warmed him in a special way. It meant a lot, hearing that Emmy had remembered his favorite treat. She'd always had a unique ability to lay her finger on the things that troubled him and those that made him happy.

A quality he hadn't found in any other woman.

Smiling, still deep in private thoughts, Riley unlocked his office. Snapping on the overhead light in the reception area, he nearly stepped on a white envelope lying on the floor. He juggled his keys and his briefcase in order to pick it up. Someone had obviously slipped it under the door after Marge had locked up and left for the day.

A payment? He dropped the envelope on her desk, and as it fluttered down, Riley noticed his name typed in upper case letters. Below it said Personal and Confidential. Curious, he rested his briefcase on the desk and slit the envelope with Marge's letter opener. A single sheet of paper revealed a short but pointed message. *Stop snooping into Emerald Monday's background or else...* Someone had drawn a crude row of black daggers, each dripping red blood.

Riley almost lost his grip on the paper. This was the last thing he'd expected. *Who? Why? When?* The questions tripped over each other. His reaction veered from anger to excitement to a clutch of fear.

Dammit, would the perpetrator of this message really kill to protect his or her secret? Folding the sheet of ordinary computer paper, he hurried into his private office. This proved he and Emmy had rattled someone's cage yesterday. "Hot damn. We're on the right track," he muttered to himself.

Loosening the tie he'd only fastened an hour ago, he telephoned the friend who'd recommended the program. "Duncan? Riley Gray here. I'd hoped to catch you at your desk. I have something to run by you. After the first day of working with that search program, I got a threatening note shoved under my office door."

The two men conversed for several minutes, tossing out cause-and-effect scenarios as they'd often done as law students.

"I think you have to take this person seriously," Duncan advised. "While some birth parents want to remain anonymous, they usually aren't violent. If I were you, my next step would be to give that letter to the local police.''

"Frankly, it looks like the kind of threat one kid might make to another. You know as well as I do that the police never take these notes seriously unless some type of action follows the threat. I'm inclined to press on with our search to see if we can smoke this person out.''

"Yeah,'' Duncan admitted reluctantly. "I'd probably do the same thing. These damned searches are like three-dimensional puzzles. Solving puzzles is why we went into lawyering in the first place. Just take it easy, pal. And watch your back.''

"I will. Hey, Duncan, thanks. I believe I'll keep this information to myself for a while and see what shakes out. I'll phone if anything develops. Bye.''

Riley sat gripping the phone until he heard Marge arrive and call out her usual greeting. He'd stored the letter and envelope in an inside pocket of his briefcase before she walked in and placed a steaming cup of coffee on his desk.

"Any luck with yesterday's mission?'' she asked, presenting him with the normal stack of outgoing correspondence awaiting his signature.

Riley uncapped his pen. "A bunch of dead ends. Reverend Briggs promised to check the church records. I'm glad you cleared my afternoon. We'd like to take the basket Emmy was found in over to the factory where they're made. Did anyone happen to call after we left yesterday, asking…oh, I don't know, anything about Emmy or this search?''

"No.'' Marge studied her boss. "But I hope you weren't counting on keeping this quiet. If so, you've failed. Last night was my standing hair appointment at the Clip and Curl. The place was abuzz and speculations were flying.''

Riley finished signing the letters, capped the pen and handed everything back to Marge. "General gossip? Or did you hear anything concrete?"

"Emmy's search sparked old stories about which husbands were sleeping around back then. As far as anyone knew—or was willing to reveal—none of the affairs resulted in a hushed-up pregnancy."

Riley didn't say so, but after the note he'd received, he was inclined to believe there was at least one illegitimate child conceived by someone in Uncertain. Someone who'd indulged in a well-guarded tryst. A tryst he or she wanted to keep hidden.

"Marge, could you get Jed Louis on the phone?"

"Shall I schedule an appointment for him?"

"No. Fielder apparently questioned him about the Granger murder again. I just wondered what bee he has up his butt this time."

A few minutes later, Marge rang on the intercom to say Jed was on the line. Riley snatched up the phone. "Hi, violin man. Where've you been lately? You and Gwyn need to meet Emmy and me down at Crazy Jake's. No reason I should be the only sap Emmy thwacks at darts."

Jed's laugh sounded strained. "I'm lying low for a while. Although I don't know what good it does. Fielder isn't looking beyond his nose. Still thinks I'm his man."

There was no need for Jed to elaborate. Riley knew he meant Logan had him pegged as Frannie's murderer. "Gwyn mentioned the old fool came by to dig his spurs in again. What this time?"

"Forensic botany identified material on what was left of Fran's shoes. Spore fibers indicate she was killed on one of the lakeside docks and later moved to the Caddo mound where she was buried. Fielder demanded I come clean about the fight I had with Frannie the day we argued about Juilliard and I took off in my boat.''

''Frannie's isn't the only lake dock. I should think one board would test pretty much like another. It's certainly not conclusive.''

''Precisely what Thorny said. But Fielder's insinuations are insulting. I'd love to knock that smirk off his ugly face.''

''And he'd love for you to do it, Jed. It'd give him an excuse to arrest you. If he had any proof from those latest tests, you'd already be looking to post bond. Stay cool, man. Don't let him rattle you. Hey, Gwyn suggested getting together this weekend for a barbecue. Is the date negotiable? I've decided it's time to patch a few wounds I've caused. First thing I have to do, though, is connect with my uncle, see if I can make some arrangements to visit. Emmy's agreed to go with me to introduce Alanna to her grandmother.''

The two old friends talked for a while about Riley's momentous decision. They signed off after agreeing to touch base later with a date for the barbecue.

Riley's first appointment arrived as he hung up. For the next four hours, he practiced the type of law that earned his keep.

Marge appeared in the doorway seconds after his last morning client had gone. ''That's it for appointments. Mr. Davidson's going to bring in those contracts he mentioned around three o'clock. I'll leave them with Mrs. Yates on my way home.''

Riley glanced up with a start. ''I forgot to tell you about her, Marge.'' He quickly conveyed the details of his housekeeper's hasty departure.

"Good riddance to bad rubbish, if you ask me. Alanna will be a hundred times better off with Emmy Monday. But, you'd better watch they don't get too attached— unless you plan to do something about making it permanent." Marge clucked like a mother hen and crossed her plump arms, staring at Riley with her gimlet eye.

"It's a shame you're so shy and retiring, Marge. But I'm squelching that rumor before it starts. Emmy's in town to find her roots, not a husband."

"Doesn't mean she wouldn't want both if the opportunity presented itself."

"Don't get any ideas." He rose and stripped off his already loose tie. "Most of all, don't put ideas of that sort in Alanna's head. Emmy's been a rolling stone for years. Who's to say she's even capable of settling down in one place?"

"Horse pucky. Any fool can see that young woman wants nothing more than to be part of a family. But if you're too blind—"

"That's enough, Marge." Riley spoke in the tone of a boss. "If you need me for any reason this afternoon, you can reach me on my cell phone."

After marching from the office and peeling out of his parking space, Riley brooded all the way home about what Marge had said. Interspersed with those thoughts were his worries over the note shoved under his door. Maybe he ought to press Emmy harder to accept his marriage proposal. What if the note writer was some kind of sociopath? He'd never forgive himself if anything happened to Emmy because *he* was negligent in taking the threat seriously enough. Why, even now some nut could be stalking her.

Riley vaulted out of his car almost before the engine stopped running. Bursting through his front door, all he encountered was domestic tranquility. The house smelled of lemon furniture polish and newly baked peanut-butter cookies. Woman and child sat on his couch, their heads nearly touching. Alanna was threading shoelaces through sewing cards Riley recognized as the ones Gwyn had helped him buy for her birthday.

"Hi!" Emmy glanced up and smiled hesitantly. "What's up, wildman? You look as if you expected to find us murdered or something."

Rising lazily, she stretched like the kitten who sprang off Alanna's lap. The move pulled tight the cotton T-shirt Emmy wore over unfettered breasts. Saliva pooled in Riley's dry mouth, but her comment grated on him like fingernails raked across a chalkboard. "You volunteered to baby-sit my daughter, yet any two-bit bum could stroll in here and snatch her. Or you. Why do you think I installed locks on my doors?"

Emmy and Alanna exchanged puzzled looks. "I forget the country's changed. I won't leave the door unlocked anymore," Emmy promised.

"Me'n Emmy made cookies. She baked bread and I got to squish the dough. When the loaves got cool, we fixed turkey sandwiches and packed 'em in the basket Emmy's taking to that factory. I've had so much fun, Daddy. Please don't yell at Emmy." Alanna's lower lip puckered.

Riley dragged a hand through his hair. "I'm sorry. It, uh, looked as if the house was empty when I drove in." He swung Alanna into his arms, and squeezed Emmy's shoulder reassuringly. Lord, he had to quit acting like a panicky fool. It wouldn't serve any purpose to worry them, yet he'd come close to blurting out the truth about that note.

Forcing his body to relax, he mustered a grin. "Fresh

bread and home-baked cookies. You ladies wouldn't be trying to bribe me, now would you?''

He didn't expect it, but they both looked guilty as sin.

"Aha," he said triumphantly, setting Alanna down so he could pull out his wallet. "Okay. How much is this going to cost me?"

"No money, Daddy," Alanna said in a tiny voice.

Emmy looped an arm around Alanna's shoulders. "I unpacked some of my old picture albums today. Alanna came across a photo of the five of us at the lake. Jed, Will, you, me and Josey. Your sister's place is right on our way home from the basket factory," she rushed to say. "She'd be off work by then, and...and, well, maybe we could stop by and take her out for pizza or burgers. Also, Gwyn phoned from Austin after you spoke with Jed. She thinks we need to cheer Jed up this weekend. I okayed the barbecue for Saturday. That means we can't go to Oklahoma."

Totally caught off guard, Riley had no option, after staring at the two eager faces, but to agree to their plan. In a way he was relieved to have a different sword hanging over his head. "Sure. I never got around to phoning my uncle, anyway. So let's be off to the basket place. When we're finished there, Emmy, you phone Josey from my cell. Just to remind you, though, reunions can be difficult or unpleasant."

Emmy considered what he'd said. "I understand your reluctance to see Josey, Riley. But I believe that, unless you strip away the barriers—unless you make old wounds visible—you can't heal."

"So be it," he said gravely. "Alanna, run up and go to the bathroom. Give me the basket, Emmy. I'll put it in the trunk."

The minute Alanna was out of sight, he managed to

steal a few kisses from Emmy. Not that he really considered them *stolen*. She cooperated without any urging.

Alanna returned, and they claimed seats in the car as a family would. They hadn't gone five miles down the road when unaccountably, Riley's cares fell away.

CHAPTER TWELVE

THEY'D EATEN their sandwiches en route, so once they reached the outskirts of Jacksonville, they were ready to follow the signs directing them to the basket company. They parked beside one of the outbuildings and Riley assisted Alanna from the back seat while Emmy retrieved her basket. She and Alanna fell behind Riley as he opened the door to the retail sales portion of the plant. They stopped just inside to examine cleverly displayed baskets lining wooden shelves. Among the baskets sat decorative jars filled with colorful canned fruits and vegetables.

Lagging a bit, Emmy read an old framed news clipping that hung on the wall. She kept an eye on Riley as he approached a woman doing ledger work at a desk.

He handed her his business card across the counter and stopped Alanna from dancing around the room. "We have a basket we believe was manufactured here a little over thirty years ago. We realize it's a long shot, but we're wondering if you kept sales records back then. I'm really asking if it's possible to identify the buyer of this particular piece."

He took the basket from Emmy and set it on the counter.

"I've only worked here ten years, but I can tell you we ship our baskets all over the world. I'm afraid this basket could have been purchased through any outlet.

Our operation wasn't as large then, but even if this was bought on-site, we don't record buyer names. I'm sorry, it does look like one of ours.''

Emmy tried not to appear disappointed, although it was difficult to conceal her reaction.

Riley sensed her struggle to overcome yet another frustration in a long chain of them. He placed a bracing hand on her shoulder. ''Is it at least possible to tell if the company shipped a limited number, or are we talking tens of thousands?''

Alanna still clung to Emmy's left hand. ''There are rooms full of baskets over there,'' she whispered loudly. ''Daddy, may I go look at them?''

Emmy looked through the door Alanna had indicated. There were indeed several rooms off the main one, rather like a rabbit warren. They were all filled with baskets of various types and colors. ''I'll wander around with you,'' Emmy murmured. She decided to let Riley pursue what was obviously another dead end. He seemed so patient, bless his heart. Her nerves were continually on edge.

Fifteen or so minutes later, he found them in a narrow upstairs room, examining chore baskets. ''I put your basket back in the car, Emmy. I wasn't able to find out much. Currently the company makes six to ten thousand baskets a day. They opened in 1924, fashioning baskets from local woods. Yours is a mix of sweet gum and elm, a weaver said. She's worked here for 35 years, and explained that baskets like yours were sold in many craft stores. She believes some stores also included instructions and material on how to turn the basket into a baby carrier. She said pink- or blue-checked linings were popular and also fancy lace edging. The bookkeeper pulled bills of lading on that stock number. They were shipped en masse to craft stores all over the state. I'm sorry, Emmy. I know you were counting on learning more."

"I wasn't. Not really. I knew it was iffy."

"Daddy, can I buy a basket for my baby doll? Look, this one's just what I need. It's sort of like Emmy's basket."

"Riley, all she's talked about since you explained how I was found in a basket is getting one like it for the doll you bought for her birthday."

Kneeling, Riley inspected the basket. He determined it was pliable and sturdy enough for a rambunctious child's toy. "It looks okay, kiddo. As I walked through the rooms trying to find you, I started thinking it might be nice to pick out a couple of decorative baskets. You can give one to Aunt Josey tonight. And later, when we see your grandmother, you can give her one, too." Riley stood again and scanned the room, apparently unsure as to whether baskets would make appropriate gifts or not.

"That's a wonderful idea." Emmy slipped her arm through his and gave him a spontaneous hug. "Alanna, remember those cute hand-painted baskets we saw in the room next to the Christmas decorations? Some of them held soaps and lotions. Others had pencils, grocery pads and notepaper. They'd make great gifts."

"Yeah, Daddy. Come see." Alanna yanked on his arm.

"Whoa. I'll trust you and Emmy to pick something suitable." Seeking Emmy's eyes, he muttered, "Are you sure it won't look as if I'm trying to buy my way back into their good graces? That's the last impression I'd care to give."

"The baskets aren't expensive, so no one would ever mistake the gesture as an attempted bribe. They'll be perfect icebreakers. If Alanna's the one to take them the gifts, Josey and Neva will have all the more reason to dote on her.''

"Thanks, Emmy," Riley said as Alanna ran ahead of them to choose two baskets. "I set out to change your mind about digging up the past. The way things ended up, you convinced me to dig into mine. That's not all. Somewhere along the way, I discovered that I'm really pulling for you to succeed. I see how excited Alanna is at the prospect of meeting my relatives. I had no idea— Well, I figured we'd be fine alone. The truth is, I've missed my family. I have you to thank for hitting me over the head.''

"Marge planted the idea. I'm happy to have played a minor role. I envy you your family, Riley. I'm afraid I've waited too long to hunt for mine," she said, releasing a long sigh.

"I'll grant you, the tracks have faded.''

"Yeah. Last night it occurred to me that people drive in from all over Texas, and even neighboring states, to exhibit at First Monday Trade Days. My mother could have come from anywhere. She might've been a transient just passing through. Did you see the old newspaper clipping they have framed in the front office? Much of this area used to be tomato farms. The article says that people traveled great distances to work on the harvest.''

Riley's thoughts flashed back to the note someone had slipped under his office door. "Possible, but probably not. Farm workers don't strike me as people who abandon their kids. And would one of them own an expensive brooch? Emmy, when you were little, did anyone in Uncertain pay extra attention to you?''

"How so?''

"Like…did an outsider bring you toys or gifts at holidays? Or as you got older, did anyone in particular stop you on the street, just to talk? Stuff like that?''

Emmy rubbed a thumb across pursed lips. Finally, she shook her head. ''Joleen came for cake and ice cream at birthdays. But she visited us a lot, anyway, usually on her way home from work. Once she gave me a Barbie coloring book. Surely you can't believe my mother would dump me, then stick around to watch someone else raise me? Isn't that pretty far-fetched?''

The note in Riley's briefcase suggested otherwise. Yet, until he figured out how it fit into the equation, he wasn't about to add to Emmy's worries. ''I wonder if Joleen would be less uptight if you went to see her without me?''

''You do think she knows more than she's telling.''

''She found you. If you can get her to take a longer look back, it's possible she might have seen someone or something that at the time didn't seem significant.''

''I suppose Alanna and I could bake a coffee cake on Monday and run it by Joleen's house. Maybe seeing Alanna will jog Joleen's memory of me as a child.''

''It's worth a try. Don't pressure her, though, and if she tries to throw you out, just leave.''

''She's antisocial, Riley. I doubt she's dangerous.''

''Maybe. And maybe she's totally off her rocker. ''

Emmy started to scoff at the idea. Only...Riley sounded so serious, she felt a ripple of fear skitter up her spine. She didn't pursue the matter, because by then Alanna had selected her gifts. The two adults helped carry Alanna's baskets to the cash register. On the way, Emmy picked up two square baskets woven from wood strips dyed in fall colors. ''I need wastebaskets in the kitchen and bathroom,'' she said. ''These are vinyl-lined. They're perfect,'' she told the cashier.

"Be sure to visit our observation deck. It's outside, around the corner to your left," the woman said. "Kids find it fascinating to watch how we assemble baskets. Today the crew is making bushel baskets commonly used by small farmers or gardeners for fruit, roses or corn."

Riley thanked her for the information.

Alanna skipped off happily to find the surveillance area. Emmy, who'd already paid her bill, collected her purchases and followed, leaving Riley to complete his transaction.

They spent half an hour watching the weavers. A man who held a clipboard and seemed to be a supervisor exited one of the buildings, saw them and volunteered to answer any questions they might have. Alanna, typical of a curious preschooler, asked dozens. When she wound down, Riley jumped in. "Thank the gentleman, Alanna. We've taken enough of his time. It's getting late. If we're going to try to catch Josey before dinner, we'd better let Emmy go phone her."

At the parking lot, Riley handed Emmy his phone, and promptly got busy lowering the car's convertible top. After that, he stowed the baskets in the trunk and helped Alanna buckle herself into the back seat as Emmy chatted away to his sister. Once, when Emmy motioned the phone toward him, Riley reached out to take it, then shook his head.

Emmy backed off, giving him an odd stare.

"That was painless," she said, disconnecting and handing him the phone. "For a minute I thought Josey was going to faint when I told her what was up, but she recovered faster than you did," she said wryly. "Josey's ecstatic. Here are the directions to her house." Emmy ripped a sheet of paper from the notepad she'd taken to carrying everywhere since they'd begun her search.

He hauled in a deep, shaky breath. "I heard you ask about pizza. I remember what toppings she used to like. What if she hates pepperoni now?" Riley knew damn well he wasn't talking about pizza; so, he suspected, did Emmy.

"She said any type is fine. I'm sure she'll be too excited to eat a bite." Emmy's eyes suddenly glistened with tears. She tried discreetly to blot them away.

"Emmy, it's thoughtless of me to make you a witness to our reunion when it's yours we're trying to bring about." They'd settled into their respective seats, but Riley turned toward Emmy, his face reflecting deep concern.

"Don't mind me, Riley. I get emotional over books and movies, and even the occasional commercial. This is real life—I wouldn't miss it for the world." Her watery smile remained firmly affixed.

Alanna reached over the back seat and stroked Emmy's hair. "Don't cry, Emmy. Daddy promised he'd find your mama. He never breaks a promise."

"Hold on, kiddo." Turning, Riley frowned at his daughter. "I promised to *try* to help Emmy. That's not the same thing as a double-dog promise."

"But you will, I know. 'Cause it's important to Emmy, and we don't like her being sad, do we, Daddy?"

Her words hit Riley like a brick between the eyes. What Alanna said was true. He'd walk barefoot over tack-strip to see Emmy reach her goal. First and foremost, however, he was committed to her safety. How serious was that damned warning? Should he tell Emmy in the hope that she might shed some light? Or was the threat directed at him for getting involved? Until he knew for certain, it might be wise to slow their pace.

"If this meeting with Josey goes well, Emmy, maybe

I'll ask Marge to cancel all my appointments for a few days next week. Josey's bound to tell Mom. How fair is it to make her wait to meet her only grandchild? We could drive to Oklahoma on Sunday.'' Riley had been struck by a notion. If Marge spread the word to her friends at the beauty shop that she and Emmy were mediating reunions with his family, it might throw the note writer off track. At least until he had a chance to have the paper tested for fingerprints and other identifiable markings.

''Can you cancel appointments on the spur of the moment? Won't you lose clients that way?''

''It's to be expected if you deal with a lawyer in a solitary practice. Marge is a diplomat when it comes to switching appointments. I often have to appear in court on short notice.''

''Well, then. All I'd planned for next week was to do fun things with Alanna. Oh, and a second visit to Joleen. I can do that any day.''

''So it's agreed? As soon as we get home, I'll phone Mom. Now, before we pick up the pizza, help me figure out some possible opening lines for when we get to Josey's.''

''Oh, Riley,'' Emmy said softly. ''Be natural. This isn't something you can script ahead of time.''

''We haven't communicated in years,'' he muttered, glancing at his daughter in the rearview mirror. Alanna had put on the earphones to her tape player. She was swinging her shoulders and mouthing the words of her favorite Disney song. Riley smiled at her absorption, but he was nervous. He reached for Emmy's hand, needing the connection.

She understood his fears and drew his hand between

her breasts. She smoothed her thumbs across his tense knuckles, softly kissing each one.

Riley felt his stress dissipate. Emmy had always had that effect on him. He smiled lovingly at her, wishing he could do more, be more, than her friend and sometime lover. While she seemed content with making love when the opportunity happened to arise, Riley wanted her sleeping next to him all night. Every night. It shook him to realize how strong those feelings were.

Emmy guessed that the sudden tensing of his muscles came from the fact that they'd arrived at the pizza parlor and minutes after leaving it, they'd be standing at his sister's door. She faced him and trailed a finger slowly down each button on the front of his shirt. Her smile held promise. "You can do this. I have a method to induce relaxation once the reunion's behind you. Once we're home again and Alanna's asleep…"

Riley jammed on the brakes and his car lunged into the parking place as if he were a teen learning to drive. "Jeez," he mumbled half under his breath as he finally jerked the car to a halt inches from the restaurant wall. "Stop it, Emmy, or this is going to be the shortest reunion in history."

Laughing, she plucked up her purse and slid out of the car. "Wait here. The food's my *other* treat for tonight."

Watching the swing of her hips as she disappeared through the door proved a bigger treat for Riley than any thought of food. It wasn't until she came out again, carrying two white boxes, that he realized Emmy's method had been highly effective in ridding him of his anxiety about meeting Josey. The anticipation of spending time in bed with Emmy—time in a real bed—had blown every other thought out of his mind. While his body was far from relaxed, his tension no longer centered on the reunion.

Grinning easily now, Riley jumped out and opened the passenger door for Emmy. He managed to plant a promise of his own on her lips before she sank into the soft leather seat. Balancing pizza cartons, and with Alanna watching alertly, Emmy's only comeback was a satisfied smile.

Riley whistled, wanting to get Emmy alone, but he concentrated on negotiating the unfamiliar streets of Marshall. He drove slowly when he reached Josey's street.

"There's her house." Emmy pointed to a neat white house with dark-green trim and shutters.

Riley pulled to the curb. "Are you sure of the number? There are two cars parked in the driveway. Do we have enough pizza if she has company?"

"That's why I ordered two large ones. She said the man she's dated for years had a rare night off. I said we'd make it another time, but Josey said you'd know him. Is his name Leon?"

"Cleon. Cleon Woldu. You know him, too, Emmy. He was Uncertain's biggest track star. Ran the half mile. Beat the state record. His senior year, he tore an Achilles tendon and blew his chances for a college scholarship. Josey always mooned over him. She took it upon herself to rehabilitate him. Taught him how to throw pots. He didn't seem the type to me, so I'm surprised he's still hanging around."

"She told me they work opposite shifts as a rule. I sensed there might be more to it, but it's really none of my business. None of *our* business."

"Is that a polite way of telling me to butt out?"

"Matters of the heart are private, Riley. You know," she said suddenly, "I do remember him. Wasn't his family from Africa? His mother was tall and elegant. She wore long wrap dresses made of beautiful fabric and matching headpieces. Turbans, not hats.''

"Yeah. Cleon's Ethiopian. His mother and dad are both doctors who did drug research for a firm in Tyler. Maybe they still work there.''

"Then I shouldn't imagine he needed a scholarship.''

"I heard the Woldus were unhappy with my sister for steering their only son into a...vocational field.''

"Ah. So they're career snobs like you.''

"Me?'' Riley reared back to stare down his nose at Emmy.

"Yes, you. You made it quite plain that you want Alanna to be *somebody*.''

Riley actually flushed. "I'll have to watch how I phrase things. Especially in front of Josey,'' he added.

"That's okay. It's an old argument. Jed and Fran fought the same issue when he wanted to be a concert violinist. *She* wanted him to be a research scientist.''

"Are we going to sit out here and let our pizza get cold?'' Alanna asked petulantly from the back seat. "If that's my Auntie Josey peeking out the window, I'll bet she wonders why we don't come to the door.''

"Out of the mouths of babes,'' Riley muttered. But he got out of the car and helped Alanna and Emmy.

Emmy expected him to hang back and let her and Alanna lead the way. But Riley surprised her. He relieved her of the pizza boxes and strode right up to the door.

It flew open immediately, giving credence to Alanna's observation that Josey had been watching through the window.

There followed a poignant and sometimes tearful reunion of brother and sister. Emmy stood back, wiping her own eyes, as did Cleon Woldu. Luckily he'd had the foresight to grab the cartons out of Riley's hands and put them on a dining table already set for five. Otherwise, the food wouldn't have survived all the hugging.

The two outsiders quietly became reacquainted on the sidelines, while Josey clung to her brother and met the niece she hadn't seen since birth.

"The refurbishing you say you've done to this room is terrific, Josey." Riley studied the bookcases as his sister found an appropriate place to exhibit Alanna's gift. "I assume you helped her with the cabinetry," Riley said, turning to shake hands with Josey's boyfriend, whom he'd pretty much ignored up to now. When Cleon nodded, Riley said pointedly, "It's nice of you to spend your free time helping a *friend*. I finished my basement, so I know the hours woodworking takes."

Cleon quirked a brow at Josey. She nervously fingered a shining dark braid coiled tightly at the nape of her neck. "I, um, we…" She cast a worried glance toward Alanna, who was busy inspecting an array of hand-painted pots across the room.

"Josey's trying to say we both live here," Cleon blurted. The chip on his shoulder was a mile wide, and the belligerence in his tone dared Riley to knock it off.

Riley's gaze swung to his sister. "Are congratulations in order? My sources aren't as good as I'd always assumed if I missed news of a wedding."

Josey coughed twice, but Cleon's eyes turned hostile. She recovered enough to slide an arm possessively around his narrow hips. "Cleon's folks are dead set against us getting married. They're holding a considerable inheritance over his head as a deterrent. He expects my family and friends to feel the same way."

Riley's arrogant expression matched Cleon's hostility.

"I never pegged you for a gutless wonder who'd put money ahead of decency."

Cleon grabbed Riley by the front of his shirt. "I'll be more than happy to go outside and settle this. You're the turkey who hasn't even called Josey in five years."

The result might have been disastrous if Emmy hadn't dived between the two men and with her slight weight, held Riley in place.

"Cleon's right," she hissed. "What business have you got coming into Josey's home now, tossing brotherly edicts around?"

Riley's shoulders relaxed, although he guiltily checked Alanna's whereabouts and was glad she'd missed the angry show. She seemed enthralled with two intricately beaded, authentically dressed Native American dolls. They looked like his mother's handiwork. "Do you like the dolls?" he called. "Your grandmother Gray Wolf used to hand-craft and sell those at holidays. If she still does, maybe she'll make you a set."

"She will, I know," Josey said immediately, obviously relieved that the situation between the men was so quickly defused. Although Cleon still flexed his fingers.

"I love the dolls," Alanna said, placing the pair back where she'd found them. "But I'm hungry. When are we going to eat?"

Even Cleon smiled at that.

Josey bustled into the kitchen, returning at once with a crisp salad. Following her lead, Cleon disappeared and brought out a frosty pitcher of iced tea. "We have milk or juice for Alanna," he said, meeting Riley's eyes squarely.

"Milk. And...I'm really sorry, man. My first reaction is to think like a lawyer. And, I guess, a brother—old habits die hard. When we leave tonight, Emmy will set me straight.'' He shook his head. ''For what it's worth, I apologize. How you two live is your business. I've been tense about this meeting all day. It's not easy to admit to being a big jerk, but the honest truth is, I've missed Josey and Mom. If you're willing, I'd like to start over.'' He held out his hand again.

Josey and Emmy, who'd both sucked in deep breaths, expelled them in a simultaneous rush when Cleon clapped Riley on the back and accepted his handshake.

The remainder of the evening went well. The couples ate and discussed old times. At Josey's urging, Riley used her phone to call his mother. If he shed any tears, Emmy didn't catch him. However, he cleared his throat a lot while talking to Neva Gray Wolf, and his voice sounded gritty when he hung up. ''I'm wiring her money for bus fare. She'll arrive a week from tonight. Until I rectify my standing with the tribal council, I'm persona non grata on the rez.''

''Mom's defying Uncle Charlie to visit you,'' Josey said. ''I won't nag you to petition for reinstatement. It'd be easier on her and me if you would, Riley. If you don't want to acknowledge where you came from, at least consider Alanna. She deserves the right to make her own decision about her heritage.''

Talk between brother and sister became stiff and awkward again.

''We should go,'' Emmy said. ''Alanna's trying valiantly to stay awake, but she's losing the battle. It's way past her bedtime.''

Riley checked his watch. ''Wow! We've been here for nearly four hours.''

Josey rose on her tiptoes and grazed his cheek in a kiss. ''I'm afraid to say goodbye. Promise we won't drift apart. I want us to stay in touch.''

Riley draped an arm around Emmy's shoulders, and he seemed steadier after she reached up and clasped his hand. "We owe Emmy for this get-together. We've talked all evening, and she hasn't even told you that we've begun a search for her birth parents. Her mom, anyway. Finding her dad would be a bonus."

Emmy lowered her eyelashes. "My search hardly seems relevant to y'all."

"Oh, but it is." Josey hugged Emmy impulsively. "As kids we talked about what your mother would be like, remember? Frankly, I wasn't about to approve of a woman who'd dump her kid. But now that I've experienced family separation, I realize sometimes there are extenuating circumstances. Oh, Emmy, I wish you all the luck in the world."

"Thanks, but we're not having any yet," she responded glumly.

Riley tucked Emmy tightly under his arm. "Sometimes it only takes one break, sugar babe."

"Are your adoption records sealed?" Cleon asked.

"I wasn't adopted. I remained forever in foster care. It's easier to access records from adoption agencies, I think."

Cleon turned on the porch light and walked them to the curb. "Wouldn't all the agencies who place kids keep records? You were born somewhere. Even indigent moms go to hospitals or birthing centers."

"Emmy's case isn't typical. Ask Josey to explain." Riley struggled to get a sleepy Alanna into the back seat and buckled in. He held the passenger door for Emmy. "We had a nice time, you guys." Riley directed his remark to Cleon. "We'll reciprocate at my place one night while Mom's in Uncertain."

"If you're including me," Cleon said, "Josey has a list of my nights off. Generally I work swing shift."

"Of course you're included," Riley said firmly, tapping Cleon on the arm. "Emmy's watching Alanna tomorrow," he said, turning to his sister. "Phone her with dates. Mom gets here next Friday, around noon." He bent to remind Alanna to say thank you, but she'd already fallen asleep against a pretty, hand-appliqued pillow Josey had given her.

Riley straightened and took Josey's hand. "We enjoyed tonight. And, sis, thanks for giving me this snapshot of Lani. I'll have it blown up and framed for Alanna. However, I still prefer to wait until she's older to open any discussion about her mother's beliefs."

Josey nodded. "I know anything concerning Lani is hard. I'm proud of you for taking this first step. It's the right thing to do, Riley."

Emmy concurred.

The four adults spent another half-hour chatting before Riley finally started the car and drove off.

"You weren't kidding, were you?" Emmy said when they'd driven in silence for several miles. "You had a good time and you're glad you went?"

"Did I sound insincere?" He acted surprised. "I meant every word. I just wish I hadn't jumped to conclusions about Cleon. He's a nice guy. Am I wrong to think Josey would rather be married?"

Emmy gave a negligent shrug. "While we were clearing the table and putting things away in the kitchen, she said they're in love and committed. The deal with his inheritance has to do with custom. As the first-born son, Cleon's apparently entitled to a sum his parents put in trust when he was born. He should have received it automatically. Josey said the Woldus tacked on conditions because they wanted him to get a college degree, and they don't want him marrying out of his race."

"He said he's taking one college class a semester. Maybe his parents will give him the money when he graduates."

"It's not about the money. His parents reneged on a tradition."

"Family customs and traditions can sure cause a lot of grief. Are you sure you want to locate your family, Emmy? Maybe you're well off and don't know it."

She smiled and slid a hand along his thigh.

A tingle shot up Riley's leg, and his groin tightened. But there was a heaviness in his heart. "I think a union between a man and woman should eclipse any family custom. Isn't that what's meant by the vows about forsaking all others?"

"I'm hardly an authority on wedding vows." She withdrew her hand from his leg.

Riley didn't want her turning a deaf ear. "Emmy, two people join out of love, pure and simple, not for anything that is or isn't in their background."

"Individual personalities are made up of lessons learned and family genes." Emmy's features, in the light of passing cars, appeared strained. "I'm not doubting you love me," she whispered. "The freedom to love comes with knowing yourself, Riley, a luxury I've never had."

"Sweetheart," he said earnestly as he parked in his driveway, "come inside with me tonight. I'll prove that what's between us transcends genetics."

Emmy released her seat belt and threw herself into his arms. "Yes," she breathed. "I want to believe love can change destiny."

Desire pulsed urgently between them as they carefully

carried Alanna into the house and readied her for bed without waking her.

So great was their need for each other, they left a trail of clothing on the floor after crossing the threshold into Riley's bedroom. His bed was wide, warm and comforting. When he covered her peaked nipples with his big hands, sending shivers of pleasure slamming through her, it was easy for Emmy to believe her life would be different. That Riley could vanquish the clouds from her past.

He whispered all the right words over the next hour, and brought a flush to every square inch of her. Physically they were attuned. Perfectly matched. Emmy had no doubt of that because they rocked the world, their hearts hammering as one before they drifted together into mindless oblivion.

But as Riley fell asleep holding her tight, Emmy lay awake staring at the moon-splashed walls of his room. Riley's love for her, and hers for him and Alanna, filled part of the empty space inside her. But she still felt...unfinished. How could she explain that to Riley when he was offering her his soul? She lay there wrestling with her private demons, selfishly drawing on his warmth until the last night owl at the lake hooted and went to roost. Heart-heavy, she finally climbed out of bed and collected their scattered clothing. After donning hers and folding his neatly on a chair, she slipped down the stairs and out the front door.

She stood on his porch a moment, shivering in the cool morning mist. A car rounded the bend of the road. Worried that some sharp-eyed client of Riley's might see her stealing from his house at dawn, Emmy struck boldly out for the lake as if she were taking an early-morning walk. The automobile slowed to a crawl.

Who would be out driving on a back road this time of morning? Emmy's shivers increased. Only after she heard the car's automatic transmission shift to a higher gear did she vault the fence and race into her house.

She chided herself for letting her nerves take over. She and Riley were both adults and unattached. "There's absolutely nothing to stop us from having an affair," she said aloud.

It was the word *affair* Emmy had difficulty wrapping her tongue around. Because what Riley wanted was marriage.

Didn't she, down deep, want the same? Hadn't she always imagined herself married to Riley Gray Wolf?

"Yes," she cried, clutching her middle. But he deserved a whole woman. One with a past, a family history. One who could give him babies with a clear conscience.

She paced the floor and decided that when he brought Alanna over later that morning, she'd find a way to tell him she *did* want to marry him. But she couldn't—not until her questions were answered.

CHAPTER THIRTEEN

EMMY'S NEWLY INSTALLED bedroom phone rang a little after 6 a.m. She knew it had to be Riley. He was the only person who had reason to call so early. She didn't even get the *hello* out of her mouth before he began a sexy scolding. "I'm disappointed you left without waking me. I know you don't want Alanna catching us, but next time I want a chance to kiss you goodbye and also to see you to your door. It may not be far, but things go bump in the night. So humor me, okay?"

"Riley, last night was wonderful. Better than wonderful—"

"The feeling's mutual," he all but purred in her ear.

"You didn't let me finish. I was about to say but—"

"There are no buts about it, Emmy. We're in sync."

"Yes, we mesh like…like two halves of a locket. But lockets need pictures to be complete. Pictures of the family."

"That's bunk! Why can't I convince you? We can get married and still look for your birth mother."

"I…can't. The unknown is too…too great an enigma."

Riley expelled a sigh that sounded both frustrated and helpless. "Sugar babe, I'm trying to understand. Just don't give up and disappear on me again. I'll find your answers. I swear."

"If you only knew how much I wish a genie would

just show up and give me the facts—the truth about my past. I really do," she cried softly.

"It's okay, Emmy. It's okay. Do you need the day to run down leads? Alanna woke up not feeling well. I'm not sure if she ate too much pizza last night, or if she's caught a bug. I called to see if you'd watch her here. If you'd rather not be tied down, I'll phone a domestics temp agency and get them to send someone out. I need to go into the office for a couple of hours. There's a brief I have to file in court on Monday."

"I wouldn't dream of leaving you in the lurch. I thought I'd phone the records office of the foster-care program as well as area hospitals, like Cleon suggested. Let me gather a few things to help entertain Alanna and I'll be over in a jiffy. Oh, by the way, she noticed my painted toenails while we were buying baskets. She's dying for me to do hers. If I use a soft color, is it okay?"

A sudden, vivid memory of how Emmy's pearly pink toenails had looked in the glow of his bedroom lamp rose up to smack Riley between the eyes. As she'd wrapped her long, naked legs around his waist, he'd caught a glimpse of small butterflies. He remembered thinking he'd ask how long it took to glue them on. The fleeting thought left him the moment she opened like a flower and he buried himself inside her. He struggled to keep mind and body connected, to return to the here and now.

"Honestly," Riley heard Emmy saying from a distance. "I understand if you object. She is young for nail polish. On the other hand, girls her age love playing dress-up. I thought after we baked Joleen's cake, I'd let Alanna indulge in a little make-believe. I have some glittery dresses and heels I wore at the casino. I've been meaning to toss them out. Forget the polish. I'll bring a few bangles and beads to use if she gets to feeling better.

It's one thing Mom Fran and I did on rainy days. Stuff like that's what good memories are made of...." Emmy's voice trailed off, as if she'd drifted back to her own childhood.

Riley cleared his throat. "She'll love you forever. Mrs. Yates never had the imagination or patience for anything like that. Bring the polish. And Emmy, thank you. It's these kinds of treats Alanna's missed not having a mother. I've been too closed-minded up to now to see it."

Emmy barely heard him say goodbye and that he'd see her shortly. She'd retreated into a comforting memory of Fran dragging out a trunk filled with outdated dresses, floppy hats, shoes and cheap rhinestone earrings. Emmy had spent many an afternoon preparing style shows for a properly appreciative audience. Frannie Granger was also great at having impromptu tea parties with a lonely girl.

Emmy's hand shook as she jerked herself from her reverie and hung up the phone. Could Riley possibly have hit on the truth when he'd suggested that her background, at least the important part, had been formed by Fran and not genetics? That those early years of love and security were what counted? It was a sobering thought. One that stuck even after Emmy made herself at home in Riley's house and stood at the window watching him get into his car. Just as she'd do if he were her husband.

EMMY WEIGHED heavy on Riley's mind as he climbed the stairs to his office and searched for his key. He couldn't rid himself of a picture stamped on his brain—how much he liked seeing Emmy puttering around in his kitchen this morning. In spite of not feeling well, Alanna had perked up the minute Emmy set foot in the house. She belonged there, dammit.

He stepped right on a plain white envelope that lay on his reception room floor. It looked identical to the earlier warning. This time he took greater care picking it up. He shook out his clean handkerchief and lifted it by one corner. The only lab he knew in town had close ties to the sheriff, and he wasn't ready to include Logan. He wondered what made him think the person sending these notes was even known to Fielder.

A lawyer's instinct.

Exhibiting the same care with which he'd retrieved the envelope, Riley sat at his desk, opened and read the note. Letters cut from magazines staggered drunkenly across the page. *Pay attention, Gray Wolf. Accidents befall nosy people.* A childish-looking skull and crossbones had been drawn at the bottom of the page.

Gray Wolf. Riley had been Gray since opening his practice in Uncertain. The composer of this tripe had know them when they were kids. He or she had thrown this together in anger and haste, forgetting that Riley had shortened his name.

Riley leaned back and swung his chair from side to side, as he did whenever he had a tough problem to solve. His money was on Joleen Berber. The old girl was batty. *Or cagey,* the voice of reason nagged.

He snapped forward in his chair, picked up the phone and called Jed's lawyer. "Thorny—Riley Gray here. How are you, sir? Glad I caught you at home."

Riley listened to the prominent attorney's greeting. "I'm not calling regarding Jed," he explained. "Far as I know, he's still Logan's target. The sheriff's got a lot riding on this case. He'd like to retire before the next election. I doubt he wants to go out with an unsolved murder on his record. I'm calling about another matter." While he gazed savagely at the crude warning, Riley explained how he'd received the two pointed notes. "My prints are all over the first one," he admitted. "I'd like to ship this cleaner one off to a lab. Since the sender seems informed about Emmy's and my investigative probes into her background, I'd rather have this handled out of our area."

The man at the other end of the line rattled off a technician's name and his laboratory address. Riley scribbled it down. After he rang off, he booted his computer and typed up the request. He had no reason not to trust Marge, but he wanted this on the q.t. He wouldn't even mail it locally.

Marge didn't come in on weekends. Riley put together his package, closed the office and got back into his car.

Operating on a hunch, he stopped at Joleen's house. Several minutes of pounding on her door finally roused her. She looked ghastly and sounded worse. "What do you want?" she croaked. "I've had the flu since the day you were here. I told you, I can't help the girl—Emerald," she added after a fit of coughing. Joleen gathered her robe under her wattled chin and began closing the door.

"Wait. Have you seen a doctor?" Riley asked politely. He really wanted to know if she'd been out of the house. If so, she could conceivably have gone by his office and delivered the warnings.

"I phoned my doctor. He said it sounds like I have a virus that's going around. Nothing to do except push fluids and sleep. I've been doing plenty of that. If you don't mind, I'd like to get back to bed. I get vertigo if I stay up for more than a few minutes."

"I'm sorry," Riley muttered. "Emmy plans to visit you again. Meanwhile, is there anything you need from the store? Tea? Juice? Chicken soup?"

The old woman raked a liver-spotted hand through untidy hair. "Just tell her to stay away. You young folks think you're invincible. A body lives a long and healthy life by keeping to herself and not doing anyone any favors." Although she looked as if she'd topple any minute, she shut the door quite firmly in Riley's face.

He gazed at the weathered wood, mulling over her parting statement while he considered the information he'd been handed. It was clear she was in no condition to leave the house, let alone tackle the stairs to his office. Her odd advice puzzled him, though, as it had come on the heels of his saying Emmy intended to visit.

Maybe it was just that, being a retired nurse, Joleen thought people who'd willingly expose themselves to her flu bug were stupid.

"Hellfire!" Riley stomped back to his car. Now he didn't even have one good lead as to who wanted Emmy's background to remain a blank. He considered his options. They'd arranged to do the barbecue at Jed and Gwyn's tonight. Next weekend, his mother would arrive. Neva might be able to help, he suddenly realized. Somehow, without raising Emmy's suspicion, he had to find a way to tap his mom's memory. Uncertain wasn't so large thirty years ago that illicit affairs and illegitimate babies could successfully be hidden. Someone was nervous about the prospect of Emmy finding her birth mother. It could only mean that in so doing, she'd expose some fact the note writer would go to great lengths to keep under wraps. As before, the big question remained: to what lengths was the perpetrator willing to go? All the way to murder? Did these notes tie in with Fran's death?

Riley wrangled with the problem while he drove to Jefferson and back. All roads seemed to lead to the unexplained death of Emmy's foster mother, and that worried

Riley. But short of bringing the notes out in the open, involving Logan Fielder and scaring Emmy half to death, he didn't know what to do. At this point, the notes were cowardly but not dangerous.

Back in his office again, he elected to wait a while longer—to wait and watch. Maybe take a second look at the computer search program. There wasn't any reason he couldn't devote a few more days to the search without involving Emmy. Anyway, all the warnings had been aimed at him.

THE GROUNDS, patio and surrounding rose gardens of Beaumarais were glorious to behold on a summery eve. Riley had hired a sitter for Alanna, who still wasn't feeling completely well. He and Emmy decided they needed a rare night in the company of other adults. Tall, citronella torchières flickered at the lake's edge and at strategic points on the patio to ward off mosquitoes, which tended to move into the region after the spring monsoons abated.

Riley stood next to Jed at the barbecue, holding a long-necked brew. Both men had worn khaki shorts and navy cotton pullovers. Gwyn went by and teased them about looking like twins.

Jed aimed a smack at her butt and missed. Grinning like a man in love, he turned the steaks and took a sip from his beer. "Why don't we do this more often?" Jed's eyes darkened with regret. "We never used to let work and everyday responsibilities interfere with our good times."

"Careers and family place demands on a man." Riley leaned an elbow on the brick wall that separated the patio from the fragrant flower garden.

"I'm spending an unbelievable amount of time thinking about Frannie's case. A case that shouldn't even involve me, except as a family member of the victim,'' Jed muttered. ''An unofficial family member. Hey,'' he said, brightening, ''Gwyn tells me Emmy's busy tracking the whereabouts of some thirty baby girls born in the county on or about the date Frannie listed on Emmy's quasi birth certificate.''

''Yes. What I find amazing is how many she's been able to locate. I believe that yesterday she exhausted her list.'' He gazed moodily across the patio to where the women sat at an umbrella-sheltered table.

As Riley watched them laughing and chatting, Gwyn topped off their glasses with a fine red wine.

''So you identified all girl babies born in the area around the time you were found?'' Gwyn asked as she returned the wine bottle to its terra cotta cooler.

''Either talked directly to them, or to someone who knew where they were.''

''Hmm. A little while ago, you said you were going to question Joleen Berber about the Caddo pearl and emerald brooch.''

''I had to put that off. She's been ill with that awful flu. Riley heard it somewhere. From Marge, probably. That woman has all the poop on everyone in town. Except she hasn't got a clue in my case, of course.''

''The thing is, you need information to get information, and you have almost nothing to work with. Speaking of that, we haven't heard jack from the military as to whether Will joined up or not.''

Emmy released a sigh. ''Darn. Nothing's coming together. I combed my memory for every detail I can remember Fran giving me about that brooch. I drew a facsimile based on what I recall of her descriptions. Riley's going to copy it and we'll send a flyer to all the jewelry stores from here to Canton. There are a lot more than you might think.''

''Can't you phone and weed out the ones that haven't been in business thirty years?''

Emmy perked up. ''That should eliminate some.'' Her smile faded. ''By the same token, I wonder how many have gone out of business since I was born?''

Gwyn patted her hand. ''I didn't say it would be easy.''

''One break is all I ask for.'' Emmy threw out her arms in a dramatic gesture. ''The more time Riley and I spend together, the closer I'm getting to Alanna.'' She inspected her fingernails. ''To say nothing of him.''

''Anyone can see how crazy they both are about you, Emmy. Not that I've known Riley long, but Jed says he hasn't been this happy in years. It's none of my business, I realize, but couldn't you guys get married and still work together to find your birth parents?''

''He asked me that, too.'' Emmy pushed a lock of hair away from her face, sad eyes straying to where Riley lounged against the wall. ''He's also made no secret of the fact that he wants more children. Siblings for Alanna.'' Emmy turned back to Gwyn, her expression anguished. ''I love Riley too much to subject him to all the unanswered questions in my background. Look at everything he's had to deal with from his first wife's family. Mine could be way worse.''

''Nonsense,'' Gwyn was quick to say.

''But if it's true, what then? If my mother turned out to be a common whore and my father some sleazy John, you think it wouldn't affect Riley's professional life? What if either of my parents had some mental or physical infirmity or some inherited disease? What if my mother was raped by a serial rapist who's now spending his life behind bars? Can anyone guarantee news like that wouldn't be thrown back on Alanna at school?''

''My parents are filthy rich. They're on every list of who's who in the world of money. They're cold, unfeeling and probably unethical. I happen to believe that I learned from what I saw and rose above it. When Jed and I get ready to have a baby, I won't spend one second worrying whether they'll be anything like my mother and father.''

Emmy kept shaking her head. ''Money has a way of whitewashing a host of other sins, Gwyn.''

''Not from my perspective. But it's your life, Emmy. There are people who can't understand why I married Jed with the murder hanging over him.''

''That's different. He's innocent, and you know it.''

''What I know is that I loved him too much to wait until this mess is resolved. It could drag on for years. Think of the time we'd have wasted.''

Again Emmy's gaze drifted to Riley. She'd loved him since they were kids. Right now her heart turned to ice as she considered the possibility of her search taking years. ''Life's so unfair,'' she managed to choke out.

''Is it? Or is it anything we make it?'' Gwyn's tone remained light, but with enough steel underneath for Emmy to study her again. She unabashedly admired Gwyn for her strength and her courage in standing by Jed.

The men walked over, saying the steaks were done to perfection. Riley set a pan of foil-wrapped grilled new potatoes in the center of the table. Gwyn jumped up to go inside for the salad Emmy had brought, effectively ending their conversation. Talk turned to other things. Gwyn's recent trip to Austin, Riley's reunion with Josey.

His mom's upcoming visit. They avoided unpleasant topics like Logan Fielder's investigation and Emmy's failure to learn anything of relevance in her ongoing search.

During a break in the conversation, after they'd eaten their fill and Emmy had helped clear away the plates, Gwyn said lazily, "June concocted this absolutely decadent, totally sinful chocolate layered dessert. I put decaffeinated coffee on to perk when I went into the kitchen earlier. I hope everyone saved room."

Jed nabbed one of her auburn curls and playfully tugged her toward him for a fast brush of their lips. "Chocolate is Gwyneth's big weakness—maybe her only weakness outside of me," he announced, winking at the others. "Now, I'm guessing the only reason she didn't share that tidbit before we overindulged on meat, potatoes and salad, is she figured to save more for herself."

She batted his hand away. "Shame on you, Jed Louis. You watched June pop that into the fridge. *He's* the chocoholic in this family. Not me."

Emmy sat forward, drawing away from the arm Riley had thrown casually around her shoulders. "Boy, does she have your number, Jed. I used to hate it that you could consume a huge chocolate bar every day without gaining an ounce. Every time I begged so much as a bite from you, I added a pound and my face broke out. In the name of vanity, I stopped asking. At night I tried to figure how I could weight the scale you stepped on every morning of your life."

A funny look crossed Jed's face. "So you weren't the one who raided my candy stash on a regular basis?" He listened to her vociferous denial. "I'll be damned. Will did it. That little sneak swore it was you."

"You two haven't changed one iota," Riley mused

aloud. "Maybe Will's punishment is that he's fat and bald now."

Emmy snorted. "Dream on. Will had the kind of thick, honey-blond hair most girls drool over," she said for Gwyn's benefit. "He was a fanatic about working out. Will was built like a brick...you-know-what," she said, glancing up and blushing.

Riley sat forward in his chair. "Here I always thought you were the one girl in town who didn't have a mad crush on Will McClain. Maybe I should hope Gwyn's letter of inquiry *doesn't* turn up old Will."

Emmy bristled. "I had no such thing as a crush on him, you goof. From the day he and Jed walked through Fran's door, I claimed them as brothers. Next to you, they were the best-looking guys at school, though. Don't think I didn't get a lot of mileage out of that. Girls who couldn't see me before suddenly started hanging around me. It did my heart good each time the guys turned down a date with one of those snobs."

"I recall you were plenty ticked at Amanda," Riley said, dragging a teasing finger down the bridge of Emmy's nose. "During more than a few of our darts lessons, I got an earful about how you'd love to mess up Ms. Jennings's pretty face."

"That's just it. She's *not* pretty. I don't know what you three ever saw in her."

Gwyn turned to her husband. "Ask Jed, he took her to the prom."

"We all dated her at one time or another," he said defensively, including Riley in the quick circle of his hand.

"At least he's honest," Emmy said. "Maybe you can get out of Jed what the big attraction was." Emmy aimed her suggestion at Gwyn. "Lord knows none of them confided in me. And believe me, I did my best to worm the truth out of one and all.''

Riley and Jed exchanged a quick, very masculine smile, assuming blank expressions when Emmy and Gwyn both reached out and smartly struck their shoulders.

''Don't you ladies feel a little sympathy for Amanda?'' Riley asked, the picture of innocence. ''She's had three bad marriages and has dated a string of losers since. She's our age and back living with mommy and daddy.''

Emmy climbed to her feet. ''I think I'll pass on dessert. Riley's obviously sweet enough for both of us. Sympathy for Amanda, indeed! Anyway, we're approaching the hour he told the sitter we'd be home. The agency triples the price if we're late.''

''Next time, try Cassie Morris, used to be Ames,'' Jed said to Emmy and Riley. ''She waits tables at the café. Anyway, her oldest daughter baby-sits. Cassie's kids strike me as nice. They're certainly hardworking. But you don't often leave Alanna in the evenings, so maybe you're not interested in a referral.''

''I like Cassie,'' Emmy said. ''But she's a terrible gossip. The fewer people who know…uh…that Riley and I are dating, the better.''

''So it's a secret?'' Jed frowned.

Riley said no at the same time as Emmy said yes. Gwyn and Jed swiveled their heads between the two. After an awkward moment, Riley shook Jed's hand and thanked him for dinner. Emmy did the same, hugging Gwyn and Jed before she started around the house toward the car.

They'd almost arrived home when Riley turned to Emmy with a serious look on his face. ''I don't care who knows we're dating.''

"We're, uh, more than dating. I thought we agreed it'd be best if Alanna remained unaware that we're sleeping together. If there's gossip around town, she'll hear."

"Dammit, that's where you're hung up. I'd marry you tomorrow and I don't care *who* knows we're sleeping together."

Emmy laid a hand on his muscled forearm. "Let's not argue, Riley. We had such an enjoyable evening with Jed and Gwyn. Why spoil it with an argument that has no possible end? At least not an end in sight."

Riley expelled a long breath. "Will it ever?" he muttered.

Emmy had worried about the same problem earlier when she and Gwyn talked. She let her palm slide off his arm and scooted to her side of the car. As soon as they reached home, Emmy didn't wait for Riley to open her car door. She climbed out unaided.

"Your mother's arriving next week, Riley. I think I'd better start sleeping in my own bed. I'll come over tomorrow and throw the sheets in the wash. I haven't left much in your bathroom, but I'll do a clean sweep there, too."

Riley opened his mouth to object. Taking note of the determined set of her jaw, he inclined his head. He wondered if he should tell her that Marge had heard talk among the tellers at the bank. Speculation as to whether he and Emmy were having sex. He thought better of it. Knowing Emmy, she'd march down to the bank and knock a few heads together.

Damn, he wished he could make some headway in finding out who'd given birth to Emerald Monday. After Marge had mentioned the gossip she'd heard at the bank, he'd gone there to see if any of the tellers were the right age to be Emmy's long-lost mother. They were all too young. Another dead end. But one day someone would slip up. Then, he wondered, would Emmy still find excuses to not marry him?

CHAPTER FOURTEEN

EMMY HAD no more than reached her bedroom when the bedside phone rang. She picked it up hesitantly and was surprised to hear Riley's voice, considering they'd parted badly.

"I don't like us being at odds," he said before she'd finished a shaky greeting. "What if I promise to quit pressuring you to marry me? Can we call a truce?"

"It's not that I don't *want* to marry you, Riley. You know that, I hope. I—I—just can't. I have to choose between what feels good and what feels right. I care too much for you and Alanna."

"She's the second reason for my late call. She waited up to see you, positive you'd come in with me. It seems the sitter taught her some string tricks. Alanna was dying to show us cat's cradle, Jacob's ladder and a couple of others." Contrition crept into his voice. "Without thinking, I promised she could show you tomorrow. Then she told me how anxious she is about meeting her grandmother. Emmy, she's counting on you to go with us on Friday to pick Mom up at the bus depot."

"Tell her I'll go. I'd love to see Neva again. She always made me feel welcome in your home. After that frightening move to Houston, I lay awake nights picturing every detail of Mom Fran's house and yours. Especially your mom's kitchen. I never felt a part of my new foster family. Those memories were my comfort."

"God, Emmy. I wish Jed and Will and I had forced the agency tell us where they sent you. Why in heaven's name would they rip you away from your only friends?"

"At the time, it seemed painfully cruel. Looking back, I believe the social workers hoped a clean break would make the transition easier to bear. Maybe if I'd been younger..." She let the thought go unfinished.

"I'd give anything to erase those years, Emmy."

"I know," she said softly. "You're a good man, Riley. Every morning I cross my fingers that this will be the day we find out I'm woman enough to match."

She heard his sharp intake of breath. "I promised no more pressure, Emmy, but one day I'll remind you of this conversation. Listen to me—you are exactly right as you are. Sleep on that," he urged in a voice rough with feeling.

Emmy held her breath and felt the faint click of his hanging up echo through her trembling fingers.

She slept surprisingly well that night.

THE FOLLOWING FRIDAY, the meeting between Alanna and her grandmother brought tears to Emmy's eyes. Neva Gray Wolf's beaming round face was as open and friendly as ever. She might have added a few laugh lines around her black eyes, and her coiled black braids had a smidgen more gray, but her warmth and generosity of spirit remained constant. Because of that, Emmy felt the loss of Mom Fran even more acutely.

Neva brought Alanna a set of the handmade dolls the girl had admired at her aunt's. Better, she had Caddo legends to go with the dolls. Alanna sat beside her at a bench in the bus station, enthralled, all anxiety forgotten.

Emmy thought Riley felt pleased with how their re-union was going. He gave his mom a brief hug after stowing her suitcases in the trunk. "We thought we'd eat lunch somewhere before we go home," he said, as they left the depot. "Do you have a preference?"

"All day, my taste buds have been primed for Carlita Santiago's green corn tamales. If it's no trouble, I'd love to see her and catch up on what's happened with all her kids."

Riley's grin couldn't have been bigger. "Emmy and I have talked about going to Santiago's. We haven't made it yet. I do legal work for Carlita, so I see her on occasion and the girls. Since Rico moved back and took over Doc's practice, all he does is work. Layla, too. She runs the marina."

"Rico Santiago and Will McClain thought up more mischief than ten boys ought to. And to think Rico's a doctor now." Riley's mother chuckled. Her tone took on more somber aspects as she turned to look at Emmy, who sat in the back seat with Alanna. "Josey phoned me when that archaeologist found Frannie. I'm sorry you came home to trouble, Emerald. And to have Jed under suspicion must be killing you and Will."

"No one's heard from Will. And Jed is innocent," Emmy said fiercely. Forcing herself to calm down, she mustered a smile. "Thanks for your condolences. I'll pass them on to Jed. We'd feel a whole lot better if Sheriff Fielder would let us hold a decent burial."

"My word, I should think so." Mrs. Gray Wolf started to add something, but Riley interrupted.

"I wonder if Jed's thought to ask Rico about Will. They were best buddies. Maybe they've kept in touch."

"Why would Will call or write Rico and not Jed?" Emmy demanded. "That doesn't make sense."

"I'm not saying he did. Right now we're all reaching, Emmy."

Riley's mother broke in to ask how Emmy's search was going.

"It's stalled. I'd planned to give you some time with Riley and Alanna before I bombarded you with questions. I know you lived in Uncertain as long or longer than Fran. Do you recall hearing any stories about me?"

"You don't have to answer immediately," Riley said. "We're trying to fill in any number of blanks. Emmy, it might help if we tell Mama what we don't know." He began listing facts without waiting for her agreement. "Emmy's not positive the birth date Frannie had is correct. We have no known religion to go by. Emmy has no idea if her parents were married—to each other or to different people. She hasn't got a single identifying birthmark or skin blemish on her entire body." Even as those words left Riley's lips, he realized he'd spoken with enough conviction to prompt Neva to raise an eyebrow.

Emmy loved the way Neva threw his lawyerly persona into disarray. "Hmm...aren't you forgetting to tell your mom about my tattoos?" Emmy's innocent smile met Riley's stunned reflection in the rearview mirror.

While he sputtered, Alanna thrust out her flat chest. "Emmy's got a neat rainbow right here on her skin, Grandma."

Total silence fell over the car until Mrs. Gray Wolf pointed out her window and began talking too fast. "Mercy. Look how Santiago's have added on and improved their restaurant. Carlita must be so pleased. Expanding was her dream."

Riley didn't lose any time hustling his party out of the car and into the busy restaurant. The owner saw them immediately and ran over with arms outstretched.

While the two old friends reminisced about the old

days, Riley whispered a promise in Emmy's ear. "I'll get you good for dropping that bombshell."

"You were sounding too much like a stuffy lawyer. And it's discouraging when you point out all the holes in my search. Do you think Joleen will be over her flu? Neva's return would provide a good excuse to visit. Didn't they chat occasionally?"

"Give Joleen a few days, Emmy. She was pretty sick."

"Okay. But I'm not kidding about being stalled. I got all those names of baby girls born around my birth date, and not a single one panned out. I don't know where to go next."

"I combed the search program for other ideas. Wednesday, I placed an ad in the personals in all the papers delivered around Canton. I described how and when you were found. I mentioned the brooch in general terms. At the end, I put my office and cell phone numbers and offered a reward for information. I hope you're not mad." He didn't tell her he'd been frantic and desperate to do something—anything—after hearing from the lab. No prints of any kind were found on the second warning note.

"Mad? Riley, you're a genius! Money loosens tongues. Oh, but let me pay the reward. I told you I have some savings put aside for my search."

"Let's wait and see if any information turns up first."

Their discussion ended abruptly as soon as Carlita discovered who Emmy was. The older woman clasped her in plump arms. "Let me look at you, *chica*. So long you've been gone. Jed must be so happy. *Por favor, es Will…?*"

Riley rested a hand on Emmy's back. "Carlita, neither Emmy nor Jed has heard from Will. Jed and his wife,

Gwyn, are trying to locate him. We wondered if Rico's heard anything from him.''

"*Nada.* If I see that naughty boy, I box his ears. For now, you eat.'' She bustled off, shouting orders in fluid Spanish to someone in the kitchen.

"She didn't ask what we want to eat,'' Alanna complained.

Riley yanked playfully on one of her braids. "She's preparing a royal feast in honor of your grandmother and Emmy's return home. There'll be samples of almost every scrumptious item on the menu.''

He was right. The four of them ate tortilla soup, chicken mole, crepes Ensenada, fresh tamales and more, until all declared they couldn't eat another bite. Carlita refused to present a bill. Riley peeled a generous amount from his money clip and dropped it on the table before they filed out, mixing goodbyes with high praise for the cook.

"I need a siesta,'' Neva declared. "If you young people have something to do, please drop me at the house and point me to my bedroom.''

"I will, Grandma,'' Alanna offered. "But... Emmy said *siesta*'s another word for *nap*. Do grandmas take naps? I thought only little kids do.''

"Ah. You have much to learn about grandmothers.'' Glancing at her son, Neva's coal-dark eyes filmed with tears. She looked back at Alanna and smiled contentedly. "I'm so very grateful to finally be granted the opportunity to teach you.''

Riley hardened his jaw. "Thank Emmy.''

"No, it was Marge,'' Emmy interjected swiftly. "To be honest, Marge said my asking Riley to conduct the search into my background is what persuaded her to...give him a lecture. About family...''

"That was no lecture. Marge blasted me with both barrels."

"Whatever led to my son's change of heart," Neva murmured, "it's an answer to my prayers. Emerald, you're far too modest, I think. Riley always had a special glow about him whenever you showed up at the house." Neva inspected him closely with a mother's eye, adding with satisfaction, "He has the look again. So tell me you're going to make an old woman's life complete. While I'm here, will I be shopping for a mother-of-the-groom dress?"

Riley tossed that ball to Emmy, who turned brilliant red, stuttered, stammered and finally spit out a feeble, "Uh...no."

He'd entered the lane leading to his house, and parked the car before coming to her rescue—if it could be called a rescue. "Mama, that's the weakest denial I've heard out of her yet. You have my permission to keep nagging while you're here."

Emmy slapped his shoulder. "Mind your manners. Your mom wants to go inside and rest. And I have to shop for tonight's barbecue."

At his blank look, she elaborated. "Don't tell me you ate so much at Santiago's you forgot we'd invited Josey, Cleon, Jed and Gwyn over at six? For barbecued chicken, your special baked beans and coleslaw?"

His groan said he had indeed forgotten. "Give me a minute to carry the bags in and get Mama and Alanna settled. I'll tag along and provide a strong back."

Emmy faltered. She imagined how it would feel to engage in the simple domestic chore of grocery-shopping with Riley. Somehow, the task seemed more intimate entered into as a couple. As though they were married.

She shook off a longing that struck out of nowhere—

a desire to belong to this family. She reminded herself a man and a woman didn't have to be married to be a couple. "Sure," she said at last. "Honk when you're ready to leave."

He did.

And they got through the store without incident. They were at the cash register when his cell phone rang. Riley mimed to Emmy that he'd be outside talking. He'd clicked off by the time she pushed her shopping cart out. "You look funny. Nothing's wrong at home, is it?"

"No. That was a woman answering my ad. A retired social worker who was on the intake desk the day Joleen Berber came in with you. She refused the reward I offered, even though she said two interesting things. Joleen handled you like a pro for an unmarried woman who didn't have kids—which could be simply because she was a nurse. But she also said Joleen was unusually attached to you. To the point of making a real stink over the possibility that you might be placed with someone other than Fran Granger."

"What do you think it means, Riley?"

"Sick or not, I'm for questioning her again. I'd like to hear what she has to say in defense of those odd actions."

"So would I. Except Joleen already said she was worried about Fran's grieving over the loss of her husband. Are you doubting Joleen's friendship?"

"Probably not. Put that way, you make what she did sound logical." Still, Riley turned the car and drove straight to Joleen's.

She answered the door after only one knock, appearing recovered—although she was less than happy to see who stood on her porch. "You *must* leave me alone."

"Why?" Emmy blazed. "I'll leave you alone if you'll

come clean and admit you're my mother." One of Emmy's oldest questions spilled out uncontrollably.

Joleen gasped and turned florid. "Where did you get that preposterous notion?"

Riley explained what he'd learned, keeping his source private. Joleen shook her head vigorously through his entire monologue.

"Yes, I pressured the agency to give you to Frannie," she told Emmy, remaining visibly upset. "Frannie wanted to follow her husband to the grave. Nothing I said helped. Then you dropped into my lap, like a sign from God."

Emmy's face fell. "Which means Mom Fran wasn't my birth mother, either."

"She wanted kids. Couldn't have them. You can verify that with Dr. Barr's son. He has his father's OB-GYN practice. Fran suffered from severe endometriosis. She never could get pregnant. It's all in her medical records."

Riley felt the shiver of disappointment course through Emmy. He slid an arm around her shoulders. "Easy, sugar babe. We'll find your mom. It's a cinch you weren't delivered by the stork."

Joleen glanced furtively up and down the street. Hurriedly withdrawing, she gripped the door tight. "Why can't you be happy with the upbringing you had? Fran loved you like a real mother. Let that be enough." Joleen slammed the door shut before either Emmy or Riley could comment further.

"Come on." Riley urged Emmy toward the car, tugging with gentle hands. "We'll get nothing more from her even if she knows something else."

"Joleen acted like she was afraid a troop of Klingons would zap in from outer space and blast her with their phasers or something."

"Hey, you remember all the Trekkie trivia I taught you!" He grinned, then gave a deep sigh. "That's great, but hardly applicable. Joleen's a phobic old woman. It's sad, really, how she's shut herself away from the world."

"I guess that's all it is." Emmy climbed in the car after one last look at the house. Sunshine glinted eerily off the foil-covered windows. Hiding secrets, Emmy thought.

AT RILEY'S LATE that evening, Emmy listened to the banter going on, but didn't join in. Midway through the evening, Jed noticed. He sank into the empty lawn chair beside her. "You're quiet tonight, Emmy-M. Did you and Riley have a fight?"

"Uh-uh." She listlessly retold what had happened at Joleen's house.

Jed rolled his bottle of beer between his palms. "I always thought she was an odd duck. Fran gave her free run of the house. Will caught her in our room once, snooping through our drawers. I know you thought we installed that lock to keep you out. We let you think it because neither of us wanted to tell Fran her friend was the real reason. Joleen never trusted Will. He figured she hoped she'd find drugs."

"Hmm. I must have been used to her. From my first memories, she made herself at home whenever she dropped by."

"I guess we ought to be thankful she worked two jobs, or she'd have spent even more time ordering us around."

"I didn't know she worked two jobs. I rarely saw her in anything but a uniform. What else did she do?"

Jed hunched both shoulders. "Nursing—weekends and a few nights a week at a street clinic in Tyler. I know

Fran worried about her. She complained once that winos and degenerates hung out where Joleen had to park."

"I suppose she saw a lot of dope users. That's probably why she snooped in Will's dresser. He did sneak cigarettes. Maybe she was afraid he was smoking pot."

"I guess." He shrugged again. "Fran didn't have family. Joleen was the closest thing she had to a sister."

"Hey, you guys, quit talking and listen up."

Jed and Emmy raised their heads and realized Josey had stood up and clapped her hands to gain everyone's attention.

When all talk had stopped, she hurried over to Cleon, who sat talking to Neva. Grabbing his hand, she pulled him to his feet. "This is kind of a celebration for us tonight. After work on Wednesday, we stopped at the J.P.'s and...well, we got married."

Shock rippled through the audience. "Married?" Emmy was first to emerge from her stupor. "But...last week you said—"

Josey nodded, suddenly shy. "That's what started Cleon thinking. He said Riley's right, I'm more important to him than any inheritance. So...here we are." She pulled a set of sparkling rings from her pocket and handed them to Cleon. He gazed at her like a lovesick hound as he slowly worked them onto the third finger of her left hand.

Riley whooped, and pounded his sister's husband on the back. Alanna danced circles around Gwyn, who'd jumped up to congratulate the happy couple. Jed joined her, as did Neva.

Emmy was slower in climbing to her feet. While she was happy for her friend and thought they'd made a wise decision, she also dealt with pangs of jealousy. As the evening wore on and turned into a wedding party, she despaired of ever finding her own roots so she'd be free to marry Riley.

Miraculously, she made it through the evening. And through seven long days of the next week, with Riley's mother taking every opportunity to issue not-so-subtle hints on the subject of marriage. Specifically, Emmy's marriage to Riley.

The following Sunday, the women stood side by side at the bus depot. Riley had taken Alanna outside to watch luggage being loaded onto a bus. Neva made one last attempt to strong-arm Emmy. "Josey cheated me out of my one and only chance to do what mothers of brides get to do. I've pictured shopping for gowns, flowers, invitations, oh—all that storybook wedding stuff. Since you haven't got a mom, I'd be more than willing to assist you."

Inured by now, Emmy smiled. "Riley told me he was going to ask you to move in with him to help care for Alanna."

"He did, and I'd love to. But my brother's health is failing. He needs me more than Riley does. What my son needs is a wife, Emerald. Alanna needs a mother."

Emmy sidestepped that direct shove toward the altar, and harked back to Neva's previous statement. "Riley doesn't talk about his first wedding."

"That girl," Neva said acerbically. "I hate to speak ill of the dead, but her uncle lives in a different century, and he had way too much influence on her. He performed his own version of a wedding ritual. If Riley hadn't asked my brother to have tribal headquarters file his marriage with the county, it wouldn't have been legal."

"Legal or not, he'd still have Alanna. Neva, if I were ever to marry Riley—and please don't get your hopes up, because I need to find out who I am and where I came from first. But if I did...you should know I'm not big on pomp and ceremony, either.''

Emmy was saved from the lecture Neva was sure to deliver by Riley's return. Alanna raced up and threw her arms around her grandmother's hips. "Your bus just came in, Grandma. I wish you didn't have to go home." She started to cry. "Everybody always leaves me. If you stay, I'll be a really good girl."

Emmy forgot her own dilemma in the midst of consoling the brokenhearted child. Still, it made her nervous to hear both Riley and Neva assure Alanna that she had Emmy, who'd always care for her.

"Emerald's not going anywhere," Neva declared stoutly.

The knot in Emmy's stomach coiled tighter the minute Alanna transferred her full allegiance from her departing grandmother. The child placed her small, sweaty hand in Emmy's, and gazed at her with such trust, Emmy panicked. All her life, she'd been a nomad, an outcast who belonged nowhere and to no one. Was she afraid that would always be her condition—forever an outsider? Or did she fear not measuring up, being unable to meet a child's needs. Or a husband's...

She hung back, letting Riley and Alanna escort Neva to her bus.

On the final leg of the drive home, after they'd stopped for dinner at one of the lake lodges, Riley leaned close to Emmy's ear. "Please," he said in a voice too low for Alanna to hear, "spend the night with me."

Identifying in his voice a mixture of love and the same desperation she wasn't handling well, Emmy accepted. If stolen nights were all she was going to have with the man she loved, then she'd grab them without qualms.

They didn't rush into the house and jump directly into

bed, although each could see it was precisely what was on the other's mind. Emmy ran Alanna's bath. Both adults sat beside her on the bed as Riley read her a bedtime story.

Even after the little girl fell asleep, they didn't rush off to Riley's bedroom. It was as if each knew that prolonging the inevitable would heighten their excitement. "I bought a bottle of real champagne to drop by Josey and Cleon's. If you'd like, we can indulge and I'll buy them another."

"What's the occasion?"

He took her in his arms and kissed her long and deliciously. "*We're* the occasion," he whispered, kissing her earlobe. "Don't get me wrong, I'm glad I patched things up with my family. But do you know how many days it's been since I've had you to myself?"

The tightness which had taken up residence in Emmy's stomach unfurled a little. "Our lives have been a bit of a whirlwind." She smiled. "I never realized your mother was such a shopping machine."

"I don't want to talk about my mother."

"Oh? Okay." Still smiling, Emmy crossed her arms and skimmed her sweater off, leaving her blond hair a flyaway mess of curls. She wore nothing underneath the sweater. Her reward was the gleam of lust that darkened Riley's eyes and brought an immediate heavy droop to his eyelids.

"To hell with the bubbly." Growling low in his throat, he scooped Emmy into his arms. In three long strides, he'd entered his bedroom. After two more steps, he dropped her in the middle of his bed. "I intended to have a civilized discussion with you about your search. What our next strategy should be," he said in a muffled voice as he yanked his knit shirt over his head and hopped on one foot to shed his jeans.

Emmy, meanwhile, had kicked off her capri pants and her lace bikini panties. Just for tonight, she didn't want to talk about the disappointing progress of her search. She held out welcoming arms.

Riley sank into her softness. If any strategy remained in his head, other than coming up with new ways of pleasing her, he uttered no words to that effect.

Thoroughly loved and completely sated, some hours later they clung together and drifted into slumber.

EMMY AWAKENED with a start. Shaking cobwebs from her brain, she slid out from under the muscled arm Riley had draped across her middle. A breeze blew in the open window, rustling white sheers that held the darkness at bay. Suddenly thinking she heard a car door shut, Emmy got quietly out of bed.

Aided by the glow of the bathroom night-light, she threw on her clothes before dashing to the window. If local kids were messing around Riley's convertible, she'd wake him up. But if the noise turned out to be her imagination, she'd let him sleep.

The area near his car was dark and quiet. The same with her pickup. *But wait.* A car at the end of the lane had just switched on its headlights. A big dark car that squealed its tires in a U-turn and sped toward town. Emmy didn't get enough of a glimpse to make any kind of identification. What she saw in the bright flash of the car's high beams was a square paper flapping on her screen door.

According to the clock on Riley's nightstand, it wasn't quite five. Time for her to sneak out, anyway, or run the risk of Alanna waking and catching them in bed.

Taking care not to disturb Riley, she slipped into her shoes and crept downstairs and out the door.

It wasn't until Emmy had ripped down the note and gone inside and turned on the kitchen light to read it, that she realized it was a warning. Someone had used the stick-on letters available at office supply and craft stores. Her hand shook. Terse and to the point, the note said: *Drop your search ASAP or I'll see to it that Gray Wolf and his kid will have a nasty accident, too.*

Emmy read "nasty accident" to mean something horrible and permanent, like had happened to Mom Fran. Crushing the paper to her chest, she found it hard to breathe. She loved Riley and Alanna so much. If anything happened to them because she'd twisted Riley's arm to help her dig into her background, she'd never be able to live with herself. Drenched in icy sweat, she ran to her bedroom.

The only solution, she decided on a panicky spur of the moment—was to pack a few clothes, grab her cat and leave town. With her gone, whoever found it necessary to make threats would surely back off. Stifling sobs, Emmy haphazardly tossed shirts and jeans into her treasured basket.

She was in the middle of frantically stuffing the cat carrier into her truck when sanity of sorts descended. Hadn't she suffered the anguish caused when someone disappeared without a word? *Jed.* She'd tell Jed and Gwyn that she was going. They didn't need to know the reason. Let them think she and Riley had quarreled.

Yes, it was the right thing to do. By the time Jed circulated the message that she'd dropped the idea of finding her birth family, she'd be long gone. Riley and Alanna would be completely safe. Their safety was all that really mattered. *Why would someone threaten them?*

Leaving Riley, leaving Alanna. It hurt so much.

Emmy scrubbed at tears coursing down her cheeks. Tears that stung her eyelids, blinding her as she backed out, sobbing a second unheard farewell to the only man she'd ever loved.

CHAPTER FIFTEEN

EMMY DROVE through the gates of Beaumarais before the sun had broken through the mist rising off the lake. She expected to have to drag Jed from his bed. But there were lights on in the house.

He answered the door, fully dressed in black jeans and matching cowboy boots. "Emmy! What a nice surprise. Gwyn and I are having breakfast in the morning room. Go on back and join us," he said, shutting the door.

Gwyn glanced up from her meal as Emmy preceded Jed into the room.

"Get Emmy a plate and silverware, would you please, Gwyn? I'll pour her a cup of coffee. Sugar, right?" he asked, lifting the carafe as he reached for the sugar bowl.

Gwyn wrapped her hand around Jed's wrist. "Jed, wait. Emmy's been crying."

Emmy tried to act as if dropping in unannounced at the crack of dawn was nothing out of the ordinary. "I need to talk with you for a minute. I'm not hungry."

Jed set down the carafe, a troubled frown replacing his smile. Taking Emmy by the hand, he forced her gently into the wicker chair that sat empty next to Gwyn. "Now, Emmy-M, what's this about?"

"I'm going away. Today. Right now." Unable to meet either pair of probing eyes, she nervously separated and twisted a lock of hair. "I woke up and…and saw how I'm wasting my own time and everyone else's. I've lived thirty-two years without knowing my real identity. I can go on doing that. Anyway, my search went nowhere. I've gotta hit the road before the sun gets too hot. I have the kitten, and my air conditioner's on the fritz. I saw your lights and figured you wouldn't mind spreading the word that I've taken off.''

"Like that? Going where?'' Jed shared a puzzled glance with his wife. Gwyn picked up the carafe and poured a clean cup full of coffee. She set it in front of Emmy, and slid the sugar bowl closer.

Emmy reached for the cup. Her hand shook so hard she spilled the sugar.

Gwyn left her seat and threw an arm around Emmy's bowed shoulders. "Have you and Riley had an argument? Is that why you're leaving? Emmy, the man *loves* you. Nothing could be so terrible that discussing it rationally wouldn't patch things up.''

"What did that knucklehead do?'' Jed demanded. "I'll phone him right now and read him the riot act.''

"No, don't,'' Emmy said in a strained voice as she catapulted from her chair and grabbed the cellular phone Jed had flipped open right out of his hands. "Please give me an hour's head start before you tell Riley. Please.'' Tears streamed from pleading eyes. She let them run down her cheeks and drip on her blouse without even trying to rub them away.

"No mere argument would cause you this much pain,'' Gwyn declared. "I think you'd better tell us the truth, Emmy.''

Jed pried his phone out of her white-knuckled fingers. "Gwyn's got a point. There's no way I'd let you on the road in this condition. You're an accident waiting to happen. And don't give me any crap,'' he added sternly. "As a kid, you always twisted your hair like that whenever you tried to get away with telling a whopper.''

"All right.'' Emmy capitulated with a huge sigh. Digging in her pocket, she pulled out the crushed note. Gwyn and Jed grouped around her to read it. "Now do you understand?'' Emmy cried. "Some birth parents don't want to be found. Ever. I know Riley. He'd insist on tracing this note. He's stubborn and very protective. I hate to think what he'd do if he found the person who left it. I'm just not willing to take a chance. Would you?'' She put her question squarely to Gwyn.

Gwyn shook her head and hugged Emmy closer.

Jed still held the crude warning. "If I thought this was just a scare tactic, I'd agree with Riley. But what does this joker mean, adding the word *too?* I don't like what I feel in my gut. Far as I know, the only other dire 'accident' in Uncertain happened to Frannie. I'm inclined to hand this over to Thorny. In fact, I'm going to call him now.''

Gwyn brought a hand to her mouth. Both women huddled together wide-eyed and mute as Jed punched in his lawyer's number. Thorny answered at once. Jed paced the perimeter of the small breakfast room while he listened and occasionally talked. "I have the note, yes. Emmy's prints are all over it, and now mine. What do you mean does it match the notes Riley got?'' Jed whirled and flagged a brow at Emmy. When she shrugged, not comprehending, he reeled off more questions. Clicking off at last, Jed sank into a chair and stared blankly at the women. "Thorny says Riley talked to him about two similar warnings he's received. He gave Riley the name of an independent lab to have the paper checked for prints. Thorny agrees the word *too* in the note seems significant. It could tie the author to Frannie's death.

He'd like to sit down and talk with you, Emmy. He asked me to find out if Riley will let us all meet in his conference room today at ten.''

Emmy's color drained. ''If Riley received threats, why didn't he tell me?''

Gwyn thrust the cooling cup of coffee into Emmy's icy hands. ''Like you said, he's very protective. You didn't want to worry him. He probably felt the same.''

''He can't put an end to this nonsense. I can. By simply taking myself out of the equation. The only way is for me to leave Uncertain, don't you see?''

''No. Like it or not, Emmy, I'm phoning Riley. The notes obviously worried him,'' Jed insisted, punching in Riley's number. ''Or else why would he have asked Thorny for an out-of-town criminal lab?''

Emmy placed trembling fingers on her lips. Objecting wouldn't have mattered because Jed already had Riley on the phone and was telling him to hustle himself over to Beaumarais.

''Egypt's caged in my pickup,'' Emmy told Gwyn. ''Do you mind if I bring him in? Frankly, I'm not too keen on going back to the house by myself. The person who left that note drove off in a big dark car. It could be anyone. What if they're watching my house? Or Riley's? I can't risk placing him and Alanna in greater danger. I won't.''

''I'll ask Josiah, June's husband, to fetch the cat. Josiah's headed around the house to clip the roses. We'll put Egypt in with his mother. They can have a high old time getting reacquainted.'' Rising, Gwyn left.

She returned as Jed signed off from talking with Riley again.

''He's on his way. I jolted the poor guy out of a sound sleep. It seems Alanna overslept and Riley hadn't set his alarm." Jed slanted an amused glance at Emmy. "He was most shocked to learn you were with us, having coffee. Riley gave the distinct impression he fully expected to find you sleeping in his bed...Goldilocks."

Emmy tried but failed to swallow a guilt-laden reply. She was still hemming and hawing in embarrassment fifteen minutes later when Riley stormed through the front door. He carried a sleepy-eyed Alanna, still wearing her angel nightgown and bunny-face slippers. Riley's shirt wasn't buttoned right. His shoes were untied and his hair stood up in tufts.

"Emmy, what threatening note was Jed talking about? And why is the back of your pickup half-full of moving boxes?" His dark eyes blazed a mix of fury and betrayal.

Gwyn reached for Alanna. "Would you like me to fix you a bowl of cereal, honey?"

Yawning, Alanna lunged into Gwyn's arms. Emmy waited until their footsteps faded before she explained to Riley. "This morning, at dawn, someone outside your house shut a car door and woke me up." She twisted a lock of hair. "I thought kids might be messing around with your car. If I hadn't taken time to dress, I might've seen who tacked this note to my screen. As it so happened, I only glimpsed a dark car. He backed all the way down the lane before turning on his headlights. Or hers. I don't know if it was a man."

"What was the model and make of the car?" Jed asked.

"I don't know. It was big. It could have been blue or green or black." She watched Riley as he bent over the note. "It wasn't light yet and I wasn't fully awake," she said nervously. "Riley, why didn't you tell me you'd received other notes?"

He spun, almost knocking over the cup of coffee Jed

had poured and was trying to hand him. Waving away the cup, Riley rubbed his right thumb over the streaks of dried tears on Emmy's cheeks. "I knew how important the search was to you, sugar babe. I figured if I said anything, it'd worry you so much you'd give up. By then I wanted answers as much as you did. Maybe more. You'd made it plain you wouldn't marry me until you had access to at least your medical history."

Crossing her arms, Emmy shivered. "With good reason, it seems. Obviously one of my parents is a real sicko."

"There you go, making assumptions we can't substantiate." Riley threw up his hands and turned to appeal to Jed. "All parents have skeletons in their closets, right?" He demanded backup from his friend before arguing with Emmy again. "Look at Jed and me. We turned out okay."

"And Gwyn," Jed said. "Her family isn't exactly The Brady Bunch."

Gwyn and Alanna walked into the room in time to catch Jed's remark. Gwyn held a bowl of cereal and a frosty glass of milk. Alanna had a spoon and several napkins. "Alanna wants to eat in here. Why don't we postpone this conversation and finish breakfast? June's just come in. I'll ask her to make a fresh pot of coffee."

Emmy shook back her hair. "It doesn't matter how much you guys try to assure me that all of you came from dysfunctional families. I'm canceling my search. I want it made crystal clear to people all over town. Tell Marge and Cassie to spread the word through their gossipy pals. I don't want the deranged person who wrote this note thinking I'm going to continue the hunt long-distance."

Riley froze. "Long-distance?"

It was all Emmy could do to square her shoulders and nod. "I may not know if there's sick stuff in my background or what it is, but I'm not a person who'd stand by and let people I love be hurt on account of me. I won't."

Riley let out a whoop, pulled her toward him and kissed her soundly on the lips. "Thank you for making my point," he said, releasing her a fraction. "Fran Granger was your *real* parent. She molded your character, not the faceless people who happened to be your biological parents. You think I'd let you go now that I've finally got you back? Emmy, what kind of man would I be if I couldn't keep my daughter and the woman I love safe?"

Pressing her into a chair, Riley sank down on one knee, and in front of everyone in the room, said softly but boldly, "Stay. Complete my family, Emmy. Thumb your nose at whoever dares threaten what we have together. Marry me."

Alanna turned, her milk mustache curved in a smile. "Grandma said if you marry my daddy, Emmy, that means you'll be my mom. Say yes, *please*." Climbing from her chair, she threw her arms around Emmy's neck.

Tears sprang to Emmy's eyes again. This time, she combed her fingers through Alanna's tangled dark hair and blinked them away. "Ye-s," she said slowly. "I will marry you, Riley. On one condition. I still want it made clear that I'm no longer interested in my past. Emerald Monday will cease to exist. Hereafter, I'll be Emmy Gray."

"How about Gray Wolf?" he asked in a soft voice, gathering both Emmy and Alanna into the circle of his arms. "Emmy, you've helped me sort out who I am. My life changed when I was a young boy and my dad died.

I was angry at him for not coming home. So angry I swore I'd find a way to quit being his son. I decided I was going to be like Jed and Will. Thanks to you—urging me to make peace with Josey and Mom—I've come to appreciate the Caddo legacy left by my dad.''

Emmy skimmed her fingers lightly over his beautiful bronzed face. ''You've got much to be proud of, Riley. Your people are strong, wise and talented. So are you.''

''I don't know about wise. Subconsciously, I think my final rebellious act was to marry Lani and show I could change her, too. I'll forever be sorry for that. Taking back my real last name is a step in the right direction. Another...I'm requesting reinstatement in the tribe. It's time, don't you think, to drop all pretexts? Especially, if you and I are going to begin a new chapter in our lives.''

''Oh, I love you so much, Riley.'' The radiant smile Emmy flashed Jed and Gwyn shone from her heart and soul.

Those two had drifted together and linked arms. Gwyn nudged her husband's ribs. ''We should have the wedding here, don't you agree, Jed?''

''Absolutely. The house and grounds have never looked better.'' He bestowed a loving glance on his wife. ''Gwyn has all the contacts. She amazed me, the way she planned every detail of our wedding. Is having it here amenable to you three?''

Alanna beamed happily at being included in the decision. ''My Emmy and Miss Gwyn can help me buy another party dress.''

''I appreciate the offer, Jed. My only stipulation is, the sooner the better,'' Riley declared, tightening his hold on Emmy. ''I'm not letting her sleep in Fran's house one more night from now on.''

Emmy blushed, and poked him, rolling her eyes toward Alanna to scold him for talking openly about their sleeping arrangements.

"What?" Riley played dumb.

"Whenever you can arrange it is okay," Emmy told Gwyn. "Riley's mom is dying to help plan a wedding. I'd prefer we keep it small, though."

"Small can still be elegant." Gwyn separated from Jed and went to rummage in the sideboard until she found a pad and pen. "We have some time before meeting Thorny at Riley's office. Let's draw up a guest list."

The two couples batted names around for twenty minutes. It was tough when all Riley seemed interested in was kissing Emmy every chance he got.

"So is this it?" Gwyn finally said, extending a clean copy she'd rewritten to Emmy and Riley.

Emmy scanned the list while Riley looked over her shoulder. Jed did, too. "If you don't have anyone else in mind to escort you, I'd be honored to play the proud papa." He rubbed his chin thoughtfully. "Too bad we haven't been able to get a lead on Will. Wouldn't it be something if we could both walk you down the aisle?"

"Oh, Jed, I'd love to lean on you. And if Gwyn struck out finding Will in the military, I'm afraid we've lost him forever."

"Hey," Riley chided. "Our wedding will still be a memorable occasion. No long faces. Gwyn, tell me what needs doing and someone in the Gray...uh, Gray Wolf family will get it done. Right now, though, Emmy and I had better run Alanna by the house to get her dressed. If we're meeting Thorny at ten, that is."

"Yikes, we are," Gwyn agreed. "Egypt can stay here for the time being."

"No need. I'm moving Emmy lock, stock and cat litter into my place."

Not a soul in the room argued with Riley's set jaw.

"In that case—" Gwyn grinned at him cheekily "—maybe you won't mind sticking the rental sign back in the cottage window for me. In the interests of propriety, how about if we set the wedding for next Saturday? And all you have to do, Riley, is come up with a romantic place for the honeymoon."

"Not too romantic," Emmy cautioned. "It needs to be someplace fun for kids. Maybe it sounds offbeat to y'all, but now that I've finally found a family, I want us to be together."

Riley kissed her so thoroughly and for such a long time that everyone else in the room grew fidgety. "Fun it is," he whispered huskily once they broke apart.

Gwyn snapped her fingers. "Arlington isn't far. It's close to a Six Flags amusement park and a Wet N Wild."

Arching an amused brow, Riley herded his brood out of the room. Pausing at the threshold, he leaned back inside. "I think I can be a little more creative in combining a romantic getaway with entertainment suitable for Alanna. In fact, a travel brochure on New Orleans just came to the office. Four days, three nights. Does that meet with your approval, Gwyn?"

She elbowed Jed. "Delightful. Isn't he some friend, Jed? Riley's inviting us to go along on his honeymoon."

Riley thumbed his nose at her. Gwyn just laughed, tossing him a thumbs-up before Emmy reached back for his arm and yanked him out of sight.

EIGHT ROUND TABLES were grouped under a rented canopy on the gently sloping back lawn at Beaumarais. Each groaned with an abundance of food. Bouquets of roses cut from Jed's garden added color to the center of each pristine white tablecloth.

Emmy would have settled for paper plates and balloons.

Gwyn and Neva Gray Wolf had something more elaborate in mind when they set out Gwyn's best china and silver and her gleaming lead crystal Waterford champagne glasses for the wedding guests.

Gwyn's pale-peach dress magnified the red highlights in her hair.

Alanna looked like a princess in a frothy blue organza dress that her grandmother had taken delight in buying. Neva herself looked regal in a tea-length, beaded beige gown.

Emmy hadn't been keen on wearing anything frilly or white. But even she had to stop one last time to stare at herself in the hall mirror. The cream-colored dress with its sweetheart neckline and short, flirty skirt showed off her slim figure and golden tan. Neva had risen early in order to French braid both Emmy's and Alanna's hair. Emmy now covered Neva's handiwork with a hat Josey had woven and trimmed with a net veil. A veil too short to hide Emmy's ear-to-ear smile.

Jed slipped up behind her and handed her the bridal bouquet. "Ready?" he asked, lifting her chin with one finger. "I wish Fran and Will could be here to see you." His voice sounded gritty. "You look all grown-up and beautiful, Emmy."

"Stop," she chastened. "Gwyn will kill both of us if you make me cry before the ceremony and ruin the makeup she spent an hour fixing." She straightened his already straight tie. "You're looking pretty hot, yourself." Her tone changed abruptly. "Jed, I'm scared. I keep thinking the person who wrote that note is going to burst in here and expose me as the daughter of some lowlife. The last time I was this happy, Mom Fran disappeared and my whole life fell apart." She let her forehead rest against his broad chest.

"Shh. Nothing's going to happen, Emmy-M. Hey, I can't call you that anymore, can I? Emmy G. W. doesn't have the same ring."

Jed's teasing restored her balance.

"Come on, I hear the music," he said. "That's our cue. Big smile now. Riley's waiting. If it's any consolation, I think he's twice as nervous as you are."

Emmy heard Jed, but from the moment they stepped outside and she saw Riley turn and gaze at her with love and focused intensity, any fear that she might not be doing the right thing disappeared completely from her mind. Nor did doubts return at any time while she and Riley exchanged their vows.

Later, she enjoyed their reception too much to let adverse thoughts enter her head. So much, she let it pass when Jed, Riley and Thorny withdrew to a quiet corner of the yard to engage in serious conversation during the few minutes it took her to toss her bouquet.

"Look," Riley growled at the other two men, "I know it's probable that the fool who wrote those notes lives in Uncertain. But I promised Emmy I'd scrap the search, and by God, I'm not starting my marriage lying to my bride."

"We wouldn't want you to," Thorny emphasized, sliding a reassuring hand over Riley's tuxedo-clad shoulder. "Jed and I thought if there's a possibility of some connection to Fran Granger's murder, you wouldn't mind sending the search program off to me. Plus a list of all the leads you two have followed up on."

"Yeah," Jed seconded. "I'll pay Thorny to do the

digging from here on, and it's out of your hands alto-gether. What do you say, Riley? If those threats relate in any way to Fran's murder and ultimately expose her killer, I know Emmy would change her tune."

"Maybe." Riley shoved his hands in his pockets, rat-tling his ring of keys. "Okay, but here's the deal. I don't even want Marge suspecting what you're up to. And I'm leaving on my honeymoon in less than two hours." He pulled out the key ring and peeled off two keys. Slapping them into Thorny's hand, he muttered, "Everything we've gathered to date is in a folder in the bottom right-hand drawer of my desk. Including a copy of the flyers I mailed to area jewelry stores hoping for a lead on the brooch Emmy sketched. I've heard back from two. Both negative."

"What about responses that come in while you're gone?"

"Sorry, Jed. You'll have to call the stores on the list and give them a change of address. As of now, Emmy and I are no longer part of this dog-and-pony show."

The older lawyer slapped Riley on the back. "I un-derstand your need to keep your family safe. If I turn up any pertinent information on your wife's birth parents, I'll run it by you before telling anyone."

"Don't. I don't need to know. There isn't anything in Emmy's background that'll make one bit of difference to the way I feel about her. And if the SOB writing those notes is related to her, she's better off not knowing. At first I was sure Joleen Berber was behind the notes. She'd acted screwy the day Emmy and I went to see her. The old lady even mistook Emmy for someone else. I thought it might be significant, but my suspicions didn't pan out. Joleen was bedridden, sick as a dog, when the first note was delivered."

"Hmm. Might be worth rechecking, anyhow. I'll be in touch again if I find anything, Riley—just to see if your feelings have changed. Otherwise, I'll take this opportunity to wish you much happiness in your marriage."

"I can't think of anything that would make it much happier, unless you prove Jed's innocence."

"I fully intend to," Thorny said without modesty. "Put the whole mess out of your mind, Riley. Go have fun in New Orleans. Start this marriage on a positive note."

"You bet. Any bad luck is behind us. The other day, Alanna asked if she could call Emmy Mama. I've never seen Emmy more pleased. Later, she said to me, 'Funny, all this time I thought my life was missing a foundation. It's not. I carried it with me. It's Mom Fran, Jed, Will and you, Riley.'"

Looking up, away from the men—across the room to where his wife stood with the other important people in his life—Riley met Emmy's eyes. And nineteen years worth of love coalesced for them both. *Nineteen and counting,* he thought happily. The truth was written on her face. Emmy had everything she needed to make her life complete.

Turn the page for an excerpt from

A MAN OF HIS WORD

by Eve Gaddy,
the third book in the

RETURN TO EAST TEXAS

trilogy.

Tessa Lang found Fran Granger's remains
at the archaeology site she's been working.
And Tessa's life has been on hold ever
since. Just when the police were about to let
her return to the site, Texas Ranger Will
McClain puts a stop to things. Will's
investigating the murder now and his
interest is more than professional—Fran
was his foster mother and the chief suspect
in her murder was once like a brother to
him. Nothing—certainly not Tessa's
protests—will stop Will from finding Fran's
killer, and along the way he just might
uncover the answers to other mysteries—like
who Emmy Monday's parents were...

"Ms. LANG."

The sheriff drawled her name. Tessa didn't make the mistake of thinking he meant any respect.

"Well, what can I do for you?" He stood aside and motioned her in.

As if he didn't know. They'd played out this same scenario about a hundred times in the past few weeks. "Sheriff Fielder, you know why I'm here. Surely you've had time by now to gather all the evidence you need."

Fielder settled into his chair, leaving Tessa to perch uncomfortably on yet another hard plastic piece of misery.

"Well, now, that depends. You're mighty anxious to gain access to the murder site, aren't you, Ms. Lang?"

Duh, she thought, barely stopping herself from rolling her eyes. "Yes, sir. As I've told you—" a zillion times, she thought darkly "—it's very important to my thesis that I be allowed to finish the dig started in that area." Choking on the need for amiability, or at least civility, she itched to wipe the smirk off his face. Too bad she couldn't think of a way to do it.

Fielder pursed his lips and shuffled through some papers on his desk. "Then this must be your lucky day, Ms. Lang. I'm about convinced we've got all the evidence to be gained from the site. I've decided to allow you to resume your dig."

"Like hell she will," a deep male voice fired from behind her.

Tessa whipped her head around. A stranger filled the office doorway. A very large, very intimidating stranger. From her vantage point, seated in a low-slung chair, Tessa thought he stood about seven feet tall. Mid-thirties, she guessed, with a fallen-angel face she bet earned him more than his share of female attention.

Tessa tore her startled gaze away to glance at Fielder. His mouth opened and closed. No sound emerged, but his face reddened and his harsh features looked even more unaccommodating than usual. Suddenly she felt sorry for Deputy Masters. She doubted the sheriff appreciated his letting the stranger through.

"Who the hell are you?" Fielder asked.

The man strode into the room to stand in front of him. Tessa sucked in her breath at the power that entered along with him.

"Will McClain." Pausing a beat, he reached into the back pocket of his well-worn blue jeans and pulled out a leather case. He flipped it open and added, "Texas Ranger."

If possible, the sheriff's face darkened even more. "McClain?" His brows drew together until they met over the bridge of his nose, then flattened again. "Not—my God, you couldn't be. Not the McClain—"

"The very same," he said, his voice laced with amusement. "Small world, isn't it?"

Tessa shivered at the diabolical smile he offered Fielder, glad she wasn't on the receiving end of it. Still, this business had nothing to do with her. Gathering her wits—which seemed to have fled with the Ranger's entrance—she turned to Fielder and spoke briskly. "Excuse me, but what's going on here? I thought you were in charge of the investigation?''

Ignoring her, he rose jerkily, staring at the man in revulsion and—she could have sworn—a hint of fear. ''What kind of bullshit is this? Show me that badge again.''

McClain shrugged and flipped it to him. Fielder inspected it, his face paling as he did so. He glanced at the Ranger, then back at the badge. After a long pause, he handed it back and said heavily, ''I don't believe this.''

''Believe it,'' McClain said, his voice silky, dark.

Fielder shook his head, as if trying to clear his mind. ''What are you doing here?''

''If you'll recall, the Rangers never signed off on this case.'' He pocketed his badge and nailed the sheriff with another hard smile. ''I have orders to finish it.''

''Finish it?'' He drew himself up and glared. ''I've practically got it sewed up. I didn't ask for the Rangers, and no piece of—'' He hesitated, eyeing McClain's stony face. ''No Texas Ranger is going to come in and lay claim to a case I've already figured out. I don't need your damn interference.''

The Ranger looked almost amused now. ''Yeah? I'll be sure and tell my captain you said so. In the meantime, fill me in on what you've got.''

Fielder's jaw tightened. He and McClain stared at each other while Tessa grew more puzzled and irritated, and damn it, curious, by the moment.

Turning to Tessa, Fielder said, ''Ms. Lang. I'll have to get back to you on that other matter.''

Tessa sprang to her feet to gape incredulously at him. ''You must be joking! I need access to the area, and you just promised it to me.'' She waved a hand at the man beside her, realizing that though he was big in comparison to her five foot three, he wasn't quite the giant she'd originally thought him. "Everything was fine until he came in. Are you just going to let him order you around?" From what she knew of Fielder, she couldn't imagine it.

"This is a murder investigation," McClain said, his voice deep with a hint of gravel. "And that site is pertinent to the investigation."

"No joke," Tessa snapped. "Since I'm the one who discovered the bones, I think I'm aware of that."

"Then you should also be aware we can't allow you to disturb the site any further." His gaze assessed her dispassionately, his eyes a cool, cynical gray. "Not until I'm assured all the evidence pertaining to the murder has been collected and logged."

She couldn't believe what she was hearing. Hands on hips, she jutted out her chin. "This is an outrage! If you think I'm just going to go meekly away—"

"File a complaint," McClain told her, taking her arm. Escorting her out with a firm hand under her elbow, totally ignoring her sputtered protests, he added, "I'm sure the deputy will be happy to assist you."

Their gazes locked for a brief moment, and a reluctant smile twisted his mouth. Then he shut the door in her face.

Tessa stared at the closed door, unable to believe what had just happened. "You wait, Ranger McClain," she threatened, regaining her power of speech. "You haven't seen the last of me."

In July 2001

New York Times bestselling author

HEATHER GRAHAM

joins

DALLAS SCHULZE

&

Elda Minger

in

TAKE5

Volume 3

These five heartwarming love
stories are quick reads, great escapes
and guarantee five times the joy.

Plus

With $5.00 worth of coupons inside,
this is one *delightful* deal!

HARLEQUIN®
Makes any time special ®

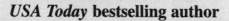
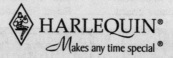

HARLEQUIN *Super*ROMANCE®

To celebrate the
1000th Superromance book
We're presenting you with 3 books
from 3 of your favorite authors in

All Summer Long

Home, Hearth and Haley
by **Muriel Jensen**

Meet the men and women of Muriel's
upcoming **Men of Maple Hill** trilogy

Daddy's Girl
by **Judith Arnold**

Another **Daddy School** story!

Temperature Rising
by **Bobby Hutchinson**

Life and love at St. Joe's Hospital are as feverish
as ever in this **Emergency!** story

On sale July 2001
Available wherever Harlequin books are sold.

HARLEQUIN®
*M*akes any time special ®

Visit us at www.eHarlequin.com   HSR1000